Hal Brognola nodded.

"But there's also a renegade force in Norfolk, Virginia," the President continued, "being funded and supplied by the People's Republic of China and Saudi princes."

"All we know right now is that an Idaho white supremacist group has targeted European tourism," Brognola replied.

"I've got people keeping a lid on the La Palma volcano threat," the President said. "But according to my staff, posts are popping up about that damn Jeopardy white paper."

"Jeopardy is an American company, so if anything does happen, it will lead back to us. No amount of money is going to cover it up."

"The livelihoods of millions of Americans will be destroyed by a superwave, and *we're* going to take the blame for the damage." The President narrowed his eyes. "Stony Man can fix this, right?"

DON PENDLETON'S

STONY

AMERICA'S ULTRA-COVERT INTELLIGENCE AGENCY

MAN®

SEISMIC SURGE

A GOLD EAGLE BOOK FROM

W🦅RLDWIDE®

TORONTO • NEW YORK • LONDON
AMSTERDAM • PARIS • SYDNEY • HAMBURG
STOCKHOLM • ATHENS • TOKYO • MILAN
MADRID • WARSAW • BUDAPEST • AUCKLAND

Recycling programs
for this product may
not exist in your area.

First edition October 2012

ISBN-13: 978-0-373-80435-1

SEISMIC SURGE

Special thanks and acknowledgment to
Doug Wojtowicz for his contribution to this work.

Printed in U.S.A.

SEISMIC SURGE

PROLOGUE

Bernie Jackson stowed the spare blank forms inside his folding metal clipboard, then adjusted the top inspection sheet until it sat squarely on the cold, bare metal. There had been a few too many incidents for the Occupational Safety and Health Administration's liking at the Heyerdal Hull Company, and the Norfolk, Virginia, plant was shut down for the day, pending the results of his OSHA team's observations.

Seven men had died already, and twenty more were injured due to mishaps at the plant. Heyerdal's owners, the Jeopardy Corporation, had requested that they be allowed to clean their own house, utilizing one of their security contractors. These promises had held off the federal government's agents. The fact that Heyerdal was behind some large defense contracts, developing new hulls for a low-profile patrol craft that could be used by the Navy and the Marine Corps, had been enough until the most recent "accident" left two dead and seven wounded. Local constituents were demanding in Congress that the government take a closer look.

The Jeopardy Corporation tried to muddy the waters with claims of outside interference, suggesting saboteurs or espionage agents were responsible for the mayhem and death. Jeopardy owned private military contractor companies that had provided security for the U.S. government overseas in Iraq and Afghanistan, as well as for allied Middle Eastern governments. As such, they claimed that they could deal with all of this on their own.

That suggestion bubbled up in Jackson's memory and he had to strangle down a snort of derision.

"Like that's going to come up kosher," he muttered.

"I told you, these damn corporate bigwigs act like their shit don't stink," Gerber said. Whereas Jackson was an older African-American man, thick around the middle with the weight of advancing years and too many desserts, Gerber was in his thirties. Jackson's partner was, in his old Virginia way of saying things, all knees and elbows with a ginger head balanced atop a skinny neck. There was a noticeable disparity between the size of his skull and his slender frame, which was further enhanced in its awkwardness by ears that stuck out like jug handles.

Jackson looked his young partner over, shaking his head. "The old military industrial complex—MIC— conspiracy again?"

Gerber nodded avidly, his serious glare looking out of place above freckled cheeks. Jackson and a few of the older men noted that the kid, by their perspective, was what could have been the love child between two timeless comic-book teenagers. Any mention of Arch or Jugs, however, had gone over Gerber's head, the references eliciting a blank response.

Of course, knowing the history of those comics, Gerber had probably developed a selective memory loss after having been needled over the similarity from other guys in the Navy, especially his instructors.

"Collusion and corruption in those areas do still exist," Gerber replied. "You wouldn't believe the stuff I saw back in the Navy."

"But if you told me, you'd just have to kill me," Jackson concluded, rolling his eyes. The others, eight total, laughed at the end of this particular segment of the "Bernie and Gerb" show. Jackson didn't mind Gerber's constant conspiracy theories, and their seeming Moebius Strip of argument and counterargument added some spice and variety to a job that could end up a drudgery as it devolved into rote observation and paperwork.

"Get the camera, Gerb. Document anything you can find," Jackson ordered. Neither Gerb nor the other cameramen on the inspection teams really needed to be told this, but it was the best way that Jackson knew to turn off his partner's manic running commentary.

While Gerber was normally a motormouth, when he was recording footage of safety violations, he had the steady focus of a laser beam.

That professionalism, as well as Gerber's entertainment value, went a long way to helping Jackson forgive the younger man's many quirks.

Now it was time to go to work.

"BERNIE! BERNIE!" Gerber shouted, his big green eyes wild and wide as he rushed back to Jackson's side. He wondered what could light such a fire under his coworker's ass like that when a sudden bout of stammering answered his unspoken question. Jackson could recognize the symptoms of too many ideas competing to get out of Gerber's mouth. Something that the jug-headed man caught on camera had led him to believe that he had conclusive, documented proof.

"Look! Just look!" Gerber squawked, pushing the LCD screen of the digital camera far too close to Jackson's face. "I knew that the MIC was behind these accidents! Heyerdal is making weapons to provoke a world war!"

Jackson reached out, trying to still the camera so that he could get a better look. "Then let me look at it, dummy!"

Distant laughter from the closest pair of inspectors reached Jackson's ears through the excited chatter and dancing of Gerber. Finally, he was forced to snap the camera out of his partner's hands. "What the hell are you on about, son?"

"They killed workers who had stumbled on that dilapidated old hulk," Gerber exclaimed. "Once those men saw the submarine pens, they had to die, so they wanted to lay proof about sabotage before we got here."

The glow of the liquid crystal display showed the interior of a gutted freighter and small docks low in the water and designed for slender craft less than a quarter of the width of the hulk. They would have gone unnoticed had it not been for all of the recent accidents and the diligence of a young inspector with a head full of ideas. The dead freighter didn't look out of place in a boatyard, as many shipbuilders found that good, extant hulls were a basis for updated craft. However, the footage showed a hull without a keel and small hydraulic doors at the front.

"That *is* damn strange," Jackson muttered. "Especially since Heyerdal doesn't have anything in its records about designing submersibles, just light seacrafts."

"Told you!" Gerber snapped, all excited. "Secret submarines!"

Jackson pinched the skin at the bridge of his nose. Whenever Gerber got a hair up his ass, he was nearly incomprehensible. What a secret berth had to do with a conspiracy involving the government and Heyerdal's deck designs would take forever to straighten out in an intelligible manner. But first he had to calm Gerber down, and right now, unfortunately, the kid had a gallon of adrenaline to burn off before he could make any sense.

"Gerb! Focus!"

"This could be used to sink international ships and draw the U.S. into another stupid, bloated war," Gerber continued. "It's the *Lusitania* all over again!"

"Gerb, they must have had weeks to clear anything out. Why would they even leave that area unlocked for you to stumble upon?" Jackson asked.

Something gave the older man pause.

Their two friends, though they had only been about a hundred feet away, close enough to laugh out loud at Gerber's renewed antics, were now nowhere to be seen. That didn't feel right, and Jackson's scalp tingled as if his close-cropped gray-white hairs were all trying to stand up at once.

"Hey, Jake! Ned! Where'd you two go?"

Gerber's agitation seemed to drain away, as if someone had cut a hole in the bottom of a tub. The call to their coworkers hadn't seemed to calm the young man, but it had silenced him for the moment.

Gerber snatched back his camera and pulled his phone from his pocket. With a device in each hand, Gerber's left thumb flew across the touch screen, his lips moving silently as if quietly narrating his own actions. "This is bad."

"What are you doing?"

Gerber spoke up. "They don't want witnesses." This time his manic energy had disappeared, and his voice was flat and serious. The thrill of discovery had been shocked into submission by the dread of some realization. "Got to get the footage out."

"Because Ned and Jake are probably smoking on government time?" Jackson asked. Even as he spoke the words, he lost faith in his rationalization. Something could have been wrong; he could feel that in the air, even though logic dictated that the deaths or disappearance of ten OSHA inspectors would actually invite even more intense scrutiny to whatever secrets lurked in the boatyard. Such a loss would probably involve the FBI or the Department of Homeland Security, so any top-secret construction projects would simply be uncovered in the wake of foul play. They were simply too high profile to warrant any harm, even by the most desperate businessman intent on concealing his shady dealings.

Submarines? he thought to himself.

Why the hell would that be so important to kill witnesses? Sure, there were cases where companies, if they had failed at bribery, sometimes resorted to violence, but there had been no interaction between the OSHA team and the Heyerdal company. There should at least have been a man at the gate with an envelope full of cash.

As much as he tried to dismiss his fears, Jackson couldn't quiet his nerves. He could sense a predator stalking in the shadows. No one had been allowed through the gate for the past week except for the OSHA team, not even the usual security guards hired to baby-sit the shipyard. He just couldn't shake the feel of being stalked, the weight of malevolence hanging in the air.

"It's out." Gerber sighed with relief. "They can't keep this shit quiet."

"What? Where?" Jackson asked.

"App on my phone and built into the camera. It can read off the memory and then upload it to a backup site," Gerber explained. "Better than the little piece of garbage in the usual cell. This transmits good, crisp images."

"Why?" Jackson continued.

"Safety for us. Keeping my documentation of their secrets kills any incentive for them to do the same to us."

Jackson looked around.

"Kill us? Try to silence us? No go," Gerber said. He let loose a nervous titter. "Their dirt is now in the Cloud.

The whole conspiracy sphere knows and is breathing this all in now."

"Gerb, they wouldn't kill federal inspectors," Jackson countered. His strength ebbed, and he added in a softer, more nervous tone, "Would they?"

The red-haired ex-Navy man pocketed his phone after frowning at its screen. "I wish I had brought my knife."

That was all Gerber had to say for Jackson's sake. The older man brought out his walkie-talkie and keyed it. All he received was static, unfortunately. He tried again, but the radio was working; it just wasn't receiving or transmitting any usable signal.

"Hey! Anyone's walkies still working?" Jackson yelled as he transferred to his own cell. "Ned?"

"All the phones are out, Bernie," Gerber said, deadly serious.

In the distance he could hear spasmodic coughing erupt. A silhouetted form, Jackson couldn't tell who, staggered into view, then clutched his throat and chest, toppling over. Sudden bright flares, vomitous blossoms of flame, erupted throughout the area. Smoke billowed from multiple sources, obscuring the scene as at least two men screamed their last.

"Gerb, you think you can swim?" Jackson asked, his mind racing.

"Hello! Navy submariner!" Gerber replied. He waved to the hulk, where no flames had erupted yet. "Come on!"

Jackson followed blindly, sweeping the boatyard around him for signs of impending death or onrushing danger. He hoped that Gerber, in all of his paranoia, knew what he was doing. The coughing brought to mind choking smoke, but the men appeared to be suffocating even before the flames erupted and thick, strangling clouds spread out to suck the breath from them.

Now all he could see behind him were yellow splashes of glow that burned through black roiling darkness that flowed into the air. Getting to the water was the means to get to safety, a place to duck from the fury of blaze and asphyxiation.

Jackson tabbed his phone again, dialing 9-1-1, but there was still no signal.

It didn't make sense. Only moments before, Gerber had transmitted a call, sending data to the internet. Maybe he'd done that, or now Jackson was hot on the heels of a delusional freak, not a former military man who showed the foresight to upload conspiracy documentation.

Gerber led him to the hull of the dead freighter, and as they passed through a door, Jackson stopped cold. What he saw was something out of a James Bond movie, a wide, empty interior dock with spaces for four submarines, two on each side of the hull, with loading cranes above to supply the subs with their gear. The covered docks were empty now, but there was no other explanation for the catwalks and support equipment inside the empty ship's corpse.

It was crazy.

Or was he just influenced, mentally contaminated by the ravings of his jug-headed friend?

Gerber pointed to the water. "We can dive out through there!"

Jackson followed Gerber, but only visually. His feet had been rooted to the spot thanks to fear and indecision.

That momentary pause extended the OSHA inspector's life and allowed him to see that Gerber was right. The younger man tripped, having snagged a small wire.

A loud hiss erupted immediately, and Gerber folded over, agonized as he passed through what must have been a cloud of poison. Gerber coughed, kicked, gurgled, then his limbs fell still.

Behind Jackson, the boatyard was a blazing inferno, hot flames racing up the gangplank they'd left behind. On instinct, Jackson threw the hatch shut, hoping that the steel would delay the inevitable blast of heat. He then looked back at Gerber, lying twenty yards away, forever stilled by an invisible hand that crushed the life from his lungs.

Jackson looked around. Surely there must have been some other way out. He couldn't sit still forever, but there was an unseen assassin that killed instantly in front of him, or there was the slow, agonizing demise of burning alive behind the hatch, which was swiftly growing warmer, even as he leaned against it.

There was a railing ahead and a twenty-yard drop into the water. Maybe he could make it through the invisible poison gas, swim beneath it and reach the small locks that emptied out into the harbor. Jackson had little else to choose from, so he hurled himself forward, vaulting the rail.

Instead of sailing into the water with grace and speed, an agonizing spasm contorted him in midfall, his lungs feeling as if they had been filled to the brim with hot sauce. He didn't know how much of the gas he'd sucked in, but it didn't matter. His change in pose, midfall, granted him one small mercy.

Dropping twenty yards to the water headfirst, without his hands breaking the surface, resulted in his neck shattering, bones driven deep into his skull.

Instantly dead, Jackson didn't have to worry about drowning or suffocating from the effects of the nerve gas released inside. The waters also would preserve his corpse for a month as the inferno melted steel, rendering the submarine pen an utterly unrecognizable stack of twisted, deformed and charred metal. In the cold waters off Norfolk, Bernie Jackson's lifeless form entered a long sleep, never seeing the light of day until thirty days hence.

NATALIE CHASE COULD ONLY imagine the string of luck that had got her this cruise of the Spanish Canary Islands with some of the most beautiful men she'd ever seen. She ran her fingers through her blond curls, calling attention to her face as the guys walked past. Their eyes were agog with all of the women in bikinis who were out on the deck. There must have been two dozen guys, all of them with washboard abs. Not a single extra chin in the bunch.

The crew of this yacht kept their eyes on everything, the one small hindrance to Natalie's admonition that the way to really pick up people was to go topless, leaving nothing to the imagination. The captain of the yacht was a handsome man, if likely twice Natalie's age of twenty-five. She couldn't tell what kind of body he had under his uniform, but he was tall, square-shouldered, with a disciplined, finely groomed beard and piercing eyes.

He was the most tantalizing item on this oceangoing all-you-can-eat buffet of beefcake. Captain Raul Espinoza was classically Spanish, with dark hair, skin sunburned to a pleasing even tan, and clear, cool blue eyes. He was still virile; the salt and pepper of his beard and hair gave proof to that, in Natalie's eyes.

The young men around her were fit and trim and handsome, but there was an aloofness to Espinoza that made her feel as if she needed to get to him. He didn't have wealth, but he had every ounce of manliness that Natalie could imagine.

There were still the other crew members, swarthy, scruffy, dark-eyed, seeming more as if they belonged in a pirate movie than working on the decks of a miniature cruise ship. They had scars, and hands that looked made more of callus than flesh and bone. Their knuckles were especially distorted, swollen with pads of skin that seemed liked the armor plate on some movie superhero's suit than the result of working on engines and such.

"Come up to the deck," Espinoza said, interrupting Natalie's thoughts. "And this time, it's captain's orders. Everyone topless. No excuses."

Natalie pursed her lips, trying to decide whether she was ready to walk half naked on deck. Espinoza's voice had held the lilt of self-satisfied humor. Could she do it?

Over the past two nights, at least four men had seen the goods, and Natalie knew they hadn't been disappointed.

Captain Espinoza was going to be there, from the sound of things. She could endure the leers of the scraggly, battered-looking pirates if she could present herself to him.

"Comin', Nat?" Derek, one of her recent conquests, asked. His gaze didn't meet her at eye level. He wanted a repeat performance, and Derek, all dimples and bright white smile, would be an absolutely great consolation prize. He had just the right amount of "man pelt" on his upper chest, neither a thick hair shirt nor the smooth, overly waxed self-conscious shiny pectorals. His trail was all but unbroken, from clavicle down into his board shorts.

Natalie nodded.

Derek's smile couldn't have been more obvious if it had been put up in neon.

Natalie reached behind her, undid the string holding her top on and slid out. It was warm, sunny, and the kiss of the sun on her not-yet-tanned tits was something new. Something fun. She could get used to this kind of attention. Natalie wasn't going back to Indiana with a single tan line. That was it.

She got up and spotted something on the water, just past Derek's shoulder. It was everything the yacht they were on was not. It was dirty, grunting out smoke, with rust all along its sides. She could see the nets on it. A fishing boat.

And more sea men, no doubt.

Natalie began to have second thoughts about displaying her wares for not one but two boatloads of men. Derek slid his arm around her waist, his lips brushing her cheek.

"Come on, beautiful. We have a special party to get to," he told her.

Derek's nearness, the strength of his arm holding her around her waist, the smell of his just-washed hair, pulled her worries away from the boat. She gave his muscular shoulder a nibble, and he reciprocated by leaning down for a warm, passionate kiss.

"Time's wasting, beautiful people!" Espinoza announced once more.

The two jogged toward the deck.

There, Espinoza stood on a railing overlooking the party deck. All fifty of the passengers were here, and Natalie hadn't seen such a collection of smooth, unlined faces, flowing hair and tanned skin in her life. There were more than a few with pale patches where they had avoided going topless, as well, but in those same faces, she saw the giddy excitement of an experiment with sexual freedom and the dismissal of traditional bans on nudity. One girl looked as if she were a sneeze away from ripping off the thong that covered the few inches of her flesh that weren't exposed.

"Ladies and gentlemen, I welcome you to our ship," Espinoza said. He began to unbutton his jacket, sliding out of it. The rest of the bridge crew was there. They were younger and in fairly good shape, as well, though as they peeled out of their shirts Natalie could make out the scar tissue on each of them. Captain Espinoza was especially marked up, but that only made him even more interesting. He had lived a life of danger and peril, and her imagination ran away with her…. The brave, blue-eyed captain risking life and limb, battling smugglers and rescuing half-nude maidens from wicked pirates, bringing them to the safety of his bed and the warmth of his strong arms….

"You think that you are quite lucky to be on board this ship," Espinoza said. "But you each have been chosen to come here for one specific purpose."

Natalie watched him, but lost herself more in his chest, broad, with salt-and-pepper hair where scars didn't leave bare patches. He was muscled, but not overly so. Lean and tall, he had lived a life of activity, showing in how he was tightly built without taking on the obscene distortions of a bodybuilder.

He took out a small nylon pouch and began handing out syringes to his bridge crew. He pushed the needle into his pectoral muscle and squeezed the bulb. There was a slight grunt of discomfort, and then he resumed talking.

"We needed your identifications, your luggage, your general appearances," Espinoza said.

Natalie looked to the fishing boat, growing ever closer. There were women on the deck of that ship, as well as men.

"This was an excuse to get you all together in one spot, with a minimum of cleanup," Espinoza said.

Suddenly people to Natalie's right began coughing, jerking spasmodically. The wave of those falling ill spread quickly through the crowd. Natalie took a frightened breath, then she lost control of her hands and arms. Her head snapped upright and she could feel her teeth tear open her tongue as her jaws clenched violently shut like a bear trap. Blood and froth oozed over her lips as her legs gave way and she slumped to the deck. Derek was beside her, vibrating as if he were some child's doll malfunctioning. The only signs that he was even alive were the spurts of blood through his nose, broken as he'd fallen onto his face, as his lungs tried to suck in fresh breath.

Vomit burst from Natalie's stomach, and she felt her bladder release, as well.

"The Sendero Luminoso thanks you for the donation of your lives," Espinoza's voice echoed in her ears. "We promise to use them well, you spoiled little children."

Natalie winced, reaching up as Espinoza glared down at her. Her specifically. Those blue, cool eyes she'd once lost herself in were now cold, hard, angry.

Darkness settled on the girl as the nerve gas finally took full effect.

Minutes later, gloved hands would hoist her over the rail, dropping her and the other young murder victims onto the ocean floor.

CHAPTER ONE

One month later

The cold waters of the harbor beyond the boatyard looked inhospitable to Hermann Schwarz as he walked through the wreckage of what used to be the Heyerdal Hull Company. A month ago, this place had been torched in an act of terrorism by a radical antiwar group. The incident had been investigated thoroughly by the NCIS and Norfolk police and fire departments due to the nature of Heyerdal's naval contracts and the extensive fire damage. Someone with a lot of skill had torched the facility, incinerating what hulls remained and leaving bodies almost completely unrecognizable in the conflagration.

Schwarz was here with his Able Team partners, Carl Lyons and Rosario Blancanales, and together the three of them were looking for connections. Across the Atlantic, thousands of miles due east, the Canary Islands were experiencing one of the most unusual hostage crisis situations the world had ever seen.

La Palma was one of a scattered assembly of volcanic islands that formed the Spanish Canaries, a dot in the Atlantic that was home to eighty thousand souls and a tourist destination for millions more. It also, strangely enough, was the lynchpin in a white paper about a mega-tsunami that would devastate the East Coast of the United States, as well as the British Isles, Spain, Portugal and potentially the nations ringing the Mediterranean.

Because Heyerdal had been owned by the Jeopardy Corporation, which had also sponsored the white paper, it was a slim lead for Stony Man Farm and its efforts to suss out the situation. While the world's eyes were locked on a vacation paradise under siege by madmen, the men of Able Team were looking for a handle on why La Palma was the focus of such interest.

Schwarz cast around, realizing that something was wrong but unable to put his finger on it. There was wreckage extending out into the water, the most spectacular of which was a gutted freighter that had been devastated by fire. He kept being drawn back to this, and noted that Carl Lyons, a former Los Angeles P.D. cop, also was focused on the strange vibe.

Schwarz was as comfortable with the metaphysical as he was with the very solid and real world of electronics and computer systems, and one of the things he strongly believed was that the human mind was attuned to pick up data that was outside of the realm of the five ordinary senses. He had been present when Lyons spoke of "the feel" of a crime scene. This was before the popularization of forensic psychology, and Schwarz had always been certain of some more-than-standard instincts displayed by his partners.

"What do you have, Ironman?" Schwarz asked.

Carl "Ironman" Lyons, the leader of Able Team, remained still, his gaze focused on the gutted hulk. "What did they say was in here?"

"Wreckage. It was gutted by the fire," Schwarz explained. "But you already knew that. You went over the files three times on the trip over here."

Lyons nodded, his face a grim mask.

"And you're wondering why someone would start a fire inside a hulk like that?" Schwarz asked.

Again the silent nod of agreement.

"They only found nine of the OSHA team, too," Schwarz said.

Lyons looked at a temporary gangplank that had been erected for investigators to look within the wreckage. Schwarz followed him up and overlooked the carnage within. Plenty of high-definition images had been taken of the madness left over from the arson inferno.

"Did they bring in divers?" Lyons asked.

"I'm not going to be Watson to your Holmes, homes," Schwarz quipped. "They moved in as far as they could under the docks, but the wreckage made it impossible to get inside the hull here."

"And they didn't drop anyone down into the water here," Lyons muttered, looking through the doorway. There was no latticework left to stand on, though he could see a small shelf where one of the bodies had been recovered. The flames had been insanely hot, yet there remained a small bit of surviving human tissue, carbonized, that could mark the OSHA inspector's corpse.

"Underwater metal. Not a safe place to go high diving," Schwarz returned.

Lyons nodded. He stared at the lifeless, black reflective pool beneath. Schwarz didn't like the intensity of his friend's focus.

"I said…" Schwarz started, his voice rising.

That didn't stop Lyons. He took one step through the door and plummeted into the water below.

Schwarz reached out, his throat tight as his friend splashed down, twenty yards below. A sixty-foot drop was something that was akin to making the same jump sixty feet to concrete. The standard limit for Olympic-class diving was off a ten-meter board, and while the record was 172 feet documented, he didn't believe that Lyons had the kind of training for that, not when he was jumping into a tangle of twisted metal. For a ten-meter dive, the FINA—Fédération Internationale de Natation—recommendation was four and a half to five meters of depth to allow for a glide to a halt.

Lyons went in feetfirst, as far as he could tell. Maybe that would help.

"Carl!" Schwarz called after him.

Lyons's head, blond hair matted dark brown against his scalp after his dunking, broke the surface and he spit out water.

"Come on in, Gadgets," Lyons returned. "Better yet, go get a rope."

"You are a complete freak, Carl," Schwarz snapped. It took him ten minutes to locate some rope, by which time Rosario "Pol" Blancanales, the third member of the team, had joined him. Blancanales didn't seem surprised in the least that their leader had done something as stupid as Schwarz claimed. Lyons didn't think he was indestructible, but he also knew that sometimes you had to push your limits to accomplish a task.

"Brought two spools, in case you found the tenth body," Blancanales called down.

Lyons nodded. "Toss down that rope first, then anchor it. I'll help with bearing that weight."

"We'll need a tarp. He's been down there for thirty days," Schwarz mused.

"It's not pretty," Lyons said. He held something up. It was small, metallic and red. "Got a present for you."

"Think it'll work after a month in the drink?" Blancanales asked. "In salt water?"

"Depending on how secure the SIM card was, I could recover data from it," Schwarz returned. "All depending. I've got a reader in my Combat PDA. We all do."

Lyons surfaced once more, and both men could see that he'd tied an x-harness around the shoulders of a dead man, his skin shriveled, body seeming like a mummified prune. He then waved for the next rope.

With that, Lyons was back up after a minute of climbing the knotted line.

"How did you know you'd be all right down there?" Blancanales asked, helping their drenched partner to the top of the gangplank.

"I had my combat boots on. Reinforced ankles designed for parachuting, so I figured that if I hit anything feetfirst, the boots would at least keep my feet and shins from exploding before I flexed," Lyons answered. "Wouldn't have been something a dive crew leader would authorize…"

"You do realize that your health insurance, in that

case, would have been a 9 mm slug through the head, right?" Schwarz asked.

Lyons shrugged, then produced the cell phone from his pocket. "Here you go, Gadgets."

Blancanales set off to obtain a tarp for the body of the OSHA agent.

Blancanales's jog slowed, though. A sudden deceleration that was all the warning Schwarz and Lyons would need.

An instant later the two men hurled themselves down the gangplank, diving for cover as a stream of automatic gunfire ripped the side of the incinerated hulk.

Able Team had arrived and had only incidentally recovered potential evidence of what had happened during the firebombing here at the boatyard. But now, when a shadowy group of assassins opened fire, their original plan had succeeded. Acting as nosy investigators, they had drawn conspirators out of the woodwork, conspirators who might actually have information about the deadly group who had seized control of an entire island.

Now all they had to do was to survive the hard contact.

CARL LYONS DIVED INTO a shoulder roll, bullets zipping past him. The assassins were firing high because they'd started shooting when he and Hermann Schwarz were at the very top of the gangplank, and never got a chance to catch up. As it was summer, he and his allies had been clad for the warm Virginia weather, alleviated slightly by being on the Norfolk waterfront where boatyards caught the cool breezes off the Atlantic.

Unfortunately such warmth restricted the amount of firepower each could carry beneath their windbreakers that had been emblazoned with the letters DOJ in deference to their cover as Justice Department deputies following up on an arson investigation. The size of their weaponry was limited to enticing whatever death squad was on hand into believing they had the upper hand, an overwhelming advantage.

It was a Hail Mary strategy, a blind toss accompanied by a wild prayer, and it was one that Able Team had not only grown used to, but had also perfected. As such, they had come fully prepared for a war.

As much as the trio would have loved to have kept full-blown assault rifles and rocket launchers on hand, they needed to lull the conspirators behind the Norfolk arson into believing that they were ripe and easy targets, armed with nothing more than the standard Glock 22s issued to federal service deputies. The choices in that regard could be limited, if Able Team hadn't had the services of John "Cowboy" Kissinger, one of the world's best weapon smiths.

As Lyons, Schwarz and Blancanales reached their cover, the three partners made a quick visual verification that the team was whole and unharmed.

"No hits?" Lyons asked.

"Nope," Blancanales returned. Schwarz simply grunted agreement.

"Not even on the body armor, not that we'd have been able to handle it. Those are five-five-six they're pumping out," Schwarz added. "They missed, but now they know how quick we are."

"So we go sneaky," Lyons returned, unleathering the machine pistol stored in a shoulder holster under his windbreaker. Long ago, Able Team had learned the benefits of carrying fully automatic handguns with folding foregrips for better control and utility. In the early days, these had been Beretta 93-R machine pistols. Now they opted for the Heckler and Koch MP-7. The bonus of the compact machine pistol was the fact that it not only had a vertical foregrip that could be folded to fit in a shoulder holster, but it also had an extendable stock to give it riflelike stability. Lyons wasn't much of a fan of the MP-7's 4.6 mm projectiles, but they moved at a blistering, Kevlar-defeating velocity and were still bigger than the rounds of a Heckler and Koch G-11 autorifle, which was much larger and bulkier

The three Stony Man warriors snapped out the collapsing shoulder stocks, folding down the forward grips. The folding iron sights were propped into place so that they resembled the precision sights of the M-4s and M-16s they normally utilized. As they did so, the team shifted among the wreckage of the arson-gutted boatyard, seeking better cover and concealment, even as enemy rifles crackled, trying to pin them down.

"These bastards are getting on my nerves," Blancanales snarled as a spray of debris splashed against him from the impact of a dozen 5.56 mm rounds. "Especially since this seems like amateur hour."

Lyons and Schwarz heard their partner over the hands-free communicators that they wore. Lyons spoke into his throat mike. "Confirm...low training?"

"I'm still here, and I've given them two clean shots at me," Blancanales replied. "Do the math."

"No fair, Pol," Schwarz interrupted. "Ironman can barely do math in a classroom, let alone when he's getting shot at."

Lyons flipped off Schwarz. "All right. New plan."

"Fall back and kill?" Blancanales asked over the headset.

"No. Just cover me," Lyons said. He handed his machine pistol over to Schwarz.

"Bluejay," Schwarz muttered.

Lyons pulled out one of his handguns, a Smith and Wesson .45, and held it between his thumb and forefinger. "Stop! Stop shooting!"

His voice was shrill, terrified. It was a completely alien sound compared to all that the other two members of Able Team had heard before, but this was completely new to the men trying to shoot at them.

"I'm just an accountant! Stop shooting!"

"Throw your gun out!" one of the shooters shouted in response.

"Paper jockey!" Schwarz snarled out loud. He waylaid his MP-7 and fired his pistol, intentionally missing Lyons, but that elicited a wave of precision covering fire immediately.

Lyons tossed the Smith and Wesson on the ground, without a care, just like an inept desk worker would. He stumbled out into the open, arms wavering in the air, his eyes cast downward.

The Bluejay ploy was a simple one. One member of the team would feign injury or incompetence to call the attention of the enemy away from the others. So far, the three of them were aware that their opponents were only pretending incompetence on their own. Lyons's use of himself as bait had not drawn enemy fire because they had some other agenda. When the prisoner that offered himself had come under fire from Schwarz, their precision shot up to deadly levels of effect.

Whoever these conspirators were, they were sharp and alert, but they were also curious about the trio of men who stumbled around the boatyard in Norfolk. That meant that they wanted and needed answers. If Lyons could get close, he might have a chance to take one while they were still in prisoner-acquisition mode.

And if not, well, Lyons still had his Smith and Wesson .357 Magnum in its shoulder holster. Lyons was an old-school LAPD officer, and his side arm had been a grandfathered revolver, either a Colt Python or its Smith and Wesson counterpart. Sure, the Colt 1911 had a lighter trigger and a faster reload, and it sat flatter beneath his concealment garments, but Lyons had a trigger finger that was trained for fast and deadly double-action revolver shooting. This wasn't just any .357 Magnum, either, it was a Military and Police R8. It not only had the unusual five-inch, Picatinny-railed barrel, but it also was fed from an eight-round cylinder—matching the capacity of a 1911, but not the .45 auto he'd discarded, and was rendered portable by an alloy frame.

Recoil in rapid-fire with his preferred 125-grain jacketed hollowpoints was quite easy, thanks to a set of rubber finger-grooved grips and "enough" mass. Lyons could draw and fire the R8, a name referring to its being an 8-shot revolver, and put all eight hits inside of a playing card at fifteen feet, or hit four different targets twice in the space of five seconds.

It still wouldn't help much if he were directly under the gun, but Able's version of the Bluejay ploy counted on a full team effort.

Right now, Lyons could tell that there were three sets of sights on him directly, but judging by the hail of fire that started this off, the rest were pretty well out of his line of sight, at least since his hands were up.

Fortunately for him, he had two highly trained combat veterans on his side, and thanks to his earpiece, he was picking up the pings from their laser "painters," which gave him a relative range and position for each of the enemy crew.

There were nine of them, three for each team member, at least those who were in sight. Lyons figured on at least two more drivers, plus security guns for their vehicles. His best guess put thirteen against them. It wasn't the worst that Able Team had faced, but if this death squad was worth its salt, Lyons was in for one hell of a fight and he was going to start it standing out in the open.

"Who the hell are you?" the commando who had addressed him previously snarled.

Lyons kept his hands up at the level of his ears, his face wrinkled and masked in fear. He could only imagine the ribbing that he would receive later from his partners about his acting. That didn't matter. Lyons simply had to confuse the enemy for a few more moments, not win an award for best actor.

"I'm just an accountant, I told you that already! Please just let me go."

In the open, Lyons could better make out the uniforms of the gunmen and the gear they were packing. The man who was talking to him wore a dull, nonreflective helmet with bullet-resistant wraparound goggles. So clad, he was relatively safe from a head shot. The rifleman's torso and shoulders were no less vulnerable, polycarbide shells shielding his shoulder joints and the heavy load-bearing vest betraying its built-in trauma plates. Whoever had sent these men to ensure that the Norfolk boatyard's secrets remain buried beneath ash and submerged in the cold waters of the harbor was not taking any chances by sending the killers in with secondhand weapons and armor.

Blancanales's voice hissed through the earpiece of Lyons's hands-free communicator. "All right, Ironman, we've got the measure of these assholes. It's all up to you. Give us the signal and we mop these idiots off the deck."

Lyons simply nodded, maintaining his facade of fear. Thanks to the observations of Schwarz and Blancanales, he had a good idea of where the enemy had set themselves up. Right now he knew that there were two killers just out of his line of sight but in position to pop up and riddle him with bullets. However, since they had been sighted by his partners, they were far less of a threat simply because either Blancanales or Schwarz already had them targeted. The hidden gunmen were only a secondary threat compared to the grim, armored figure who was already addressing him.

This was going to have to be done the old-fashioned way. "My arms are getting tired, can I put them down please?" Lyons whimpered as he spoke.

"I don't want any funny business from you, motherfucker," the cleanup crew killer snarled in warning. He didn't lower the muzzle of his rifle, a SIG 556 folding-stock assault rifle. Lyons knew that his body armor couldn't take a point-blank volley from the killer; Kevlar might just as well have been gossamer for all the good it would do him. "Leave your damn mitts in the air."

Lyons noticed a jutting steel I-beam that had the mass and durability to deflect the storm of rifle fire, and it was just within a few yards of his position. Just to be certain, Lyons mentally measured the distance once more, and then with an explosion of power he leaped into the shadow of the I-beam. Even as he dived for cover he clawed the N-frame .357 Magnum from its hidden holster. The enemy commando opened up with his SIG, but Lyons was no longer where the muzzle of the weapon was pointing as he pulled the trigger. A swarm of buzzing hornets whipped through the air, close enough that one of the bullets plucked at the sleeve of his windbreaker. Regardless of how close the enemy's fire had come to ending his life, Lyons was shielded and down once again.

From his right, Schwarz and his MP-7 entered the fight, the little machine pistol's 4.6 mm bullets zipping to catch one of the ambushers in the back of his head. The gunman's helmet deflected much of the glancing burst, but the single projectile hit dead-on, its reinforced point punching through the Kevlar helmet and into the skull of the would-be murderer. An explosion of skull fragments, glass and spongy dollops of brain matter sprayed to the air close enough to Lyons that it peppered the left shoulder of his windbreaker.

Lyons didn't mind brain stains on the Department of Justice windbreaker. He was far more concerned with the rifleman who was trying to burn him out of cover with extended bursts from an assault rifle. Lyons must have annoyed the killer because he had abandoned fire discipline and was shooting without regard for how much ammo he had in the weapon. In only a few seconds the sniper would run out, and once there was a lull in the firing, Lyons was poised to make his move.

The enemy rifle went silent and Lyons could hear a muffled curse coming from the angry commando. Too late the shooter realized his error and was torn between fumbling a new magazine into the weapon and ducking behind cover himself. That pause allowed Lyons the time he needed to whip around the I-beam, center the front sight of his Magnum on his enemy's goggles and milk the trigger of the revolver. Punching out of the barrel at over 1500 feet per second, Lyons's shot smashed into the tough ballistic glass of the killer's eyewear, breaking through it and crushing the forehead beneath.

From Lyons's left, Blancanales had already entered the battle with a quieter opening gambit. The wily old Able Team warrior had fast-balled a fragmentation grenade hard enough at the head of the third assailant that it popped straight up into the air over the dazed gunman. As the handheld bomb reached the apex of its bounce, it exploded. A sheet of fire and shrapnel rained down, scything into the helmet and shoulder armor of the man. Heavily protected, the gunner was unharmed by the fragments thrown off by the grenade, but the pressure wave struck him like a baseball bat and even the protection of his helmet couldn't keep him from staggering dazedly into the open.

Blancanales hated that he had to be so ruthless toward the stunned foe, but the armored assassin still had a firm grip on his weapon and would recover his senses within a few moments. Taking aim, Blancanales opened fire and peppered the gunman's chest with a full-auto salvo. While the action was tactically sound, despite its ruthlessness, Blancanales was not being unnecessarily cruel. He was simply stopping a would-be killer from continuing to target federal investigators.

Just because Able Team was undercover as Department of Justice employees didn't mean that they weren't actual Feds. This was as much self-defense as rooting out the truth behind who initiated the assassinations of the OSHA investigators. Nine innocent men, all unarmed, had died by fire to keep a secret here in the Norfolk boatyard.

Clearly the shooters who had arrived and immediately opened fire were not police officers. Furthermore they would definitely know what was going on and who had likely been behind the others' deaths.

Blancanales held off moving on to another target, keeping cover between himself and the other gunmen. These shooters were wearing armor, so he waited to be sure that the 4.6 mm bullets from his machine pistol had been able to punch through to his enemy's vitals.

It turned out that Blancanales had made the right choice, because the staggered killer scrambled back to his feet a second time, but he wasn't standing still to be the target for further full-auto hammering. Even as the gunman retreated, two more riflemen opened up, their rifles chattering and pelting the hunk of rubble that Blancanales used as a shield. Unfortunately for them, they missed, bullets smashing against mass too dense for their 5.56 mm rounds to penetrate, and Blancanales had mapped out a line of retreat in case he was attacked from that vector.

Blancanales paused just enough to unclip another of his grenades from a small fanny pack. He plucked the cotter pin and released the spoon, igniting the blaster's fuse before hurling it toward the rattle of enemy weapons. There was a brief pause in the shooting, accompanied by an almost comical cry of "Shit!"

The humor of the moment was punctuated by the earth-shattering roar of the grenade's detonation, body parts spiraling away from the source of the well-placed blast. A distant explosion hadn't been able to shred through a steel helmet and trauma plates, but the enemy commandos didn't have that kind of hard shell on their legs. Even if they did, a sheet of kinetic force severed the limbs where the joints in the armor were weakest.

"We're hoping to get one or two alive, remember," Schwarz said grimly.

"Acknowledged," Blancanales replied. "Let's hope they have the same orders."

The stunned and wounded gunner, having survived two attempts at putting him down, became Blancanales's focus. He was leaving a blood trail, which meant at least one of the prior attacks had caused him injury. Once hurt, he'd be easier to take down.

With his target in sight, Blancanales rushed forward, keeping out of the fields of fire of the enemy gunners, zagging toward the downed commando. He reloaded the MP-7 on the run, the magazine-in-grip design making it easier for his left hand to find the well that his right was wrapped around. It was so easy he could do it blindfolded, and since he hadn't run the SMG into slide-lock, he knew he had a round chambered.

A gunman edged into the open in front of the wily veteran commando, looking to cover his fallen friend. He also happened to have a device that was decidedly not an assault weapon in his hands. Blancanales only barely had a few instants of warning before he dived beneath the twin barbs of an underbarrel-mounted Taser. The wires fell across his shoulders, but as they were insulated to contain the voltage that had been directed toward whatever had been stuck by the pair of darts, the charge in the slender threads was impotent against him.

That couldn't be said for the weapon atop the Taser, an M-4 assault rifle. The killer figured that if he couldn't take Blancanales as a prisoner, then he'd simply open fire and remove him as a threat. Blancanales didn't sit still for this, however. He rolled onto his back, getting himself out of the path of the initial burst of rifle fire, triggering the H&K MP-7 at the man's shins. The 4.6 mm bullets didn't contain a lot of mass, but as they were composed of dense slugs launched at more than 2400 feet per second, they struck the enemy gunner hard, splintering bone and muscle everywhere between his knees and ankles.

Without the ability to stand, the gunman collapsed onto his stunned friend, going from rescuer to restraint.

"Ironman!" Blancanales called. "Cover me! Two prisoners at four o'clock."

Lyons would know that Blancanales would always put his position at two hours fast; it was one way that Able Team was able to engage in out-loud communication of their location without actually betraying where they actually were in relation to each other. Lyons opened up with his big .357 Magnum, firing three shots rapid-fire, drawing heat away from his partner even as his rounds tagged an enemy in his body armor. Trauma plates deflected the more lethal portion of Lyons's salvo, but it was enough to convince the gunman to retreat back behind cover.

Lyons grimaced as he snapped open the cylinder, ejecting his spent brass and feeding in a special 8-round .357 Magnum speed-loader. The gun was back in action in two seconds, but before he left cover, Schwarz was at his side, handing him the MP-7 he'd ceded earlier.

"We don't need to use kid gloves anymore. Punch through the armor and finish this fight," Schwarz said.

Lyons smirked. "Never would have thought of that myself."

He snapped open the stock and folded down the fore-grip on the machine pistol. A 20-round magazine sat flush with the bottom of the grip, so he dumped it and slid home a 40-rounder. "What's the estimate on how many left?"

Schwarz scanned around. "Three here, but there are still the drivers and vehicle security who could be coming in as backup."

"That's why you dropped off my MP-7," Lyons said.

"Gonna head them off," Schwarz said.

With that, the electronics genius disappeared from sight. Whatever the brilliant Schwarz had in mind, it would be explosive and deadly.

"They secure?" Lyons asked Blancanales through his headset.

"Roger that."

"Keep your head down, too," Lyons ordered.

With that, he lobbed a pair of flash-bang grenades in the direction of the enemy's fire. They had split up, two in one group with a long gunner trying to flank. Lyons knew that he wouldn't have much of an opportunity, even with the blinding and deafening force of the twin shock bombs. The headgear they wore would mitigate much of the force, but Lyons's throws had been true. He was counting on a close-range burst of light and sound to buy him a few seconds.

He was up and firing, catching a fleeting touch of the bang. The two gunners he'd targeted as one clump were staggered where they stood, and Lyons poured on the heat from his machine pistol. The 40-round magazine disappeared in the space of seconds, but the Able Team commander had found every weak point in his opponents' armor, punching bullets deep into their vitals. The lifeless men dropped their weapons, slumping to the ground.

As they fell, the last of the gunners was recovering from the concussion grenade that had rocked him. That mercenary was on Lyons's flank, right in his blind spot. With a clear shot and no other enemies in sight, the rifleman took an extra moment to line up on the "vulnerable" Lyons when the thunder and bellow of Blancanales's Smith and Wesson .45 erupted from ground level.

The shooter dropped his weapon as two 230-grain slugs struck him in one hip, shattering bone and snapping his pelvis. The twin slugs mushroomed on impact, going from just under half of an inch to a full three quarters of an inch of blossomed lead and copper. The duo of hammer blows tore an ugly, brutal channel through the gunman's groin, breaking his other hip on the way out.

Paralyzed, he collapsed, almost face-to-face with the prone Blancanales.

One more stroke of the trigger, and the ambusher's face disappeared, imploding under the thunderous impact of a third .45-caliber round.

Lyons knew that Blancanales had a line of sight on the last of the gunmen, having dealt with the men he'd take prisoner before backing him up.

In the distance, the unmistakable roar of plastic explosives split the air.

"You done there?" Lyons asked Schwarz via the headset.

"Grab a prisoner and rendezvous," Schwarz answered. "We toss our guys into the back of our van, and Pol drives it to the safe house. We grab the other vehicles and bring them in and rip them apart for forensic evidence."

"Sirens," Blancanales said. "We made a hell of a lot of noise."

"Grab one of these fools and let's go," Lyons suggested. "Hopefully the Farm's screwing with police communications so we have a route out of here."

"If so, good. If not, I'll cut us a path without hurting any cops," Blancanales replied.

"I'm counting on that."

With that, Able Team rushed away from the Norfolk boatyard, prisoners in tow. They were gone with only seconds to spare when the police arrived, looking upon the carnage wrought by their explosive presence.

In the upcoming days, the Norfolk Police and the Naval Criminal Investigative Service would wonder what caused this brutal spat of violence, but would soon be distracted by yet more violence. Able Team was on the case, and they were up against a deadly conspiracy that was bringing far more to the fight than just guns.

CHAPTER TWO

Calvin James and Rafael Encizo checked over the scuba kits of the three partners, David McCarter, Gary Manning and T. J. Hawkins, even as the silo the five men stood within filled with seawater up to their knees. James was a scuba expert thanks to Navy SEAL training, while a lifetime of maritime salvage employment had honed Encizo into a master diver. As such, they took it upon themselves to perform safety checks on the rest of the team's equipment. It was almost paranoid the way that they double-checked their partner's preparations, but neither man wanted to take a chance with the lives of their dearest friends.

"All right, Mom!" T. J. Hawkins quipped as James manhandled his scuba tank. "If you fuss any more over me, I'll miss the damn bus and you'll have to drive me to school yourself."

"Language, motherfucker!" James snapped back. "I'll wash your fucking mouth out with soap."

This back-and-forth solicited chuckles from the others even as they clamped the nozzles of their bubble lists' self-contained breathing systems between their teeth. The packs that the five men wore were larger than standard scuba gear, but the extra bulk would prove to be worth its weight. Not only would the scrubber chamber in the system recycle their air, allowing for nearly limitless time under water, but the lack of bubbles would also lower their profile, making any approach from beneath the waves even stealthier. Under water, the extra mass would be less of a burden. Any additional effort would be further alleviated by the Swimmer Delivery Vehicle or SDV, an underwater equivalent of a convertible sports car meant for cutting through the depths with the "top down" at a speed far faster than any man could swim.

The silo was full of water now, and the pressure inside was equal to that outside of the submarine, making it easier to open the hatch and less of a shock when the five men exited the nuke sub to reach the SDV. The undersea craft from the U.S. Navy had brought them close to the hospitable island of La Palma, one of the most popular tourist spots in the Spanish Canary Islands. The sub had powered across the Atlantic at its maximum speed after picking up the members of Phoenix Force when they had been transferred from a helicopter launched from an aircraft carrier just off the coast of Virginia.

For now the rest of the United States Navy was still organizing an emergency blockade around the vacation spot besieged by terrorists. Both the United States Marine Corps and U.S. Navy SEALs were on full alert and ready to engage in hostage rescue, but were held at bay by the threat of deadly charges set in volcanic fissures on the caldera that made up the heart of the island. Local hotels were also packed with thousands of captive tourists rigged to explode. In the White House, the President knew that any conventional military intervention would result in lost lives, and the same threat stayed the hands of British and Spanish amphibious forces. Fortunately for the President of the United States, he was aware of the one group capable of being able to move in quietly, with all the training and flexibility to overcome even insane odds. That was the agency known as the Sensitive Operations Group, a top-secret facility stationed at Stony Man Farm, which boasted one of the most incredible cybertechnology information-gathering services in the world and two of the most elite combat teams ever to engage in warfare—Able Team and Phoenix Force.

The five Phoenix Force operatives swam to their stealth sled. The fifteen-foot-long craft looked like a torpedo whose center had been peeled open. The two aquatic jet engines were contained in the belly of the SDV, which could push through the depths at upwards of twenty-five knots. Because of that relative speed, a huge nosecone and windshield were in place to keep the water from pushing on the riders with great force. Ordinarily the SDV was meant for Navy SEAL commandos, so James and Encizo had stowed their armaments in purpose-built compartments on the vehicle. Both Phoenix Force divers were already familiar with the controls and operation of the SDV.

The La Palma terrorists had warned that if any covert-operations teams were sighted on the island, and harmed any member of their force, the hotel jammed with upward of one thousand frightened tourists would be demolished.

Phoenix Force needed to plan their infiltration with extreme care. Though they brought with them suppressed submachine guns for later use, when hard contact was unavoidable, their most important weapons would be Manning's air rifle, an assortment of knives and impact weapons and a pair of Barnett commando crossbows. Of these so-called silent weapons, Manning's air rifle was the quietest. Unless they had disarmed the explosives threatening the tourists, any gunfight would be the absolute last resort. The darts fired from Manning's air rifle were loaded with Thorazine, which would almost instantly put an enemy to sleep. This would allow them to have live prisoners to interrogate. However, if things tended toward a worsening situation, Manning also had a supply of deadly poison darts.

James slid behind the controls of the SDV, and with a jolt the impulse jets kicked in.

Gary Manning, due to his expertise in demolitions and engineering, had been among the group of Stony Man geniuses who had run equations regarding the consequences of a detonation. The other members of the scientific team had included Hermann Schwarz, Aaron Kurtzman, the Farm's cyberteam leader, and several other Stony Man Farm experts. Every physics simulation, every math equation and every program told the same story. A detonation in the right spot along the cliffs making up the outer ring of the volcanic caldera would create a mammoth landslide, which would drop into the Atlantic with more than enough force and momentum to unleash a hemisphere-wide seismic event.

Coastal cities would be flooded as far inland as fifteen miles, and any harbor facilities would be destroyed beyond repair.

During the 2011 earthquake in Japan, the world had seen the raw, unmitigated power of the tsunami against the modern coastline. Entire towns and cities had been carved from the land, either bulldozed miles inland or sucked into the Pacific. The tsunami that would be unleashed by the landslide in La Palma would be like that, except that it would stretch to England, Spain and Portugal, and from Maine to Florida. It would be the tragedy of Japan multiplied many times with no fewer than twenty-two million estimated casualties in the United States and Canada alone.

The terrorists hadn't said what they wanted in concrete terms, just the hell that would be unleashed if a rescue attempt was initiated for the hostages. The tidal-wave plan had been discovered by Stony Man Farm only after hours of intensive search to identify the island's tactical or strategic value. Nothing else could have motivated such a hostile takeover.

All of this data had come in the form of a white paper that postulated the deadly tsunami. Written by the Jeopardy Corporation, the paper was discovered by Hal Brognola, the Farm's director and White House liaison. Brognola had the job of giving the President the vital news about the actual purpose behind the takeover. Now, the leader of the free world faced two problems, balancing the lives of thousands of tourists, many of them American, against the lives of millions of Europeans and billions of dollars of infrastructure that would be damaged. Either way the blow delivered would be catastrophic.

The Man couldn't choose to let either the hostages or the nation come to harm, so he had turned to the Sensitive Operations Group based at the Stony Man Farm. Led by Brognola, the counterterrorism teams could strike around the globe, neutralizing threats to the entire Free World.

PHOENIX FORCE RODE their SDV beneath the waves, heading into the jaws of death. Their counterparts, Able Team, were back in the United States checking the damage wrought upon the Jeopardy Corporation by an unknown force, most likely the same one that was at work at La Palma.

As the SDV powered toward the hostage island, James kept it low, close to the ocean floor to avoid being seen on sonar. They were at a depth so that even the noon sun was dimmed to the point where it was like dusk. They needed headlights, but were able to use them unseen from the surface due to the massive water above them. The Phoenix Force warriors were watching for signs of other undersea craft or magnetic antiship mines when they saw the grisly collection of figures on the seabed.

James and Encizo knew that the corpses hadn't been down here very long as there was still tissue on their bodies. Meat, especially carrion, on the ocean floor often ended up in the bellies of crustaceans or fish. Indeed, the lifeless bodies were identifiable as men or women.

The estimation of the time that the bodies had been down here was undermined by the stilled forms of crabs and small fish scattered around the bodies. The corpses had nibbles, small bites in them, but once it was learned that others who ate from the carrion died instantly, the rest of the undersea scavengers avoided the deadly meals.

This was an ominous indication of how the poor souls had died. Somewhere, likely while they had been moored on tranquil waters just above their current position, the collection of dead had been afflicted by nerve gas, most likely a type that was absorbed through skin. The deadly toxins would make the corpses a lethal last meal for the carrion eaters who normally seized upon fresh flesh drifting to the bottom.

McCarter tapped James on the shoulder, then pushed himself from his seat. James grimaced, teeth clenched around his mouth gauge. The rules of extravehicular activity on the SDV had been decided beforehand, and first among them was that no more than one diver would be apart from the sled at a time. This was a just-in-case policy, something that would reduce the risks to the Phoenix Force swimmers. McCarter's lone probe into the strewed corpses and poisoned sea life could only be supported by the swivel lamp mounted next to Encizo.

The only consolation that James had was that the SDV could linger, thanks to the oxygen recycling in the bubble-less systems.

McCarter was able to make out more detail as he swam closer to the dead. He could tell that they were all relatively young, in their twenties and thirties, and to a body, none of them wore a stitch of clothing above their waists. In life, they must have been fit, beautiful, though the cold waters had lent a bloated complexion to each of them as he took images with his underwater digital camera. He was also able to peg their nationalities as predominantly American, mostly thanks to the fact that the men wore "board shorts," surfing wear that was loose, airy and comfortable, as opposed to the European preference for tighter, more revealing swimwear.

The dead had also come from a private cruise, since the women were all topless, yet with American males. It had been a party among friends, where the girls had felt confident enough and comfortable in baring their breasts to one and all. That hadn't kept them from showing some modesty as several had gossamer-thin wraps tied around their waists.

McCarter grunted, feeling a dark consolation that these poor kids had passed quickly, thanks to the nerve gas. They undoubtedly died in agony, but they hadn't been molested before or after their demise. The bodies of the women were free of bruising indicative of rape or post-mortem activity, further evidence of the dangerous toxins absorbed through their bare skin.

He swam to the bodies of the men and began searching through pockets after he took digital photos of their slack, cold faces. One of them might have had the presence of mind to pack a wallet or some other form of identification, but instead he found seawater-corroded cell phones and unopened foil packets of condoms. It had taken five tries to get a good, old-fashioned wallet, and he also found a more modern design, a stainless-steel model that sealed money and cards inside, safe from sweat or immersion while surfing or swimming.

Having found some ID, McCarter returned to the sled, not quite happy, but nor was he despondent. The Navy would be directed to these GPS coordinates to recover the lost and perhaps bring them home for proper burial. Right now, however, he had the means of giving closure to the families of the dead.

With grim resolve, McCarter buckled into his seat. He no longer saw the victims of La Palma as an abstract. There were faces, and those faces could be turned to names. The victims of the hostage takers, no matter what their incentive for violence, had been slain in the prime of their lives. He'd seen them, touched them and knew that they were gone forever, even if their remains were pulled from the cold, dark depths at the bottom of the Atlantic.

They had come here in life, looking for joy and camaraderie and romance. Instead, they had been murdered.

It wouldn't be up to him to piece together names and faces caught on his digital camera, but he could only imagine what horrors had befallen them in the last moments of their lives.

McCarter grit his teeth tighter around the mouthpiece of his rebreather. The murderous bastards were going to pay. He may not have been the raging berserker Carl Lyons of Able Team, but he sure as hell had come close in his days before assuming the responsibility of leading Phoenix Force. Even though he was calmer now, he still held a spot in his heart for anger, loathing, soul-crushing rage against those who slaughtered helpless innocents. And he'd squeeze all of that out in bloody retribution against these killers.

CHAPTER THREE

The three men of Phoenix Force surfaced along the western coast of the island of La Palma in darkness. They paused to give the shore a good scan with binoculars and laser range finders that were carried on the SDV. Over their satellite link to Stony Man Farm, they double-checked their position and sought a real-time infrared photograph of the rocky shore ahead of them. The shore was in a province of the island called Tazacorte, which was fairly sparsely populated. There was only one post office and one school for the whole area, as well as a port, which they had surfaced near. Most of the province was unreachable thanks to a sixty-meter elevation where the cliff fell off rapidly into the ocean, but that wouldn't be a hindrance to Phoenix Force.

They were still going to land a mile to the south of Tarajal, which was a popular marina for tourists and locals alike. They wanted to stay out of sight of the native population and the mercenaries, if they were active in this part of the island. That meant that they would climb a rocky cliff and cut across the sparsely populated banana plantations that topped the oceanfront cliffs.

There were tourist-oriented beaches, such as the Playa del Puerto. A seaside promenade with restaurants and beach facilities was present. Farther south, there was Los Guirres o El Volcán, which was wild in nature, isolated, but a favorite spot for surfers who wanted to get off the beaten path. All along, they could make out the black volcanic sands that made the island so well known and striking.

McCarter joined in on the scan of the Spanish marina. "Looks like a lot of the locals got in their boats and took off."

"I don't see much in way of an armed presence either way," Encizo said.

"That means bugger all. We've got a submarine loaded with guns and explosives, and we look like bumps on the waves," McCarter countered. "And don't forget that a cruise ship turned out to be a missile-launching Q-ship that took over Santa Cruz harbor."

"That's over the spine of the island," Encizo said. "But they might have some kind of presence here, especially since we're that much closer to Cumbre Vieja."

None of the team had to double-check the map that they had memorized. Cumbre Vieja volcano was the subject of the Jeopardy white paper about how a catastrophic volcanic landslide could result in a mega-tsunami. La Palma, seen from orbit, looked something like a yolk-up egg, except that the dome was actually the depressed caldera of an ancient but recently geologically active volcano. Most of the tourism was concentrated along the lower level, southern coasts of the island.

James's frown was ever present as he checked the forearm-strapped com link that kept him in touch with

Stony Man Farm. Still nothing about the identities of the bodies seen below the waves.

McCarter noticed the grim look on James's face. "You put a few clues together to get something disturbing."

"Those were tourists dropped off shore," James returned. "We haven't gotten anything solid back from the Farm, but who else would they be?"

"And that marina is a good place for a yacht full of terrorists disguised as vacation-goers to pull in," Encizo added.

"You don't have to tell me twice," McCarter said. He had been right there, looking the corpses in their lifeless faces, getting digital photographs to upload to the Farm. "So they could have parked, leaving behind spotters."

"And they could have women terrorists on hand," James threw in. "So we can't be sure of who we're looking at, if we run across some tourists."

"Which is why we're avoiding any contact until we're sure who we're dealing with," McCarter said.

James nodded.

"You're not going to get cold feet about shooting a woman, are you?" McCarter asked.

"If they have a gun and they're trying to kill me, not a chance," James answered. "We've encountered enough murderous ladies, and I've never flinched from that."

"This is also Spain, where gun laws aren't like America. It's not bloody likely that we'll run into a lady with a concealed carry pistol," McCarter added.

"And that was what I'd worry most about," Encizo

said, nodding to James in agreement with his unspoken doubts.

"Just keep your eyes peeled," McCarter warned.

The three men swam back to the submerged vehicle, turned it to the south and continued on toward the rocky shore.

HAROLD BROGNOLA LURCHED from the couch in his office, grimacing as he felt the pinch in his neck caused by sleeping with his head on the armrest. While he was aware of the Farm's accommodations for guests—soft, comfortable beds—Brognola was more of a mind to avoid sleeping there. The couch was its own quiet alarm, its lumps and painful armrest rousing him from slumber after only an hour. If he were on a schedule that would allow a full night's sleep, he'd drag himself to a guest room and snore happily.

Awake, he made his way to the Stony Man Farm War Room, looking at the gigantic map on the wall. The display was made of several interlocked plasma screen televisions, enabling different panels to be pulled up for individual windows containing pertinent information. Right now, the screens showed a blockade around the island of La Palma in the Atlantic Ocean. Forty-eight hours earlier, the western port of the island, Santa Cruz, became ground zero for a wild, unprecedented explosion of violence, literally.

A cruise ship, what appeared to be a cruise ship more precisely, suddenly fired anti-shipping missiles from its deck and shattered the hulls of two ocean liners so that they were left malingering in the path of any other large craft attempting to get away. With the sudden blasts, smaller craft were suddenly set to flight, two speed boats with vacationers accelerating out of the harbor as quickly as humanly possible.

As they fled, smaller missiles were launched. They easily caught up with the civilian crafts and blasted them out of the water.

All of this was caught on video camera and transmitted to the rest of the world with its grim, ominous warning.

"Send forces ashore, and we shall kill thousands."

The group called itself Option Omega, and they were railing against the G8 and its interference with the natural economy of the world. Governments mismanaging taxes and regulations, they had said, were leading the world to the brink of financial collapse.

Option Omega wanted to show the world's governments how weak they truly were. La Palma was a tourist mecca, a wide-open maw for tourist revenues that kept Spain solvent.

Option Omega intended to show Spain and the other European members of the G8 simply how weak they were when it came to pushing the people under the wheels of their insane economic policies.

Brognola knew that this group was borrowing the vague, half-assed rhetoric of Occupy Wall Street and the even older Tea Party movement—two groups of American citizens who had legitimate gripes about American financial and fiscal woes—and was regurgitating it with elements of both groups' ideals. It was a hodgepodge jumble that had garnered them a modicum of "I admire your sentiments, but not your actions" lip service on left- and right-wing squawk boxes.

He proceeded to where Barbara Price, the Farm's mission controller, was working at her station, collating information as quickly as it came in.

"Anything new?" Brognola asked.

"Gunfight in Norfolk," Price told him matter-of-factly, not hiding the annoyance in her voice. "Small consolation is that it was far from bystanders, though the whole waterfront heard machine guns and grenades for miles."

"How's the Virginia news handling it all?" Brognola asked.

"They're reporting that it might be gang violence. They brought up the fire that gutted the boatyard a month ago," Price said. "And then they skimmed away when there was a fresh tweet from that actress trapped on La Palma."

Brognola grimaced. "She's still posting to the internet?"

"Nobody can get out of the hotels, but they have some pretty good internet connections," Price told him. "I wouldn't be surprised if they were letting hostages have access to social media in order to keep the world watching."

"Social media, but they're pretty good at only putting their video out," Brognola mused.

"Even smartphone video has a pretty large footprint to be intercepted," Price suggested. "Aaron told me that it would be easy for someone to monitor and purge video footage or digital photos from the stream."

"Meanwhile, social media posts adding only 140 characters at a time can get through because there's no way that a strike team could use a status update to plan an assault," Brognola grumbled.

Price nodded. "Aaron also said that our satellite coverage of the Spanish Canaries is being assailed. We keep getting spikes of interference, which means they are intent on keeping the outside world blind but not deaf."

Brognola sneered. "It's like poking a wounded hostage so that their screams weigh on rescuers, but they keep the drapes drawn so we can't take a shot in."

"But we did take a shot," Price said. "We sent in Phoenix."

Brognola nodded. "You don't sound happy."

"We got an upload of a few dozen photos over satellite laser link. They're of preserved corpses in the waters off of Tazacorte," Price said. "That was a few minutes ago, but they're of young people. We're trying facial IDs, as well as tapping some SIM cards that survived being at the bottom of the ocean."

"Tourists?" Brognola asked.

"McCarter and James both suggested that in texts to us," Price answered. "Mode of dress was summer casual, very casual. Everyone was topless."

Brognola grumbled at this suggestion. "Meaning that if they were on a boat, they left the majority of their clothing and personal identification in their state rooms."

Price nodded. "James sent that as a follow-up after they came up. There were some yachts still docked at the marina in Tarajal."

"What have we got on those faces and cards?" Brognola asked.

"Still checking on it," Price told him. "But we've got the fastest fingers on the East Coast working on this."

Brognola looked immediately over to Akira Tokaido, who was running through multiple images on his computer screen. They were flashing through too fast for Brognola to follow, but Tokaido had been born with a nervous system that seemed to have a quad-core processor. Brognola was still in abacus world when it came to technology, and he barely knew what *quad-core* meant, but it was fast, and Tokaido was that quick. He could look at those faces and run through code at lightning speed.

There was a quick whoop as Tokaido made a connection. "Barb! I have IDs."

"That was fast," Price said. Brognola accompanied her over to his station.

"We've been looking for signs of trouble since the first explosions," Tokaido said. "That meant going back months."

"So missing persons reports?" Brognola asked.

Tokaido nodded. "A bunch of twenty-somethings gone missing, but they said that they were staying on some extra time."

"Email contact?"

"And new photos and videos up on social media," Tokaido added. "So that's allaying most of the suspicion."

"Who isn't buying this?" Brognola asked.

"Young lady, Cathryn Lopez. She was due to ship out after her vacation," Tokaido said.

"Where?" Brognola asked.

"Marines. When a female Marine doesn't report in for duty, it raises some flags. Especially if she's still posting online," Tokaido said. "As her last port of call…"

"The USMC is doing part of our intel for us," Brognola mumbled. "There was a face in that batch?"

Tokaido shook his head. "But Lopez was on the same boat with Bryce Jennings. And his SIM card was recovered by McCarter."

"Bryce Jennings?" Price asked. She shook her head. "Was he a porn star or something?"

"No, it was his real name," Tokaido said.

"They slipped ashore disguised as tourists," Brognola murmured. "Does our satellite coverage have identification on any of the boats?"

"We're getting interference," Tokaido returned. "And any IFF we have on the ships show nothing on the yacht that these kids were supposedly on."

"So they're anticipating us," Price mused. "They're anticipating something."

"Are we getting anything at other marinas on that side? Or just Tarajal?" Brognola asked.

"No fine details in Tarajal, so that means that particular marina has some craft inside that's jamming us," Tokaido mused.

"And keeping watch on that coast," Price added.

"You can fit a bit of surveillance equipment on a yacht," Brognola said. "Radar, telescopes, satellite communications…"

"And Option Omega scouts," Price noted.

"Option Omega has very little history except as an

Idaho-based splinter of a white-supremacist militia," Huntington Wethers, another member of Kurtzman's cyberteam, interjected. "As to being a splinter, we're talking a top membership of a dozen."

"No other references?" Brognola asked. "Because—"

"I've been quite thorough," Wethers told him. "Option Omega has the computer skills and resources to launch attacks on any other group usurping their name. I've tried a couple of runs at their main website, and they are not only pro-La Palma takeover, but they are vehemently anti-G8."

"Idaho is a long way from Norfolk," Brognola said. "And it's even farther to the Spanish Canaries."

"Traffic to their site has risen exponentially," cyberteam member Carmen Delahunt advised. "As has the mention of them on BBSs. They appear to have been recruiting heavily."

"Appear?" Brognola asked, aware that Delahunt was referring to computerized Bulletin Board Systems.

Delahunt shook her head. "It doesn't feel right. Especially since they ratcheted back their angry militia rhetoric and pumped up the antigovernment bile."

"Like they switched horses midstream," Price mused.

Brognola nodded. "Someone either usurped the leadership or is influencing them."

"So Option Omega has become a sock puppet," Wethers offered. "Maybe they were inspired by the supremacists who threatened the G8 before, utilizing orbital launched rods. I can't see much in way of La Palma's significance as a strategic target, outside of the Jeopardy Corporation's white paper."

"If they've got enough resources now to transform cruise ships and assemble a large enough army to control an island, they're going to have some kind of money trail," Price said to the distinguished African-American cybernetics professor. "Dig deep, Hunt. If anyone can find even an infinitesimal trace of outside influence, it's you."

Wethers took out his pipe, then clenched it between his teeth. "I shall be thorough."

Wethers was an educated man who had been working with computers for decades. He had the appearance of a college professor, and many of the mannerisms of a highly intelligent, cultured man. One thing, however, that made the job worthwhile at Stony Man Farm was fighting against groups that victimized innocents. On those occasions when they went up against intolerant bigots, he took special satisfaction in being of assistance in slamming the lid on their plans and machinations. Especially against white supremacists, men who considered him no more than a talking ape, rather than a brilliant mathematician and programmer.

He turned his attention back to his workstation and dived in deeply.

At the same time, Carmen Delahunt took her cue to return to her work, checking for Option Omega's links to prior white-power groups that Stony Man had recently encountered.

There had been a sudden surge in activity among the Christian Identity and White Power movements, where lots of money had been raised. The most violent of the groups' splinter elements had been involved in multiple other crises, which meant that there was someone who wasn't putting their eggs in one basket, or maybe some manipulators were seeing the near success of others as their chance.

With the right words, the right equipment and the right money, things could be attempted that could rock the world, to the benefit of one or another cabal.

Either way, the monsters behind the scenes were nearly as insidious as the general thugs who were manipulated into committing murder for the profit of their puppet masters. In some ways, even worse, as they rarely caught the full attention of law enforcement, or were well hidden behind the shields of treaties and diplomatic immunity.

Brognola grumbled this time, and knew that he was going to have to do something to bring down the headmasters of this particular escapade in terror.

He pulled Price aside and spoke with her in confidence.

This was going to be one instance where the plotters would bleed, as well.

"WE'VE GOTTEN WORD from the Farm. Your assumptions were pretty good," T. J. Hawkins said after closing the satellite-linked field laptop that put them in uninterrupted contact with the Sensitive Operations Group headquarters back on Stony Man Farm.

"Tourists murdered so that the terrorists could take their place," James murmured grimly. David McCarter's grimace was readily apparent.

"We were expecting this," James whispered to him.

"Don't let this distract you from the lives we have to save."

McCarter narrowed his eyes, glaring at James. "I'm in control. We rescue the hostages, and stop the detonation that will cause the La Palma landslide."

The Briton grit his teeth, eyes alight. "But that doesn't mean I won't enjoy giving it to whoever we manage to catch hold of."

Manning winced, but let that flash of the old David McCarter pass. Even at his worst, the feisty ex-SAS man was hardly cruel, and was only ruthless to the point of ending a battle before it could harm bystanders. He might shoot a man in the back of the head, but only to keep a stray shot, or an intentional salvo of bullets from slaughtering innocents. When it came to handling murderers and other assorted thugs, if there was a personal bent toward McCarter's duty, he was willing to go beyond the doctrine of using the minimum force necessary to end a conflict.

"All right, does everyone have their assignments?" Manning asked.

Officially, McCarter was the team leader. But Manning had a better bedside manner with teammates, and was generally the British warrior's scientific adviser and the cooler head off which he could bounce ideas. Every member of Phoenix Force was a close friend to his teammates, but Manning and McCarter were especially close friends thanks to their cultural similarities—Canada and Britain sharing an allegiance and a loyalty to the Royal family, as well as both being original members of Phoenix Force. While Encizo, the other original veteran of the team, joked that the two bickered like an old married couple, it was their similarities and the sharp contrast of temperaments that made the two of them an effective team.

McCarter didn't look particularly happy, but he nodded at Manning, thanking him for focusing on the present.

"We've got 'em," Hawkins said.

"T.J., I'll need you to delay in hooking up with Cal and me," McCarter said. "Head to Tarajal and scope out the scene there. You can coordinate and reunite later."

"Why not me?" Encizo asked.

"I want this done from land. Someone who could fit in," McCarter said. "You're a little too memorable. T.J., on the other hand, can be completely nondescript and act the role of someone new stumbling into town."

Hawkins shrugged. "I'll take care of things. Take my weapons bag with you. If it goes sideways, I don't want to be tempted to risk overkill."

"Pistols and knife, just in case," McCarter admonished. "We'll keep a hold of the bigger stuff. If you need something with more oomph…"

"Y'all are doing it wrong," Hawkins concluded with his wry Texas grin.

McCarter nodded in assent. "We hold off on the shooting, at least until we get the lay of the land. That doesn't mean we can't kill any of these Option Omega bastards, but we do it quiet. Broken necks can be made to look more like accidents than bullet holes."

Hawkins nodded.

"One last word of advice, though." McCarter paused.

"We're planning to keep a low profile. But you know what military planning is…"

"It's what you have in mind until you actually run into the enemy," Hawkins answered.

"Stay sharp, lads. This is going to get bloody."

CHAPTER FOUR

The men of Able Team had bound and separated their two prisoners, isolated from each other by nothing more than a strip of duct tape over eyes and mouths, preventing communication between them. Rather than immediately asking them questions, the three Stony Men preferred to work smart, letting them speculate on their own about their fate.

Thanks to fingerprinting and analysis of their equipment, the trio were able to gather some useful information on the two gunmen. They got names.

One was Stephen Baxter, drummed out of the U.S. Army Reserve for selling equipment out the back gate of his base. He then worked as hired muscle for Tonberth Security. There was little surprise to the fact that Tonberth was a contractor for the Jeopardy Corporation. However, the guns and communications were not linked to any purchases made by Tonberth, and Baxter was no longer employed by the company, having been let go for the same reason as his dismissal from the USAR.

The other gunman was Emmanuel Rosca, a Mexican national, although his fair skin and blue eyes painted a picture of him as someone from a family of pure European blood. Lyons knew this kind of man, especially if he were a violent, gun-toting thug. Able Team had once fought a conglomerate of Latin American racists, the Fascist International, who felt it their birthright, by dint of their European blood, to command those who were descended from the native Central and South American Indians or those who had "sullied" their whiteness by lying down and creating generations of "mud people."

The group had considered itself the Reich of the Americas, and Able Team had waged a long, brutal war with this particular breed of bigot.

It was no surprise to Able Team, then, when Rosca's background turned up a series of dropped charges of violence or convictions on lesser crimes in Mexico, always avoiding prosecution for hate crimes or terrorist acts. Rosca had been rumored to have been a lieutenant in Los Soldados Blancos, the White Soldiers, but it was nothing that the Mexican authorities could actually pin on him. He'd disappeared about a year ago.

The correlation of the White Soldiers to Option Omega, a connection established by Stony Man Farm, was only cause for more concern.

"What's the approach?" Lyons asked Blancanales.

Rosario Blancanales had been called the Politician, or Pol for short, because of his way with words and ability to convince people to follow his suggestions, not because he was a liar who slung mud. Blancanales was one of Stony Man's best interrogators, showing an uncanny skill at delving into someone's wants and fears and utilizing diplomacy to open doors that even Carl "Ironman" Lyons couldn't kick down. "I'm going to start with Rosca."

Lyons glared at the Mexican bigot as he squirmed, wrists and ankles bound, eyes and mouth sealed off with duct tape, ears rendered numb by headphones pumping white noise.

"I know," Blancanales added, reading the enmity that Lyons held for Rosca's predecessors. Lyons had been captured, tortured and brainwashed by the Fascist International, a month-long ordeal that occurred in the wake of one of his best friends being murdered by those self-same "liberators." "Carl, I know that this is one group that you wouldn't mind resorting to killing with a thousand cuts. But we need answers."

Lyons nodded. "Don't worry about me. I don't want to hurt him. I don't even feel like executing the bound-up little bitch. Killing helpless prisoners isn't my way."

"I know that," Blancanales said. He glanced at Rosca. "Though, mind if I let you build up a head of steam before I begin chatting him up?"

Lyons smirked. "Oh, I don't need to build up a foul mood. I installed a tap for that years ago."

Blancanales chuckled. "I figured as much. Gadgets and I've been getting pints off of you for years."

"The fear of a psychopath, ready to rock," Lyons growled. His good humor only added a frenzied mania to his angry appearance.

It was time for Blancanales to begin his work at dismantling the White Soldier's defenses.

HERMANN SCHWARZ WASN'T called Gadgets as an ironic statement of his technical ineptitude. The man was an electronics engineer and innovator, having done much of the development of some of the surveillance and communications systems that kept the teams in constant communication with their headquarters in the Blue Ridge Mountains of Virginia.

Having gotten hold of the communications carried by the mercenary team that had attacked them, Schwarz was on the job. This wasn't a toil for him, either. His was the kind of inquisitive mind that had dismantled and reassembled everything from the smallest robot toy to the most complex, top-of-the-line personal computer ever since he'd developed the coordination to operate a screwdriver.

The one SUV that Able Team had captured was fitted with electronics that Schwarz could tap into. The GPS unit from the SUV was one of the best bits of intelligence that he could have collected. He was able to backtrack the path that the hired guns had taken from their starting point to the Norfolk shipyard. Schwarz downloaded everything from the unit's hard drive, gathering every destination that the vehicle had gone to and from.

While he was plotting out thousands of miles of road travel for the vehicle—he made special note of the fact that it wasn't a rental—he went to work on the communications systems that the men carried.

They were fairly standard electronics, mass-produced in Southeast Asia—Vietnam to be exact. It didn't quite jibe with the SIG 556 rifles, but Schwarz took a closer look at the assault weapons that had been utilized against them.

They were Brazilian IMBEL Model LCs, not SIGs,

though there were considerable similarities between the two weapons that could cause confusion at a distance. The fineries of weapon identification hadn't mattered in the heat of combat, just that they could tell the unique sound of a high-velocity .22-caliber round and how easily it could penetrate body armor but not solid cover. The Brazilian firearms were going to be difficult to track, but that was the point, Schwarz assumed. The electronics were similar, and he would have to rely on the skills of the Stony Man Farm cyberteam to look for elements inside of the programming for these GPS units, just in case they were utilizing proprietary software. He noticed that there were downloaded updates of coordinates that had been recently entered into the electronics, new paths updated on the fly.

Only two of the men had smartphones with them, at least as far as Schwarz could recover. He took the SIM cards from those phones to shield them from any long-range, remote nullification of the information in them. The phones themselves were just housings; the SIM cards held the most vital information for each of the mercenaries' normal use. These were business phones, though, and had very little personal information as far as he could tell.

It didn't matter, thanks to the Location Area Identity entries into those cards. Now, in conjunction with the GPS, Schwarz could track their movements for several days.

Right now, he was uploading the data from the devices to Stony Man Farm after gathering some preliminary notes. If anyone could discern what patterns the opposition were keeping to, it would be the techno-wizards at the Farm.

In the meantime, he was going through the memory on the two smartphones that had been recovered. Memos and notes had been erased, but Schwarz had them plugged into his laptop, and he brought up a drive "unwiper" that could recover lost data easily.

Blancanales rapped on the door to the room that Schwarz had set up as his tech lab. "Gadgets?"

He looked up to his oldest, dearest friend. "What's going on?"

"Carl's hit a brick wall."

"Poor wall. Or do you mean figuratively?" Schwarz asked.

"Figuratively," Blancanales replied. "You'd have felt the safe house shake if he'd actually punched a wall."

Schwarz nodded. "I've collected a lot of data already, on movements, on people called. Is he going to try to force admission?"

Blancanales grinned. "It helps to be able to say we've got someone where they've been. We need to know as much about them as possible."

"Here's the background and records pulled up from the Farm, too," Schwarz replied. "Lots more dirt on our prisoners."

Blancanales accepted the small file folder, looking it over. His lips were drawn tightly, and Schwarz could see the glint in his eyes as he was filling his brain, memorizing everything he could about the two men in their custody. It was a typical tactic, not only of police detectives, but of carnival mentalists who gave "cold" readings of their subjects.

The foreknowledge of answers to questions was a means of breaking down bricks in whatever wall the subject erected to deflect a questioner. If the questioner could provide answers to his own questions, it made any effort at keeping secrets seem more and more futile. Such a regimen was generally successful, even with the grimmest and toughest of subjects.

Interrogation—the most successful and adept interrogation—didn't come from torture or from terror. It came from shattered spirits, from the truth that nothing could be hidden from those interrogating them.

"Carl and I have gotten about half of this," Blancanales admitted. He looked up. "But we can still use this."

"Good. I'm still working with the Farm to dig deeper," Schwarz said. "Aaron's already on top of the forensic accounting for these two thanks to the smartphone work."

"That'll prove interesting," Blancanales mused. "Not enough for me to sit and watch it, but the results would be pretty damning, and useful for breaking our shooters."

"Right now I've done all that I can. I'm going to be sitting on my thumbs for a good bit," Schwarz said.

"Can't grab a catnap?" Blancanales inquired.

Schwarz spread out all of the information he'd accumulated. "Data overstimulation. I'm running things through the back of my mind subconsciously, so I'm not going to get much toward sleep."

"Multilevel intellect." Blancanales sighed. "You've

usually got at least three or four things working in that brain of yours. I'm surprised you can ever get to sleep."

"Meditation which duplicates REM sleep generally gets me through," Schwarz answered. "That or caffeine crash. Coffee actually makes me sleepy."

Blancanales chuckled. "So what's your plan? Hit up a coffee shop?"

"Unless…"

Schwarz looked down at one of the smartphones, then powered it back up.

"We nullified all of the GPS-locating soft- and hardware, didn't we?" Blancanales asked.

"I triple-checked all of that," Schwarz replied. "But you know…"

"Hang out as bait? That usually works best if you're in a team," Blancanales countered.

"You and Carl are busy. And Mack Bolan does the solo stuff all the time," Schwarz answered.

Blancanales shook his head. "We're not that guy. He's too experienced, too skilled. He's on a whole different level than we are."

"He plans ahead, he lays traps," Schwarz returned. "He thinks on damn near as many levels as I do. And he doesn't have a trunk full of nasty technology like I do."

"So double the technology and a few points of IQ will make your little ploy as survivable as him?" Blancanales asked.

Lyons entered and took the file folder from Blancanales. "Gadgets wants to suck in some more bad guys?"

"Not necessarily to get into a rumble, but I can trace them while they're tracing me," Schwarz said. "And if things do get violent, I have a plan and the awareness for all of that."

Blancanales looked to Lyons for support.

"You can't stop him," Lyons said. "His brain is afire. He's got an idea, and when he gets that, he's like me with a lead or you with an interrogation. We don't let go. We're driven."

Blancanales looked at Schwarz again, worry still present in his eyes. "At least tell me you have something that can minimize the danger. Something to even the odds."

Schwarz grinned. "I'll have Schrödinger's cat with me."

Lyons tilted his head. "That's from quantum physics, right?"

"Look at you, Ironman. Where'd you pick that one up?" Schwarz asked.

Lyons shrugged, a little embarrassed "There's a comedy about four scientists… Highly illuminating about guys like you, Hermann."

Schwarz's grin grew, even though Lyons was gently gibing him about his first name. Lyons continued. "What I don't get is what your 'cat' is all about. How does a layman's explanation about observation and uncertainty help with a group hunting you elec…"

Schwarz nodded.

"The Schrödinger's cat thing is an explanation of how the act of observation has an effect on what is being observed," Lyons said. "You've found a means of making equipment more sensitive to observation. Part one is going to be something about cloning one of their smartphones into a device with that kind of sensor."

Schwarz laughed. "Careful, Carl. I might have to have you trade in your jock card."

Lyons gave his friend a one-fingered salute. "Don't fit me for a pocket protector yet. I'm learning a lot off of you, but I couldn't build your little cat tablet."

Blancanales spoke up, a wry grin on his face. "Looks like you just buy one of those Pads, then put a kitten sticker over the fruit logo."

Schwarz looked at the older Latino. "You don't like it?"

"Able Group Investigations would never be able to market that," Blancanales replied.

"Wow, Rosario, you are getting to be as money-oriented as a real politician," Schwarz chided.

Blancanales shook his head. "I just don't want to be sued. Those guys have huge money. Besides, as David would say, we're just taking the piss out of you. Go on."

"It's more accurately a search engine and radio listening matrix that the guys at the Farm helped to work up in relation to cell-phone-tracking soft- and hardware," Schwarz answered. "What I did was make the search subject—the cat tablet in this instance—highly visible."

"So you'd be listening in on the frequencies that others would be using to track the phone," Lyons said. "The GPS signal, cell-phone transmission lines, even internet locations."

"Besides, how's this for a CAT acronym? Counter surveillance Analysis of Tracking," Schwarz offered.

"You're going to need more than a Hello Kitty label to keep Apple from ripping us apart," Blancanales said.

"I'm designing my own shell, this was just leftovers," Schwarz countered.

Lyons looked at the tablet. "So, what is your means of avoiding the ambush itself? I'm thinking a radio-controlled...helicopter? No, the tablet's too fragile, and the enemy might wonder why their quarry is rising and lowering in altitude. An RC, as in remote-controlled, car."

"Amped-up motor, capable of handling highway velocities," Schwarz returned. "I tell you, I'm getting too predictable. Either that, or you've been lying about being a caveman all these years."

Lyons winked. "Cavemen invented fortification, art and learned how to tend to fire on a long-term basis. A couple things I watched mentioned that if a virus hadn't knocked out all of the other Neanderthals, we'd currently be colonizing other planets and having pet mammoths in our yards."

Schwarz sighed. "I'm starting to miss the days when you just grunted and picked fleas out of your chest hair."

Lyons smirked. "The RC has a purpose-built brace for the tablet...and I'm going to guess you have a docking port for the RC on the Able van."

Schwarz nodded. "The tablet currently has not only the signature of the smartphone, but there was so much room in the shell that I was able to set it up to mimic multiple devices concurrently. Both phones and the GPS of our captured rental are going to be active on the CAT."

"You're probably also going to have a programmed course, which should get you to a nice, secluded location to watch for the bad guys, since it would be impossible to drive and remote control the car at the same time," Blancanales said. "Where do you have in mind?"

Schwarz pointed out the location on the map.

"Proximity sensors to keep it from being run over in traffic?" Lyons asked, curious about the type of artificial intelligence to be employed by Schwarz's RC car.

Schwarz nodded. "I've put in the AI from one of the better NASCAR simulators, with provisions for drifting under the carriage of other cars. It only has to avoid the tires and keep to its ground clearance of eight inches."

"Nice and compact," Blancanales mentioned. "Now, about your personal protection."

Schwarz folded his arms, lips drawn tightly. "Since when have I ever been underprepared for a big-ass fight?"

"I seem to remember someone on the back of a top-secret train, fighting an attack helicopter with only an Uzi."

Lyons spoke up. "Wasn't me. I brought my Konzak with slugs for long-range engagements."

"And I had my M-16/M-203 combo," Blancanales said, rubbing his chin.

"To be honest, I thought the two of you would be pulling antiaircraft duty on that train," Schwarz grumbled. "It also would have been more logical for them to have gone after a vehicle on the tracks with pickups and vans."

"Well, this time we're looking at something heavier,"

Lyons returned. "A two-SUV team with assault rifles, body armor, encrypt—"

Schwarz cut him off. "I know the technology these guys had." He motioned to the assorted components strewed across his worktable. "Oh, speaking of tech, most of this stuff is pure knockoff. Brazilian firepower, Vietnamese electronics, Korean programming. It's possible that they might have Russian MiGs, but improbable."

"Hind-24s?" Blancanales offered.

"In Norfolk," Schwarz asked. "That would have been noticed. But I promise, I'll go larger than an MP-7, all right?"

"Take the SIG 552," Lyons said. "I know you like that, and you can fit it out with an XM-26 underbarrel shotgun, which could give you a couple of magazines worth of FRAG-12s."

Schwarz nodded. "Okay. Now, don't you two have prisoners to continue interrogating?"

"Back to work. Gadgets is tired of us playing mother to him," Blancanales said.

Lyons gave his forehead a tap, as if in salute. "Good luck, bro."

"You, too," Schwarz answered.

Now it was time for the wizard to gear up for war.

GADGETS SCHWARZ DROVE HIS planned route taking himself and the CAT tablet away from the Able Team safe house before activating it. Immediately, the GPS transmitter within came online, providing a beacon for anyone who would be interested. The smartphones came online almost immediately afterward, one of them sending out a text to an address in the memory of the device, an emergency contact.

It was a simple message. "Escaped. Coast Clear. Pickup at prearrange 4."

No code, just the normal texting encryption, and the lockout function on the phone would have been impossible to crack for all but the most brilliant of computer specialists. It just happened that the mercenary's phone had fallen into the hands of such a genius.

The Schwarz CAT received a text reply, which the dashboard display of the Able Team van showed as it came in.

"Confirmation code."

Fortunately that bit of information was among the first topics that Lyons and Blancanales had covered. Utilizing the touch screen, Schwarz entered the confirmation code text easily.

He waited for the response, still figuring out dozens of ways that this could have possibly gone wrong. He'd been thorough in checking out all the means of bugging the gear belonging to the assassination team at the boatyard, but there were always possibilities, what-ifs, that could have slipped through the cracks of possibility and probability, no matter how impractical.

Schwarz tried to keep himself from looking for ways things could go wrong, but it was ingrained into his psyche. As long as there was a possibility for something to screw up, he had a part of his mind devoted to figuring out how the eponymous Murphy of Murphy's Law would come up and screw him over.

It was that level of attention to the worst-case scenario that had most likely kept Schwarz alive all these years.

He pulled the van to a halt, and watched as the CAT and its radio-control/AI-directed vehicle pulled onto gravel just inside the doors of an old, empty warehouse.

Schwarz would wait for as long as necessary.

That's when he noticed something glint in the sky, just an errant, almost totally dismissible flash of light.

Moments later, the loading dock doors where he'd parked the CAT tablet erupted under the unmistakable impact of an air-to-ground missile.

The flash came from an unmanned drone, and Schwarz called up the Able Team van's radar net.

There was an object, smaller than almost every manned aircraft in the world, and it was hanging in an orbit over the warehouse. The explosion was a gutting, powerful blast that caused sections of wall and roof to collapse, tumbling as the high-intensity shock wave tore through them.

The drone wasn't going anywhere. It was searching for targets on the ground.

It was too far up to be visible by the naked eye, let alone be in range of even the FRAG-12 grenades in his underbarrel shotgun.

But the eyes of the deadly predator in the sky would be meticulous in picking him out and targeting him.

And Schwarz didn't have a single gun in the van that could deal with this kind of a threat.

CHAPTER FIVE

The Able Team van didn't let out its alarm as late as a radar lock from the unmanned drone. Such a warning would simply be an announcement of imminent vaporization. The van's sensors, designed by Schwarz himself, picked up the prelock of the sky predator's laser illuminator, allowing him to throw the SUV into gear, stomp on the gas and break the targeting lock.

The hard reverse continued for thirty feet before he braked and spun the wheel, throwing himself into a 180-degree spin. Grinding down into drive, he accelerated to get out of the area, pausing only to hit the ELINT—electronic intelligence—countermeasures activation on the dashboard.

Somewhere in the depths of the van, a wide array of jamming signals produced a sphere of interference around the van, not large enough to take out electronics across a lawn, for example, but certainly enough to make radar locks and laser targeting almost impossible.

Almost. And then there was the simple, brutal fact that most Predator-style drones could use their cameras, or more accurately, the minicameras inside their air-to-ground missiles, to track elusive targets. Schwarz knew for a fact that American tanks had countermeasures against the missiles that they used and in anticipation for conflict with both allies and enemies who would have utilized espionage to copy American equipment. American armor development was in a war with itself as much as it was against other nations, as U.S. military designs informed the completion of Communist China's aircraft.

The Able Team van had Schwarz's own take on such anti-missile measures, but he knew that he couldn't evade the camera-guided Maverick-knockoff forever, especially if there was someone else manning the weapons systems. Even so, it wouldn't be hard for a remote operator to slave the drone itself to an autopilot while he focused on flying the loosed television-guided missile. He'd need to bring down that drone, and hope to hell that it didn't lose all of its electronics in the crash, or to a self-destruct mechanism.

It'd be an easy way to track down the enemy, provided he survived.

The asphalt behind Schwarz suddenly erupted in divots of flying rock and dust. Someone had upgraded the usual weaponry on a drone with machine guns. That kind of firepower and the use of a drone to sever an enemy lead added up to one thing—Option Omega had to have some kind of robotic support on the island, perhaps even more than just a few drones. It would explain why they suddenly had so much security.

Of course, inside the interference sphere, Schwarz was unable to communicate with the outside world. That didn't matter. The most important thing was that upon the activation of the sphere, indeed, any of the Able

Team van's countermeasures, it sent a signal to Stony Man Farm and to his partners' CPDAs.

He hoped that it wouldn't distract them from anything important, but the CPDAs were always set to vibrate instead of alarm.

Since he had come here specifically to avoid getting people caught in the crossfire in the event of an ambush, he had the unfortunate choice of having to stay in the area. He swerved hard, the drone's underslung machine guns chopping a line of destruction away from him on the ground. Schwarz hit the gas and accelerated back toward the first missile strike. The old warehouse floor would give him a tiny bit of room to maneuver without being in the enemy's line of sight.

He'd also be able to separate from a relatively large and visible object, or rather, large and visible void that would be easy to track.

Machine gun rounds hammered the back of the van as the Omega "pilot" found his range and distance, forcing Schwarz to swerve. The van was armored, but from the sound of those impacts, the sky predator was packing belts that could damage even light-armored vehicles. Able Team's van was as tough as it could be, but it was nothing compared to the rolled-composite armor of a tank or armored personnel carrier. Able Team wanted to be able to operate in traffic, without burning endless amounts of fuel necessary to move a twenty-ton turtle.

The trade for maneuverability and fuel efficiency was something that Schwarz only slightly regretted. It wasn't every day that he'd run into an air-to-ground setup assault drone.

Luckily, the drone wasn't packing .50-caliber machine guns. The awesome punch of an M-2 shell, even a salvo of standard slugs, would have gone through the back armor of the Able Team van. AP ammunition would have punched clean through and chopped down into the rear axle, rendering the vehicle useless. This had to have been a .30, either an old Soviet design and knockoff, or a NATO standard GPMG. Even as he accelerated, swerving in a serpentine pattern to get to the smoldering warehouse, the part of his mind devoted to enemy gear and tactics popped to life and identified the distant sound as a 7.62 x 54 Russian general-purpose machine gun. The 54 Russian round was the Warsaw Pact equivalent of the old Springfield .30-06, which was more powerful than the 7.62 mm NATO by dint of a longer case and more gunpowder.

The rest of Schwarz's multiple lines of thought were working in tight collusion. His aircraft and drone knowledge factored into his driving, while mathematics measured angles and anticipated the line of sight of the enemy craft. His usually subconscious awareness of the environment rose to the forefront, giving him an impression of the altitude of the deadly drone and its relative speed in comparison to the van, while his memories of his work on this vehicle were instrumental in giving him the hope that he could reach the cover granted by the blasted warehouse.

Another hard swerve had him fishtail, screeching tires and raising a burst of smoke from where the rubber met the asphalt. Schwarz kept up the acceleration, whirling in a doughnut, gushing a thick, nasty trail that created a thick mist that he spun through. He got the van back under control and stomped the gas, rocketing ahead and making for the warehouse.

The sudden stop and doughnut spin did more than raise a confusing cloud of smoke, making a missile lock even more difficult. It also forced the drone to hurtle past, making the operator fly away from the Able Team van to swoop back around. With that brief instant between losing and swinging back to target, Schwarz charged through the burning wreckage of the warehouse doors.

The impact jarred him, and he could feel even the tough, bullet-resistant, run-flat tires slashed and torn by twisted, broken and, most importantly, burning hot metal. The run-flats were meant to be immune to deflation by bullets, but against the guillotine edge of twisted, blasted and ragged metal, they were chopped apart.

Even so, Schwarz was able to control the van and bring it to a flopping stop. He threw open the driver's door, hit the seat belt release and then grabbed his rifle and his equipment vest. It was time to go extravehicular. He was out of the van and running toward a deeper part of the building. He spotted a support brace, a pair of steel girders poking up from a thick concrete base. It would do for cover, and he knew that the van was out of sight of any aerial opponent except for one literally flying in through the smashed hole.

The drone, however, that could carry such a payload would have a wingspan too wide to get through that entrance. Schwarz didn't want to discount the possibility that the drone itself still had a warhead in its nose that could be used to take out an entire building on a suicide run. Option Omega's Virginia forces had already lost a sizable investment in dead mercenaries and lost equipment, but the destruction of an up-armed battle drone wouldn't matter much more to them, especially if they had even more equipment covering La Palma over in the Atlantic.

He checked the XM-26 and saw that it was loaded with FRAG-12 slugs. They had a range of 200 meters, but if the enemy drone needed to get close enough to catch Schwarz on its thermal sensors or radar, then it would need to be that tight, especially with a high roof interceding between them. Schwarz discounted that, but knew that the Russian machine guns would need a range of less than 200 meters to penetrate the roof and get a solid kill on him.

That meant that he had a shot at taking out the drone. The SIG 552 Commando's short, 9-inch barrel wouldn't give him the ability to reach out to anything over 150 meters, not for antivehicle work. The FRAG-12 was going to have to do the job for him.

He checked his CPDA momentarily. Stony Man Farm had their own eyes in the sky, satellites that could see but not interact. However, the flash of an explosion would undoubtedly have raised alarms back at the Farm, especially on the heels of the transmission put out by the van as soon as Schwarz hit the electronic countermeasures.

Schwarz didn't like the idea of being a sitting target. Obviously there would be need for visual confirmation of a kill, which could mean that there might be one or two spotters on hand. He looked around the rafters and catwalks above the warehouse floor, grimacing as he realized that this building was exactly where the enemy would have had spotters out of sight. The 552 Commando, relatively useless at long range, would be devastating against opponents in close quarters like these. It was the shortness of the barrel that didn't stabilize or provide enough velocity to reach targets beyond 150 meters. Conversely, at close range, the 5.56 mm rounds ripping across short distances had the tendency to disrupt their course and upset violently in human flesh. Things would even get worse if there was body armor intervening as the tumbling, tearing slugs would deform even worse against soft body armor.

Only the barest of movements registered in Schwarz's peripheral vision, and he spun, plunging behind the cover of the support strut base, bullets slamming into the concrete and blasting chunks away. The enemy drone wasn't going to be making an attack from inside the warehouse, and certainly not with a relatively puny pistol-caliber submachine gun.

The derision over the power of the weapon didn't make it any less dangerous. Schwarz had killed, and nearly been killed, by 9 mm SMGs on numerous occasions. He swung around the corner of the base and triggered his Commando, ripping off a 5-round burst in the general direction of the enemy's muzzle-flash. He realized he didn't tag anything, since he didn't have a good sight picture and his trigger pull was a hard jerk, but it was suppression fire, and the enemy guns fell silent for a moment.

That gave Schwarz the time he needed to make certain his FRAG-12 shells were loaded into the XM-26 and chambered. The initial salvo of gunfire had forced his opponents to scatter so they wouldn't be caught bunched up together, and they would be looking for stronger, more certain cover. The Commando wasn't going to do the trick, so it was going to have to be the 12-gauge explosive shells. He got out his CPDA and hooked up the Firewire cable camera. He needed to look around corners, and if he did, he was sure that he'd be exposing himself as a target. The fiber-optic camera instantly transmitted the around-the-corner view, its infrared lens picking out the self-evident glows of his enemies via their body heat. There were three of them, and the camera was sharp enough that he could make out the spill of hot brass from their weapons as tiny stars strewed on the walkway.

Two were currently in motion, one of them giving cover to the others, barely visible behind something that blocked his body heat. If it could do that, then there was little his rifle could do to penetrate and catch him. He could tell by the blobs of red and yellow that made up his opponents' outlines in infrared that they were wearing body armor.

He wondered what kind of optics the enemy was using. It was sunset, and to say it was relatively dim was an understatement, as there were no lights operating in the cavernous black belly of the warehouse. He did know that if he poked his head out, he'd be visible and targeted immediately, simply showing up on night vision, thermal or infrared.

One thing all three, however, were vulnerable to was a powerful emitter that Schwarz had developed. The hand-size illuminator was along the lines of a flash-bang, but instead of one brief instant of light and sound, this would give out a blaze that would overwhelm light amplification measures across the board and do so for more than the brief instant of a flash-bang.

There was a sudden curse on the other side as Schwarz's spectrum strobe pulsed, whiting out the enemy's night vision. Now, with the cover of invisibility, he rushed to a different girder. A side benefit of the emitter was that now his scope had the whole area lit up by the powerful projector he'd deposited on the ground. As he wasn't facing it, neither his electronics nor his eyes would be overwhelmed by the harsh flare of nonvisible light, unlike his opponents'.

He shouldered the SIG but worked his index finger to the trigger of the XM-26. The enemy gunner was still mostly obscured by the steel partition he was utilizing as cover, but one tug of the underbarrel attachment's trigger and a two-inch-long explosive shell rocketed across the distance between the weapon and target. The impact fuse connected with the rolled steel and detonated, blowing a hole through the plate and sending a volcanic jet of fire and pulverized metal dust hurtling into the gunman behind it.

There was a second issuance from the throat of the blinded shooter, but this wasn't a coherent word; it was the gurgling cry of a wounded man as hot shrapnel and an explosive shock wave struck him.

"Open up! Open up!" came a hurried cry over the sound of gunfire.

Schwarz grimaced. The remaining gunmen must have decided that sticking and fighting it out with someone who brought explosive ordnance to a gunfight was not a smart plan. They were calling in their air support to cut loose "danger close."

The Predator-style drone's machine guns obeyed, bullets chewing up the floor of the warehouse, sweeping and cutting through the roof. Schwarz hurled himself to one side as the concrete he'd been standing on was shattered into a cloud of dust. Had he remained still, that gray powder would have been tinted pink as his flesh and bone would have exploded into a bloody mist to mix with the cloud.

Unfortunately, Schwarz couldn't return fire. The FRAG-12 grenade would hit the ceiling of the warehouse and detonate, but the drone, even if it weren't invisible in the skies beyond it, would be too far away to be affected by it, unlike the human who had cleaved to the steel panel for cover.

He was a sitting duck, especially if Option Omega decided to cut loose with a Hellfire missile. No amount of body armor would protect Schwarz from an anti-tank missile.

Whatever dread that Blancanales had held about Schwarz going out alone on this was coming to fruition. The segment of Schwarz's ever-active mind that studied paranormal phenomena was not surprised at such a prophetic instinct among his allies in Able Team. It was that level of awareness, bordering on superhuman, that made the warriors of Stony Man Farm so skilled. It was not so much a preternatural ability, as an instinct to listen to subconscious cues, mostly from information that one often forgot that one had.

Schwarz hoped that the others would be more prescient than he was in dealing with the opposition. They'd already mused that the enemy would have the potential for air support. An antiaircraft missile would come in extremely handy right about now.

He cursed himself for having driven so far from the safe house to maintain secrecy and security for his partners.

Schwarz looked at the catwalk and knew that his opponents were making their escape along a planned exit route. They left their wounded behind and had called down a rain of thunder and death to scorch the earth and leave nothing of their presence.

The prior group had failed at remaining unnoticed, and the cost would have been their lives if Able Team hadn't had them already in custody. These two knew that their existence wasn't worth a damn if they left a prisoner. That meant a rain of hell.

That also suggested a Hellfire missile or two. Schwarz knew that the van was going to be ground zero, the opening of this salvo. Then the wreckage of the warehouse atop the destroyed vehicle would be raked with machine gun fire, or a second missile, or a mix of both. He knew that he was going to have to do something fast, and the electronics genius had it.

Schwarz raced toward the Able Team van, knowing that he had the right tools to deal with the enemy drone even though he was going to have to cobble something together on the fly. He figured he had at least one minute to get it done before he was caught in the open and slaughtered, either by the Option Omega gunman or their air support. On the way back to the van, he paused only long enough to grab his emitter. He pulled off his night-vision goggles and allowed his eyes to get used to the increasing gloom of the empty warehouse.

It didn't take more than a few seconds for him to be able to see clearly, the amount of time it took to cross the warehouse floor back to the van.

Even as he reached the vehicle, he swung around the front of it to use the bulk of it as cover. He avoided diving in through the driver's door because he knew there were still potential enemies at his back. As he opened the passenger's door, his instincts were vindicated by the plunk and pop of enemy SMGs striking the van's armor uselessly.

Schwarz snaked into the van and slid into the rear. The van's roof was dimpled, puckered and even perforated in a few places where heavy-duty rounds had penetrated. Luckily, Schwarz kept his electronic equipment in the same heavy-duty lockboxes where Able Team stored its weapons and especially its ammunition. A sandwich of Kevlar and fiberglass formed the lockbox shells, able to prevent a lucky shot from detonating any explosives within and keeping valuable or needed electronics safe from enemy fire.

Schwarz opened one in particular, withdrawing

something that resembled the unholy coupling of an Uzi submachine gun with its T-shape and trigger with a hand-held spotlight with its large lens and D-carrying handle on top.

Quickly he braced the lockbox against his back, using its open lid and bottom components as a shield, just in case more enemy gunfire came in. Even during his run to the van, his swift brain had already determined what had been necessary, mapped out the wiring. All he had to do was to open the casings, expose the wiring and use his pocket tool to strip insulation to enable the new linkups.

Quickly, Schwarz cracked the casing on his IR and UV emitter, then broke open the light module on his bazooka. The flashlight cannon was a focused-beam laser projector, set at a frequency that would overwhelm and overload surveillance cameras, such as those used in security, or precisely the same cameras used on a Predator-style drone or its camera-guided air-to-ground missile. Both devices worked on the same principle of overwhelming enemy optics. This particular one was intended to be a quick blast of powerful light that would be invisible to the human eye, but to an electronic lens would be searing to the point of the camera equivalent of retinal burn. To get the area effect on his emitter strobe, he had put lenses all around, on four of six of its cube-face surfaces, so he could always leave an unlit side facing him, and one to rest on the ground.

The best part of this design was that he could "unfold" the petals from the omni-emitter for easier maintenance. He unhooked them and set them up parallel to the light bazooka's lens, then wound the wiring together on one trigger. Another few seconds and he had the powerful battery belonging to the emitter duct-taped and supplementing the main charge of the light gun. This setup would allow the light bazooka to increase its range and effectiveness at opposing objects even five thousand feet up.

This was a concentration-intensive process, but he'd worked out the potential for the design on the fly, and for Schwarz, he was able to compartmentalize his thoughts. He was able to feel the sudden rattling hammer of the drone's general-purpose machine guns as they hammered through the roof, one in five shots defeating the armor finally, but in punching through, they lost more energy, enough to be defeated by his equipment-locker tortoise shell.

Still, he kept his mind focused on stripping wires, utilizing discipline and will forged through countless battles and dozens of instances across the years. The lockbox hammered against his shoulders and back, but thanks to the multiple layers and the spreading effect of the lid and sides of the box, what would have been a sharp, deadly penetration was reduced to a series of harmless though highly uncomfortable slaps.

He completed the entire jury-rigging process in only forty-five seconds. Schwarz didn't have to look at his watch, yet another part of his mind kept actual time nearly as accurately as an atomic clock. Those forty-five seconds had been marked by machine guns and the Option Omega shooters firing at the Able Team van in relative futility. Even so, the roof of the van was pep-

pered, cut through in a dozen spots. He no longer heard
the lighter pop and crack of the smaller weapons firing
against the side of the van.

They had cleared out, which meant the drone was
coming around for another attack, but this time it was
with missiles. That was Schwarz's cue to kick open the
back door of the van and take off in a hard, fast run toward the original hole he'd driven through. He leaped
over the smoldering rubble, somersaulting to a kneeling
position. The drone was high above, practically invisible if it weren't for the light and image amplification
of the scope he'd removed from his SIG 552 and placed
atop the improved camera-killer.

Once again, Schwarz made himself a target. He
needed the drone's camera looking at him; otherwise
he wouldn't have the cameras exactly where he needed
them. Through the scope, he spotted the drone turn,
swinging toward him. The enemy needed the cameras
on the air-to-ground missiles pointed in his general
direction. He could see, thanks to the magnification
through the scope, that the drone had two more Mav-
ericks beneath the wings, ready to go. He pulled the
trigger on the emitter bazooka.

To the naked eye, anyone watching would see
Schwarz sitting still, kneeling and aiming an ungainly
gun upward. To anyone with light-amplification optics, a brilliant, searing cone of surging light vomited
skyward. It was as if a magnificent spotlight opened
up, torching through the air in a blazing, deadly line
that was so bright, the Option Omega drone disappeared for a moment. The burn was so bright that it

would have surprised a viewer that the drone hadn't been obliterated.

The remote operator was not working a blind drone, and he still pulled the trigger on the missile launchers, taking a shot at where he remembered Schwarz had been. Breaking into a hard run, Schwarz raced back toward the battered van. As no gunfire chased him, he knew that the enemy wasn't shooting. He dived through the rear doors he'd already opened and slammed them shut behind. He also dragged the lockbox across him.

He'd crossed fifteen yards, and even at nearly fifty feet, the thunder and roar of the two missiles shook the van violently. Luckily, no lockboxes were stacked higher than he was, but the sheer sound of the twin explosions left him momentarily deaf. He crawled away from the lockbox, kicking it off him.

Schwarz felt his communicator vibrate. He plucked it off his belt, shaking the cobwebs out of his head.

"Gadgets, we're here. And we caught two stragglers. Looks like the plan backfired," Blancanales said.

"If you caught the stragglers, no problem with that," Schwarz said.

"Yeah, but you're in a half-collapsed warehouse," Lyons returned. "Think you can find a way out?"

"The van was far enough away from the one entrance I came through that the roof didn't drop on me," Schwarz said, looking out the windows. "Farm, anything on the drone?"

"Akira hacked its controls and walled off its CPU. No one's going to erase anything, and we're going to pull it down to the Farm," Barbara Price's voice said through the earpiece. "We're going to have a hell of a time explaining an airstrike in the Norfolk metropolitan area."

"What's this 'we'?" Lyons asked. "Your work."

"Screw off, Ironman," Price replied. "Someday we'll bring you back to paperwork."

Lyons chuckled. "I hope I'm dead before that. But it's not gonna be today. We'll clear out."

"The less contact with cops, the better," Price agreed. "Makes my job a little easier to do. Just get out of there, Gadgets."

"Crawling behind the wheel," Schwarz answered.

He put the van into drive and plowed through a door on the far side of the warehouse.

CHAPTER SIX

Gary Manning and Rafael Encizo pedaled the bicycles up the trail toward the caldera of Cumbre Vieja. They had "borrowed" the off-road bikes from a rental depot. There were rental kiosks for automobiles around the island, but there weren't any major roads that would reach everywhere necessary for sightseeing, and fewer cars meant less gasoline to be imported to the resort.

This was also a side bonus for the two Phoenix Force experts. Their off-road bicycles were far more quiet, yet still quick enough to get them across the island's back roads easily. As such, they had the stealth to sneak up on enemies, simply by coasting and not exerting energy. Lack of motors meant not only an unlimited fuel range, within reason, but a lower heat signature and a smaller metal content, lowering their visibility on infrared and radar, as well.

Neither Manning nor Encizo had worries about becoming winded. Not only were they the most muscularly dense members of Phoenix Force, but they were in fine athletic condition. Encizo used bicycling to keep up his aerobic endurance for the sake of increasing his time free diving, going under water without the use of oxygen tanks or a snorkel. Manning, on off days, made it a point to jog for miles to keep up his physical conditioning.

It was night, but they had more than enough light to see the road, making it easy for the two men to bike along. Neither was burdened with more than a small day-tour backpack, keeping with the cover that they were tourists, not commandos. Both men were armed only with pocket pistols, Walther P-22s to be exact. Loaded with eleven rounds of subsonic ammunition, the Walther would fit the bill as being the quietest handgun without a suppressor—as a silencer meant a professional strike team—as well as being the kind of handgun that a legitimate owner would take along for plinking and recreational shooting. Subsonic .22 long rifles weren't exactly the hammer of Thor, but in the hands of Encizo, a longtime Walther aficionado, and Manning, a consummate outdoorsman, they would be enough to keep an armed exchange from stopping Phoenix Force cold.

Anyone that happened upon the scene of a conflict between Encizo, Manning and an Option Omega patrol would have assumed that some local Spaniards would have done their business utilizing a .22-caliber target rifle, one of the few firearms that a European would have on hand in his home. The two men might have taken along a small-gauge shotgun, but at range, a .410 shot shell would not have had the killing power on a man as it would against a pigeon or rodent, and the current craze of .45 Colt or ACP/.410 gauge shotgun revolvers wouldn't be as easy to slide into a pocket as the sleek, high-capacity little .22s. Either way, hard contact was something the men of Phoenix Force had to avoid, unless Option Omega's hostages ended up being killed in the thunderous cacophony of an exploding multistory hotel.

The Walthers were, appropriately enough, carried in their jeans in slick little pocket holsters made from Kydex thermoplastic. The plastic sheaths kept the Walthers safe from sweat transferred through the pocket as they bicycled and kept them lighter than a leather alternative. Encizo had carried pocket-size autopistols and revolvers for a long time, so he was well-versed in the use of holsters for the purpose of keeping the tiny weapons from being jammed by lint and other pocket detritus, as well as keeping them oriented for a quick draw while disguising the guns as wallets or other small pocket items.

Encizo slowed his bike as he felt his smartphone vibrate against his pectoral muscle. Manning's had, as well, so the two of them pulled to the side of the road and walked out of sight into a small copse of trees.

They listened intently as a voice file, dumped via high-speed direct link to the CPDA, played. "A-side confirms sighting, capture and identification of Damascus steel versions of Star throwing knives. Be advised, and keep an eye out for souvenirs."

The file was in Barbara Price's voice, so it was direct from the Farm. The two Phoenix vets quickly deciphered the cryptic message. The high-speed data dump was a means of encryption that would scarcely have been on air long enough for it to be intercepted by Option Omega's electronics, and came in a format designed only to be translated by the Farm's audio-file software. It limited two-way conversation, which a sophisticated enemy would have the ability to monitor and thus identify Phoenix Force as a special operations team on the island.

"A-side" referred to Able Team, the first team assembled by Mack Bolan at the beginning of Stony Man Farm's existence. It was also McCarter's cockney rhyming slang for the stateside crew. "Damascus steel versions" meant that Syrian technology was on the ground, at least in Norfolk, Virginia, but if they were on the East Coast, then that meant that the occupation forces in La Palma were going to be utilizing that technology here. "Star throwing knives" meant only one thing—the "star" stood for Star of David and hence Israeli origin. "Throwing knives" translated into armed unmanned aerial vehicles. Israeli UAVs—even Syrian copies that were reverse engineered from shot-down craft that hadn't completely self-destructed—were going to be the kind of force multiplier necessary for even a small army to sew up an island.

As throwing knives referred to combat ability, that indicated that Phoenix Force, if careless, could end up on the receiving end of an air-to-ground missile or two. Even without incurring ground assault munitions, Option Omega had a set of eyes in the sky. Israel, being in a state of constant conflict with its neighbors, was on the bleeding edge of UAV technology to bolster its outnumbered, but never outfought, military forces.

The five men of Phoenix Force had come in swimming, relatively lightly armed, maintaining a low radar return signature as they'd parked their SDV under the waves, and the chill of the ocean had rendered their wetsuits as cool as the surrounding waters, effectively making them invisible to FLIR and other thermal cameras employed by unmanned drones.

Encizo sneered at the news. "Just once, I'd like for the enemy not to have its own air force."

Manning shrugged. "It beats running afoul of heavily armed assault helicopters, such as our last visit to Langley."

Encizo rolled his eyes at that thought. "I love my Walthers, but a P-22 is *not* going to do anything against a Predator-style drone. Not that we'd even have a chance of spotting one in the sky."

"We've been up against aerial recon before, and this time we came prepared. Or rather, underprepared," Manning said.

"Not underprepared. We've got the heavier firepower on board the SDV," Encizo added. "Which is within free-dive distance of the surface, so either Cal or I could retrieve it, in case one of us gets taken out of this op."

"Just remember to let incoming fire have the right of way," Manning told him. "Watching you be shot in the head once in my life is more than enough."

The Cuban wrinkled his nose, remembering the brief glimpse of a gun barrel before a muzzle-flash put him in a coma for weeks. Only the angle of the shot, the use of a round-nosed, full-metal-jacket bullet and the relative hardness of his skull had saved him from death or permanent crippling injury.

Manning looked at the off-road bikes. "I'm still glad we're using these. Their sound signature is lower than any other form of transportation we could think of, short of hiking."

"No engine except our leg muscles also keeps the IR exposure low, too," Encizo added. "Even without aerial recon, though, Omega is not going to like us, or any other tourist, biking up to whatever operation they have at work in the caldera."

Manning grimaced, then looked at a pair of inexpensive night-vision binoculars he'd drawn from his backpack. He considered sweeping the sky to look for the equivalent of a needle in a heavens-wide haystack. "They'll have security on site, no doubt about that. And there's also that we can't anticipate patrol routes for the unmanned drones."

"We won't have to worry about randomly being picked up by their cameras," Encizo countered. "What they need the UAVs for is to watch the shoreline, and caldera site security will deal with known hiking trails and paths. The drones are there for finding and intercepting landing parties."

"Like ours," Manning mused. "Except we came in as low profile as humanly possible."

"We're through. They can't close that particular door, and as long as we avoid a gunfight, even if we do have quiet pistols, we can recon and pick the best plan of attack," Encizo said. "And just hope that David and Cal can dismantle the setup threatening the La Palma hostages."

Manning frowned. "I'm almost sorry I pulled you onto my team…"

"The level of explosives necessary to start a mega-tsunami with a landslide necessitates you needing some-one else versed in explosives. Cal and David have had more than enough continuing education on explosives disposal from you and Gadgets to be on any bomb squad in America, and there will likely be another way of knocking out the trigger threatening the hostages, if any," Encizo said.

Manning stuffed his night-vision binoculars back into his backpack, obviously showing signs of stress. Encizo had seen this in his friends and allies many times before. Thousands of lives were in danger, and he couldn't be everywhere at once, doing what he felt he could do best. It was the kind of sense of duty that could be a slip into a sort of monomania in that only he could fix what was wrong in the world. Manning's intellect and phenomenal strength were the result of a lifetime spent seeking personal excellence. He'd mas-tered chemistry and demolitions, had built a successful business for himself and was in peak physical condi-tioning. After joining Phoenix Force, Manning applied his insatiable quest for knowledge and physical chal-lenge to becoming what could only be described as one of the top ten counterterrorist operatives on the planet.

It was a simple thing for Manning to succeed, but he was the type of man who could only see what he wasn't able to do, the lives he failed to save by not being there to come to the rescue.

"You are not a superman, Gary," Encizo told him. "We're doing everything we can to save the people on this island. Cal and David have the hostages' safety on their plate, and who do you know is better than they are?"

Manning frowned. "I can count them on the fingers of one hand."

"Meanwhile, I need you to help me save the East Coast, where the death toll could rise into the millions if the mega-tsunami strikes," Encizo said. "You're here to prevent a multinational disaster."

"I know that," Manning answered.

"Gadgets talks all the time about how he has his mind on a dozen different things at once but isn't distracted. Indeed, he tends to be more distracted unless he has something to occupy those different parts of his brain. You're his equal intellectually, so I can see those gears spinning inside your head. You need to focus," Encizo said. "And you usually do…"

"But the stakes on this are a lot worse than usual," Manning replied. "Even if they take out the bombs threatening the hostages, the harbor has a ship in it capable of launching missiles that will kill thousands anyway. In the meantime, we've got the caldera explosives. Sure, we could stop it, but if we prevent the explosion and landslide required for the mega-tsunami, the island itself could be in danger thanks to the volcano activating."

"Activating…you mean an eruption?" Encizo asked.

"At least on the scale of the Eyjafjallajökull," Manning confirmed.

Encizo sought confirmation. "The one near Reykjavik that shut down air travel in Europe for weeks? And that's the least problematic on your scale?"

"The potential eruption of the caldera could be an Ice Age-level event," Manning told him.

Encizo frowned. "Now I can see why you're seeing so many worst-case scenarios. A twenty-first-century Ice Age would be catastrophic. You think that the volcano could put out that large of a cloud?"

"To cast about seventy-five percent of the world into thirty to sixty days of night? It's likely. There are several super volcanoes around the planet that could produce such an eruption and planetary climate-affecting event," Manning returned. "And even so, if it doesn't go that hot, we've still got a pyroclastic cloud vomiting out of the ground with as much heat and force as a small nuke. Nothing on this island would be left standing."

"Then we have to be careful," Encizo said.

"That's an understatement."

"We've got miles to go, Gary," Encizo reminded him.

Manning nodded and saddled up, pedaling back toward the road.

Encizo patted the Walther in its Kydex sheath, then followed his friend. Even if they saved North, Central and South America's eastern coasts, the world could still suffer and thousands could die in a failed trigger. One wrong step wasn't the problem.

From here on out, every step they took had to be absolutely correct.

CALVIN JAMES AND David McCarter picked up their off-road bikes at the same time and place as had Encizo and Manning, and since they were electronically linked to the Farm thanks to their smartphones, the two men re-

ceived the high-speed voice message at the same time.
They also translated the cryptic recording, and were
fully aware of the unmanned drones that were in Option Omega's quiver of weapons.

"Maybe there's no plastic explosives in the hotels,"
James said after listening. "It makes things a little easier...."

"Yeah. All we have to do is make an amphibious assault on whatever ship Omega's got the bloody remotes,"
McCarter said. "Which is bugger-all shitty because that
might not be the Q-ship in the harbor. Those bastards
have the missile firepower to knock out naval forces,
but a Tomahawk obliterates a hotel just as easy, if not
easier, than that."

James nodded. "And we might not be dealing with
people who take half measures. They disguised at least
one yacht and a cruise ship to get people onto this island, and that cruise ship has missile launchers. They
could have more craft, but that also means that they're
a belt-and-suspenders type of crew. We eliminate one
potential way of killing a hotel full of hostages, what's
to say that they don't have an alternative?"

"So we just work our way down the checklist," Mc-
Carter said. "Unless you feel like half-assing it?"

"Hell no," James answered. He touched his pocket,
making certain that the little polymer-framed .22 Walther in it was still oriented correctly, despite the Kydex
holster anchoring it against the seams of the pocket.
Even though he had a pistol, James was not going to
rely on that to acquire something heavier in the event of
a fight. Rather, he had his G96 "Boot and Belt" fight-

ing knife sheathed against his forearm, under the long sleeve of his shirt. It was reasonably reachable, and if he couldn't surreptitiously grab that, he had an automatic knife—formerly known as a switchblade—tucked in the small of his back. The autoknife, made by a company called Benchmade, was hardly the flimsy, easily broken shiv utilized by teenage ruffians decades ago. It had a solid locking mechanism, a thick spine and its means of staying open was not dependent on the spring built into the "switch" but the metal leaf locking piece that braced against the opened blade.

Thus the Benchmade autoknife could be popped into action and used for anything from prying open a crate to eviscerating an angry pit bull in the space of an instant. James had grown up in a rough neighborhood, so mastery of the blade was the one thing that had kept him from being picked on. His time as a member of the U.S. Navy SEALs improved on that youthful brawling style, both with official SEAL training and his off-duty study of martial arts, until he was nearly as keen and clever with a sharp edge as his friend Rafael Encizo.

McCarter was less of a blade man, but that didn't keep him from learning an abundance of tricks from two of the best knife fighters that he knew—Encizo and James. He, too, was carrying an autoknife, as well as a serious knife that he had sheathed inside his waistband. Thanks to its positioning on his belt and along his leg, he was able to carry a foot-long version of one of the British empire's most beloved combat weapons—the kukri. The Nepalese weapon had been famous for its hacking abilities, but it was scarcely a compact, concealed-carry fighting knife. The Cuma tak-ri McCarter carried was a little straighter, but still had that long, curved belly and bent-down nose that duplicated the front part of the longer kukri, but without the shaft that it stemmed from at an angle. Without that middle joint, McCarter had something that he could hide away, yet still deliver wicked, brutal blows and actually stab with.

James, however, chose to stick with his old, classic favorite, the G96 design. The original Jet Aer was something he'd carried in his youth, a fearsome, wicked pointed knife, but Jet Aer no longer imported or made them, though quality copies were available.

"That old thing," McCarter prodded.

"You should talk, Mr. I carry a pistol in service since 1935," James returned, mentioning McCarter's love of the classic, pre-World War II designed but rarely surpassed Browning Hi-Power. Few autoloaders, even the team's Glocks, could match the reliability, versatility and sleekness of the old pistol.

"Oh, right, I'm the one who carries an ancient gun, Calvin Nineteen Eleven," McCarter returned with a wink. "At least I still carry my 'primitive technology.'"

The two men had exchanged these words in whispers, and each with tongues firmly planted in cheeks. Appreciation for the single-action pistols of the early twentieth century had only been one of many reasons why the Chicago bad-ass and the Cockney hard-case had gotten along famously, but it was a bonding factor. James had reluctantly given up the grand old .45-caliber 1911 Colt Commander when Phoenix Force decided to stick with 9 mm autopistol designs, for ammunition commonality, not because the gun had ever come up short in firepower or stopping ability. Even so, James still carried his Commander off duty, even recently obtaining a custom 9 mm slide and barrel for the pistol, an option he'd kicked himself for not taking years earlier, though it had only been recently that absolutely reliable 9 mm magazines were available for the 1911-pattern handguns.

Here and now, thoughts of more substantial handguns than the ones they had in their pockets were simply self-torture, and a grim reminder of the truism that if the only tool one had was a hammer, then every problem was treated as a nail. The .22s were insurance against a gunfight, both as being the last possible weapon expected by an Option Omega soldier, concealed in trousers, and an admonition against looking for a shooting solution in a hostage situation as they infiltrated.

No gun, even one with a so-called silencer, was completely quiet, and the dull, soft reports of a tiny .22 going off would still bring troops running and alert the guards that they might need to collapse a hotel and kill hundreds of hostages because of outside interference on La Palma. A single stray bullet wasn't just a treat to a bystander hundreds of yards away; it was the death knell for Option Omega's captives.

If Omega's brand of renegade white supremacists were going to die this soon into the infiltration, then they were going to have to die by the blade and be positioned so that their corpses would never be found. It seemed cruel, but McCarter and James remembered the dozens dumped unceremoniously into the ocean, and the dozens more slain when cruise ships were blasted mercilessly.

Option Omega had declared war on the world, and Phoenix Force knew exactly how brutal and lethal they had to be to prevent countless more innocent lives lost.

T. J. HAWKINS'S STAY in Tarajal would be slightly more high profile than that of his friends, but he still needed a good cover. Before entering the port town, he'd gone back to the beach and thrown himself into a tumble down a sloping path that led to a gravelly beach. This was a controlled drop, but he didn't want to come out too clean. His purpose was to render his shirt and jeans ragged and give himself a convincing set of bruises and minor cuts to support his story of being a tourist who ran for his life in the face of the terrorist assault.

He did a quick inventory of himself, utilizing a small pocket mirror, and decided he looked as ruffled and messed up as an ordinary civilian on the run. He double-checked that the Walther P-22 in his pocket was unharmed and ready to go. The Kydex holster was safe. He also looked at the two 10-round spare magazines. They hadn't been dented, and the cartridges in the top were also in good working order.

Hawkins jogged in, breathless, along the road.

He glimpsed people hidden in their homes, lights dim or out altogether, shades pulled to conceal themselves. They were frightened, and from the smell of a recent fire, he could tell why.

Hawkins called out as if he expected someone to answer him, but as a member of Delta Force and the

Army Rangers, he was well aware of the simple aspect of human nature. He was a stranger to the people who lived in this town, and of late, strangers had only brought terror and ruin to their once tranquil home.

Hawkins saw a small corner store that had its doors open. As he approached, he could see around the building and the source of the smoky air. An AGM had struck, tearing up a row of stores and bistros. The missile's explosive radius had left charred smears on the ground. There were twisted remnants of tables, and he spotted a few scattered pieces of clothing and shoes.

The missile had struck while these quaint vacation businesses were in full swing.

That thunderbolt of terror had grown into a wide-ranging sense of dread that kept people low and out of the way. He turned to enter the open store and saw why the doors were ajar. One whole wall had been vaporized, a sickly breeze wafting through, carrying the scent of roasted flesh.

Murder most foul had been committed here, and there was no rhyme or reason as to why so many had to die. It was the kind of thing that spurred Hawkins to be one of the five members of Phoenix Force. He loathed senseless violence, which might have been a redundancy to a pacifist, but Hawkins was much more realistic. Doing nothing in the face of abuse and other crime was only insurance that those who preyed upon you would continue feasting at a trough of zero resistance.

Violence was a shield against subsequent violence.

Hawkins looked around and felt his foot bump

against a plastic bottle. He picked it up and saw that it was bottled water. As much as he wanted to avoid seeming like a ghoulish looter, he twisted off the cap, took a swig then poured the rest onto his face and hair, adding to his disheveled appearance.

"Just because this place looks like a war zone doesn't mean we cotton to looting," an aged voice said in Spanish. The words cut into his dousing. Thanks to his language immersion training in the Rangers, Delta and finally Phoenix Force, Hawkins was so used to hearing Spanish that he mentally translated the phrase with his usual Texas colloquialisms. Hawkins turned to see the speaker.

"I'll pay for the water… I'm sorry," he muttered. He saw it was an older man, somewhere in his fifties, skin weathered and wrinkled by his island life. Clutched at waist level was a double-barreled shotgun, though the muzzles were small, between .410 and 20 gauge. At this range, the blast from one or both would still punch a hole the size of a human fist through his belly.

The old man glared, and Hawkins knew he couldn't draw the Walther from his pocket in time. Even if he did, the man was only defending his home in the wake of an attack. Violent self-defense may have been an option for a lesser man, but Hawkins was U.S. military, and he didn't believe in murdering an innocent man protecting himself from a perceived criminal.

The two black tunnels of the shotgun muzzle rose.

CHAPTER SEVEN

As the shotgun barrels rose, T. J. Hawkins reacted in the only way his trained and experienced body could. He lunged closer to the weapon, bringing up his forearm beneath the muzzle of the double-barrel, and using his momentum to leverage the powerful weapon up at the ceiling and away from him. At this distance, the muzzle-blast would be blinding and deafening, at least for the space of a few moments, but Hawkins and the rest of Phoenix Force had inured themselves to the painful noise and light of flash-bang "distraction devices."

The shotgun didn't roar, however. The older man jerked away from him in surprise, eyes wide. In the same swift instant, Hawkins reached for his wallet with one hand as his wrist pushed the shotgun barrels wide and away from either of the two of them. He opened it and took out a couple of Euro bills.

"I said I'd pay," Hawkins repeated himself. "No need to shoot!"

"Sorry! Don't hurt me!" the older man sputtered. "The gun was empty!"

Hawkins looked at the weapon as it dangled in the man's hands. He sighed. "Pretty foolish to approach a stranger with an empty gun."

The old man was surprised as much at Hawkins's fluency in Spanish as he was by the swiftness of his reaction to being "drawn on."

"It's a deactivated shotgun," the man said. "Stupid laws leave good men unarmed in the face of criminals in a crisis like this."

Hawkins chuckled. "I feel for you."

The old man absently accepted the money.

"Is this your store?"

The Spaniard nodded. "My name is Hector."

"Thomas," Hawkins returned. The best way to build a cover name was to have some similarity between your most commonly used name and your identity. As the T.J. stood for Thomas Jefferson, and in his youth, he was called Thomas when he angered his mother, it was an easy thing to keep straight. The ID cards in his wallet were all for Thomas Presley, fitting with one of Phoenix Force's "group identities," where McCarter was King, Manning was Roi, Encizo was Rey and James was Farrow—the five kings. The last names changed often; there was also a color set and a "Johnson" set, as well.

Hawkins pointed to the wrecked wall.

"I didn't hear any missiles while I was making my way here," Hawkins noted, building his cover story.

"It struck this morning, hours ago," Hector returned. He looked despondent. "My daughter was here, working."

"She all right?" Hawkins asked.

Hector made a sign of the cross. "She has had better days. Except for a few cuts and a bad case of the shakes, she's fine. You speak Spanish quite well."

Hawkins shrugged. "Raised in Texas. If that weren't enough, two of my best friends are native Spanish speakers."

Hector smiled. "But you're pronouncing proper Castillian style, not like the American."

"Well, it took some time. I came to Santa Cruz de La Palma for a vacation, and unlike most of my fellow Americans, I didn't want to be crude about my speech," Hawkins answered. "I'd been to Valencia a few years ago, and I got nothing but dirty looks from the locals."

Hector frowned. "You picked an unfortunate time to come to our little island."

Hawkins shrugged. "I'm just glad I got out of town."

"Santa Cruz is on the other side of the island. How did you get here?"

"As soon as the missiles went off, I started running. I didn't stop until I reached the opposite shore. I'd hoped it was safer here," Hawkins said.

Hector looked at the damage to his store's wall. "This was the only shot fired at us. This group, Option Omega, it wanted to let us know that they could reach us easily."

"So no funny business," Hawkins concluded. "Anyone hurt or killed?"

"Minor injuries. It was as if they found the one hole in our city where people weren't crowded together, that they could thread a missile in just to let us know how accurate they are, and destructive," Hector mused.

Hawkins sneered. "Pretty tame of them, but then again, they are terrorists. You can't be afraid if you're dead."

The ex-Ranger looked around. "It worked, too. No one stepped out to even greet me."

"Well, you are beat up and unarmed," Hector mentioned. "Which means you can't help us, but at least you aren't one of the Omega killers."

Hawkins restrained a smile. He *was* here to kill Option Omega's soldiers, once the island was safe enough for a search-and-destroy operation as only Phoenix Force could conduct.

"Texan. You know guns, correct?" Hector asked. He offered the double-barrel. "Maybe you can reactivate it."

"Have ammo for it, old hoss?" Hawkins returned.

Hector glanced left, then right, as if he were about to reveal a secret, but Hawkins held up his hand.

"Don't say another word," Hawkins said, stopping him. "Any other deactivated firearms on hand?"

"A few here and there across the town," Hector said. "And there are one or two that still actually work. Those are over/under shotguns at the skeet range."

Hawkins glanced over the shotgun. It was akin to an old cowboy gun, imported into the U.S. by European American Armory but built in Turkey. It was quality, and sturdy. And as far as he could tell, the only thing wrong with it, upon breaking open the action, was that there was no firing pin to go with either of the two long-eared hammers. His specialty was with more modern firearms, but he could tell that, upon pulling the triggers, there was nothing to strike the primers upon any shells within.

"I think I can improvise something. It won't be the safest thing in the world," Hawkins told him.

"Can we expect safety on an island where missiles are launched into the center of towns?" Hector asked. "Do what you can."

Hawkins smirked. "If you can, get everyone else who has a weapon of some kind. Tell them I'll do what I can to fix it."

Hector chuckled. "Thank you, Jesus Christ, for sending us a Texan in our time of need!"

Hawkins allowed his smile to grow even more. By spreading word that there was a stranger in town cobbling old weapons into fighting condition, he now had the means of flushing out anyone who was in hiding to spy on this side of the island. His cover story would be more than enough to keep it from seeming as if he were a top-secret commando sent in to raise hell, but it would draw out an Option Omega patrol, if his guesses were correct.

However, hearing Hector's improvised, excited prayer, he decided to play up his Texas birthright with the most appropriate phrase he could muster.

"Praise the Lord and pass the ammo!"

BARBARA PRICE BROUGHT her tablet out of sleep mode the moment it beeped, alerting her to the arrival of a message from T. J. Hawkins.

"'Made contact with locals,'" she read aloud. "'Playing gunsmith. Ask Cowboy if he knows how to whip up an improvised firing pin for a double-barreled shotgun.'"

Price smirked and sent a response. "That's not low

profile." She could almost sense the chuckle on the other side of the Atlantic.

"I'm not low profile. I told them I'm Texan."

The reputation of the Lone Star State was world renowned, and being good with guns was a natural assumption made by even foreigners in the deepest, darkest parts of Africa, let alone the First World tourist islands off that continent's coast.

"Don't let the islanders get into any fights they can't handle."

"It's going to be all me. Giving these people a snowball's chance," Hawkins responded.

"Fair 'nuff. Keep me in the loop," Price answered. She got on the line, dialing John "Cowboy" Kissinger's extension on the Farm.

Kissinger wasn't a man from the Wild West, but in his days as a drug enforcement agent, he'd more than earned his reputation for being "cowboy," kicking down doors despite the presence of armed thugs on the other side. In the years since, his skills and expertise had given him a position at Stony Man Farm, assembling and modifying weapons especially for Able Team, Phoenix Force and even the Executioner on occasion. His old ass-kicking ways also managed to get him some work in the field when either Able Team needed a fourth man for extra muscle or Mack Bolan needed another body, complete with razor-sharp mind, on his lone-wolf missions.

"What's up, Barb?" Kissinger asked.

"Got a free moment? T.J. decided to set up an arms

repair clinic on La Palma, and needs advice for whipping up some firing pins and other bits," Price told him.

"Seeing as how I don't expect Able to run into the field right away with these select-fire MP-45s I'm finalizing, I'll get right on it," Kissinger said. "I'll send him a schematic for whatever he needs via text attachment."

"Keep the files small enough so that Omega doesn't pick up a lot of information traffic in or out of the island," Price admonished.

"I know," Kissinger replied. "Texting T.J. now."

"Let me know how things are going," Price responded.

"You've got it," Kissinger returned.

Price hung up and checked her tablet for any further information. She glanced over at the "pit" of cyberwizards, the ring of workstations where four of the most brilliant computer users on the side of angels were in action as a team.

Huntington Wethers had an incoming message alert, and she avoided the temptation to interrupt him. Wethers would send an efficient, pared-down info dump that would tell her everything she needed to know without overburdening her concentration or cutting into time that she could otherwise utilize for coordinating with the field teams and their liaison with the White House. The lead line would give the summary succinctly, and the rest was simply Wethers "showing his work" as stated in math class.

"Forensic accounting result: after penetrating a dozen cover LLCs, narrowed down the buyer of Jeopardy Corp's shipbuilding facilities—Chinese SAD."

Price grimaced.

Stony Man Farm had encountered renegade Red Chinese operations more times than they cared to count. While they had worked alongside the Communist Chinese, as well, there were elements of the SAD—their equivalent of the CIA—that would have loved to see a world-wide Chinese empire set up. While the rest of the current regime was under the assumption of eventual Chinese superiority—an unofficial motto was China Is Eternal—there were those whose impatience would push them toward risky propositions.

It made sense. China had done a lot of work in influencing control of the Panama Canal in the wake of the United States ceding direct control of the vital waterway between the Atlantic and the Pacific. Mack Bolan and the warriors of Stony Man Farm had blunted and destroyed several efforts at conquest by proxy of the Panamanian locks, thus wresting enormous economic power. Of late, the People's Republic of China had also gained a significant advantage by virtue of the American need for fast cash to keep up its efforts in Iraq and Afghanistan. A huge debt was owed to the PRC, one large enough to cause friction within American politics and paranoia about the sudden possession of USAF similar technology.

An event that would cause massive destruction in the Atlantic would result in only minimal disruption of Chinese business and make the Pacific busier due to the destruction of East Coast and European port cities. One could also easily imagine the necessity of borrowing further funds from the Chinese government for the rebuilding of infrastructure within the stricken regions.

According to Jeopardy's white paper, the cost of rebuilding could conceivably rise into the quadrillions. America, Europe, Central and South America, and Africa, in need of fast cash and ready supplies and shipping, would need somewhere to beg. Likely donors would be the Middle East, the Russian states and Southeast Asia.

Price frowned.

"Hunt? Did you uncover anything about the Middle East in your digging?" Price asked.

"Section five has strong yet circumstantial evidence of a trio of Saudi princes involved. They have ties to international terrorism and Wahabbist extremism," Wethers answered.

Price tabbed to that part of the cyberwizard's report and read through it quickly but closely. There were two options regarding their involvement. Either they were laundering the Chinese money, or they were in support of a renegade faction of SAD, looking to make their own profits off the mayhem. She referred back to the white paper, looking specifically at the results of a mega-wave that struck the Venezuelan coast and disabled their oil transportation and production facilities.

The La Palma landslide would effectively reduce Venezuela to about ten percent of its current capacity, cutting that nation out of the business of international oil, much to the benefit of Middle Eastern petrol-commerce. She grimaced.

"Hunt, dig deeper into the Saudi angle. Akira?"

"Invade Chinese cyberspace. Check!" the heavy-metal-powered hacker returned, as if reading her mind. She wondered how he had any hearing left after the clash of screaming guitars and slamming drums, but Akira Tokaido was, like any of the rest of the Stony Man staff, an amazing human being of multiple layers and divergent skills.

Tokaido was the one whom the team turned to when it came to invading secure databases around the world. The man had the twitch reflexes of a computer gamer, which allowed him to adapt to whichever environment he cut into. Busting down the firewall around SAD's mainframe would be something he was born to do.

Price closed the document and looked for more incoming data.

Able Team had new prisoners. They'd also flattened a warehouse outside of Norfolk. Well, the destruction of a building wasn't the team's fault. It was Option Omega, with its missile-bearing UAV, that had caused the devastation. Luckily, except for members of the terrorist group, no one was hurt beyond some scrapes and bumps.

Price got on an encrypted line with the team immediately.

"Schwarz Bagels and Lox," Schwarz answered perkily.

"Where are you going to nuke next?" Price asked him.

"We were just the target," Schwarz responded with a chuckle.

"You know what I mean," Price said. "Gimme something to work with here."

"The drone is at the Farm at this moment, so there should be people there working on it as we speak," Schwarz answered, getting serious. "The hard drive and computer core are on their way to Bear right now."

One of the blacksuits arrived, as if on cue. Price took a deep breath.

"It's here," she told him.

"Great. This might give us a backtrack, provided we can keep the bad guys from finding out we caught their drone," Schwarz replied.

"You blinded it for the space of several seconds with that…whatever it was," Price returned.

Schwarz's smile was so infectious, it penetrated the cellular signal. "Something I jury-rigged. I haven't had time to name it."

"That caused the rather simple brain inside of the drone to blank out. It was deaf and dumb, out of touch with its home base," Price noted. "That gave us everything we needed to take it over."

"What about news reports?" Schwarz asked.

"We stated that a test drone out of Langley crashed into an abandoned building," Price said. "An empty shell was brought into the wreckage."

"That works for me," Schwarz replied. "Might convince them. As it is, I instructed the blacksuit crew to completely disconnect all coms from the processor and dismantle them. Hopefully that will blank things out enough, but still give us something to look for in way of electronics for their source of origin."

"Right now, Kissinger's a bit busy, so he can't check out the firepower on board, if any was left," Price said.

"One missile, and presumably the guns," Schwarz explained. "Not that it's ever really a good gauge of where they came from. We've managed to fake convincing 'local' firearms. Kissinger's done it, and he uses unbranded, untraceable brass for our ammo."

"We'll see what shakes out, Gadgets," Price said. "Anything else for now?"

"Not yet," Schwarz said. "Over and out."

Price hung up with him.

"Bear?" Price asked.

"I'm on my way to isolate the HD and go in," Aaron Kurtzman explained. "What's up?"

"Just making sure I know where all my ducks are," Price returned. "Good hunting."

"The Bear does not hunt. Hunting implies a chance of failure," Kurtzman responded in a deep, grumbling voice.

"Oh, please..." Price groaned. "Good luck anyway."

The bearded hacker nodded, then rolled his wheelchair into the "quarantine" chamber.

Two teams accounted for. One group idling, momentarily, another performing support work for a group of would-be hostages.

She wondered about the others, but knew that except for a few brief texts of absolutely vital news, such as the arming of locals, the men of Phoenix Force would have to maintain radio silence.

It didn't stop her from worrying, and continuing to pore over updated satellite imagery, though if anything happened that was large enough to register on the current resolution she was looking at, it was possible the whole world would learn about it within a few moments.

THE PRESIDENT LOUNGED back in his chair, one arm draped over the back, his brow knit in concern as he held up the report in one hand. His lips were pursed as he mentally chewed on the current batch of intel Harold Brognola had presented to him.

"So, not only is there going to be a killer tsunami that will wreck the U.S. East Coast from Maine to Florida—not only are there thousands of hostages on an island in the Atlantic—but there's also a renegade force in Norfolk, Virginia, and they're being funded and supplied by the People's Republic of China and Saudi princes," the President concluded.

"The trail is buried deep, so deep that exposing it would only appeal to conspiracy theorists. All they know right now is that an Idaho white supremacist group has targeted European tourism," Brognola said.

"I've got people keeping a lid on the La Palma volcano threat," the President said. "But according to my staff, posts are popping up about that damn Jeopardy white paper."

"Jeopardy is an American company, so if anything does happen, it will lead back to us," Brognola responded. "Idaho bigots. American corporation. No amount of money is going to cover up our blame in this."

"The livelihoods of millions of Americans will be wrecked as coastal cities are trashed by a superwave, and we're also going to take the blame for the damage caused to us," the President grumbled. "Oh, and Venezuela is going to take a hit, as well?"

"Plenty of nations will, but Venezuela is a major oil producer, which is why we believe that the Saudi conspirators are keen on this. Venezuela is no friend of the U.S., not of late."

"No," the President agreed. "People are more interested in the Middle East, but Venezuela's nationalized oil production is a result of our attempts to reintroduce democracy to that country."

"They are sitting on enough oil money to withstand a collapse of sea commerce, and their wells are on land. They just can't send it out if their ports are damaged by the tsunami," Brognola added. "We've looked into the volatility of that situation, and it's likely that there could be a shooting war if their leadership thinks that we can't respond."

"Colombia," the President agreed, nodding. He squeezed his brow. "Where we have a lot of interest already placed, including American soldiers supporting drug enforcement. Venezuela attacks…"

"Things turned bad when we acted righteously in Libya on the heels of Iraq and Afghanistan draw downs," Brognola said. "Imagine something like this exploding literally in our own backyard in the wake of an East Coast crisis."

"Your people have speculated," the President pointed out.

"I'm thinking of consequences outside of that box," Brognola returned. "Public opinion responses. Political fallout. Extremists in our own country acting out of rage…"

"We thought we were isolated from Europe over the Iraq bullshit," the President mused. "The Atlantic might as well become a wall of fire, not water."

"Global animosity will make things a lot worse," Brognola agreed.

The President narrowed his eyes. "Stony Man can fix this, right?"

"We've done it before, but that doesn't mean we won't take this as another day at the office," Brognola explained. "That's why we've won so far. We give it our all. We have a memorial for how many gave everything before this."

The President nodded. "I pray no more names are added to that memorial."

Brognola didn't give voice to his next thought. If the La Palma mega-landslide occurred, the Farm and that memorial would likely be washed away with the ensuing tsunami.

CHAPTER EIGHT

Rafael Encizo lowered his pocket binoculars after scanning the road ahead. It was the middle of the night, but the men standing watch were alert and sweeping the area with their own light-amplification optics. Fortunately, neither Encizo nor Manning was using any active illumination to observe, something that would have given them completely away.

"They're ready for intruders," Manning murmured. "I've also received a quick data dump. We can't see it, but Stony Man has satellite surveillance that's picking up a patrol drone in orbit around the entrance to the caldera."

"They haven't noticed us yet," Encizo said. "But that's going to change if they pick us sneaking past their perimeter."

Manning grimaced. "They'll have motion sensors, maybe even seismic."

"I doubt it," Encizo returned. "We are on a volcano."

"So trip wires or an infrared fence would be more likely," Manning said. "I'd go with a fence. Fewer transmitters, less electrical power, something that could be snuck up here quietly and quickly."

Encizo frowned. "Though, if they've been here for a month—"

Manning cut his friend off. "They'd still be moving this stuff in small shipments, to keep outsiders from getting suspicious."

Encizo didn't act hurt that his friend interrupted him, nor did he feel anything wrong. Manning had one of the fastest brains in Stony Man, so if there was a technical issue that had to be determined, the Cuban deferred to the Canadian. Manning had already thought out the way that a terror group or conspiracy would move heavy equipment onto the scene.

"What are you thinking they would use to start the landslide?" Encizo asked.

Manning frowned. "We've got a low-yield nuclear option, but the radiation shielding would still allow trace emissions that the satellite could track. On the other hand, properly placed fifty-five-gallon drums work quite well. That's two hundred kilograms of high explosive per barrel."

Encizo grimaced. "The paper on the landslide didn't state the location of the barrels that would set off the tsunami, did it?"

"No. I'm simply going through my own rough geological knowledge and my experience with high explosives," Manning returned. He ran the back of his fist along his chin, looking skyward. "It's all a moot point unless we find a way around the perimeter."

Encizo checked his CPDA, looking at Stony Man's current satellite imagery. "According to infrared, there's close to fifty heat signatures on hand that can be identified as human. That's out in the open, and not working underground."

"They'd need to pack the drums under the earth to form the correct fissures," Manning said. "Who knows how large that crew would be."

Encizo pulled the Walther and its holster from one pocket, handing them to his friend. He then took the spare magazines out of his other pocket and handed over the CPDA. Finally he shrugged out of his backpack, laying it at Manning's feet.

"What are you doing?" Manning asked.

"We need some HUMINT on this group," Encizo said.

Human intelligence. Manning grimaced. "So you're going unarmed?"

Encizo shook his head. He lifted his long-sleeved T-shirt and Manning spotted the metal clip that hooked one of his knives to the waistband of his jeans.

"Is that a fast-drawing knife?" the Canadian asked.

The Phoenix commando smirked. "In my hands, they all are."

"What about someone farther than twenty-one feet from you?" Manning asked. "I'm a good marksman, but if I open up with the Walther, these .22s aren't going to reach far enough to cover you."

Encizo patted a leather wristband he wore. "I've got a few things up my sleeve."

"Not the throwing stars," Manning noted. "I know you've trained hard with those, but ones of sufficient mass would not fit in that leather band."

"True shuriken, throwing spikes," Encizo answered.

Encizo had learned the art of shurikenjutsu from his

close friend and fellow original Phoenix Force founder, Keio Ohara. The skill of throwing sharpened metal in combat may have seemed rather worthless in a world of high-powered rifles, but Encizo's lessons and continued education in the wake of Ohara's death had given the Cuban an edge in situations where he would have normally been helpless.

Encizo broke from cover, with only his knives and spikes. He wanted to appear as harmless as possible, and the folding knife in his waistband was well hidden by the stiffness of his belt. A casual frisk would miss it and the other knife hanging from a thong around his neck. If necessary, Encizo could whip out these blades far faster than the eye could follow, delivering eviscerating blows in the space of a moment.

Would that be enough? It had been before, but every situation was different. All he could hope for was the sheer boldness of his plan, something to get a look at the men who were on hand, study who they were and then slink back, driven off by angry gunmen who didn't want a middle-aged civilian in their midst.

Manning settled in, and despite his complaints about the range of the Walther pistol and ammunition, he still brought it out, thumbing back the hammer for a light, concise trigger pull, which would give him the best advantage he could hope for on a long-distance shot.

After that, all Gary Manning could hope to do was to wait for nothing, but expect hell to explode in his face.

SANTA CRUZ WAS A QUIET ghost town, except for the small cadres of armed men on different, seemingly random street corners. The gunmen were acting as security, and here, in the city, Option Omega had little need of soaring their unmanned drones high in the sky.

This much was apparent to Calvin James and David McCarter as they entered the city. The drones hung low, making them harder to hit without putting bullets or missiles into occupied buildings. It also allowed the unmanned war craft to use their machine guns at a closer range, and save their air-to-ground missiles for larger, more powerful forces. Or, chillingly, the drones could simply blow hotels to smithereens, producing building collapses capable of smothering and slaughtering hundreds, even thousands.

McCarter tracked one of the drones as it wended its way down the boulevard, wishing he were in full Phoenix Force battle kit instead of the soft clothes of a civilian, packing only the smallest of pistols and a selection of fighting blades to engage in any activity against the enemy.

He looked back into a storefront window. People had hunkered down, frightened, unwilling to come out into the open after a wave of explosions and gunfire ravaged the city days ago. He could smell the sickly stench of roasted flesh in the air, meaning that somewhere nearby, humans had died in a fire. McCarter hated that scent, as it was one of the most gut-wrenching forms of death around.

Option Omega's list of murders was growing, and it didn't seem to have an end in sight.

But that's what Phoenix Force was on the ground to stop. McCarter took the anger, the spite boiling within his gut, storing those emotions, keeping them loaded like fresh magazines, just for that extra surge of strength, that spare bit of stubbornness that would mean the difference between victory and death.

He glanced back at his partner and friend. James kept an eye out for the squads and the drones while McCarter took stock of the frightened, the hiding.

"David, I don't care how many zealots the original Omega had—this is a huge operation," James muttered. "Judging by the corner observation posts alone, we're talking at least a full company or two of opposition just in Santa Cruz."

"Outnumbered, but never outfought, mate," McCarter returned. He checked his CPDA. "Text from Gary. Rafe is going to get close and personal with the guards at the caldera."

"At the caldera," James repeated. "At one road leading into the caldera. That thing is miles across. There's a reason why a volcanic eruption would be enough to—"

"Cal," McCarter interrupted.

"Sorry. Worried about Rafe," James said. "Who else am I gonna go scuba diving with?"

McCarter knew that James was trying to make light of his concerns, but if there was one thing that the men of Phoenix shared, it was a bond of brotherhood. They were so much more than a family. The death of one always struck the others hard. It had only happened twice, but each time had been an instance of dark, painful times. Even Encizo's near death had brought the men to the point of doubt, but they soldiered on.

Grief was nothing new to them. They were warriors,

and none of them expected to die of old age. McCarter's counterpart, Carl Lyons of Able Team, once said that the reason he felt he did so well in battle with the forces of darkness was that he already considered himself dead. With that philosophy, Lyons pushed himself harder, making every battle one in which he invested everything, without hesitation. Death held little fear for him.

But it was a lot easier to think of no future for yourself. It was harder to think of those you cared about suddenly snuffed out, nothing left behind except a hollow, vacant spot where once was a friend and brother.

"We have to worry about our position here," McCarter stated. He grimaced. "We can only do so much skulking and ducking every time we hear a damn UAV."

James shrugged. "The drones are flying low but fast. It doesn't look like they're actually on patrol."

"And too regularly to catch any outside activity. This is a leash," McCarter murmured. "The real trouble will be the troops on the ground."

"Not the ones at the checkpoints," James added.

McCarter nodded. "Smaller patrols. One or two men."

James took to a knee and leveled his field glasses at one of the corner mobs of Omega soldiers. They were wearing windbreakers, all of them, and there were what appeared to be weapons crooked under arms. Upon closer examination, however, James was able to make out strange details on the M-16 rifles they carried.

"Those are rubber guns," the Phoenix Force medic said softly.

McCarter focused in. "All but one. What drew your attention to them?"

"I've always been an AR-15 platform user. Those muzzles looked completely wrong, all solid black," James said. "And check out their wrists."

"Cable tied together," McCarter noted as he saw the plastic tail of one poking out. "Rubber guns and wind-breakers give the illusion of a larger force on hand in the city. But there's only one man watching this particular group."

James grimaced. "We're going to need to confirm that other groups are like this."

McCarter nodded. "Some might be hostages repurposed to look like extra muscle, but that doesn't mean all of the observation posts are ninety percent fakes."

James shook his head. "If a military force did try to storm Santa Cruz, they'd just see armed people. The better units would give them a chance to drop their weapons…"

"Which they can't, because of the cable ties," McCarter added. "They'd be gunned down."

"Making their rescuers their murderers," James grumbled. "We also have to decide if we do anything with these groups."

"We start taking out these observation posts, their central command will notice," McCarter mused. "No reports means that Option Omega will take the initiative to hit the detonators on the hotels."

"Unless that's a ruse, as well," James said. He glanced skyward. "What if the Santa Cruz situation is just a diversion?"

"It is a diversion," McCarter countered. "The real goal is the collapse of the caldera and the creation of a super tsunami. This is to keep the rest of the world from stumbling in and discovering whatever work is being done up in the volcano."

James nodded. "But what if the drones are not armed with the firepower to collapse a building, or what if the hotels aren't rigged with major explosives?"

"That still leaves the Q-ship in the harbor," McCarter returned. "They killed hundreds with an opening salvo."

"But that will still eat up time that could be spent derailing the caldera incident," James said.

McCarter looked toward the harbor. "What are you thinking?"

"I'm going to swim out to the Q-ship," James told him. "You work here and confirm whether the hotel guests are at risk or not."

"If they find you…" McCarter began.

"If they find me, who cares?" James asked. "I'll either fight my way out or raise such hell on board that I can cripple their weapons. I'm pretty damn sneaky."

"The group they chose, Option Omega, isn't going to be welcoming a black man on the scene," McCarter explained. "If you're captured, they'll put you through hell before you're killed."

James took a deep breath, tracing a scar on one of his hands. It had been the leftover from a battle against a group that had taken the Vatican hostage. Among other things, they had severed a digit from his little finger, since returned to full length with cosmetic surgery. There were still the remains of a scar where a white-hot coin had seared into his hand, part of his captors' torture. "It won't be nothing I haven't endured, escaped from or had you guys save me from. Plus, who says I won't die trying?"

McCarter grimaced. "Needs of the many outweigh the needs of the few."

"Quoting *Star Trek?*" James asked.

McCarter raised an eyebrow. "So that's where Manning got that line."

James grinned. "Trust me, as bad as things could get for me, you're not going to have it easy here. We've got millions of lives at risk. If we take this shit timidly…"

"Bring your A-game," McCarter told him. "See you on the other side."

James clapped his friend on the shoulder, and then they split up.

RAFAEL ENCIZO APPROACHED the break in the road, walking with a limp. He was glad that the shirt he wore concealed his brawny upper body.

"¡Por favor!" he shouted as soon as he was in voice range. *"¡Por favor!"*

The two guards on the scene glared at him, but neither reached for his rifle. One had the prescience to rest his hand on his belt, close to the handle of the weapon in his hip holster. The other simply looked annoyed at this intrusion on the quiet night.

The annoyed one spoke up in Spanish. "What the hell is wrong with you?"

The other guard ambled casually away from his partner. To anyone who wasn't trained, this would have been a random movement, but Encizo knew that these two were separating to keep both from being surprised by a sudden burst of violence. Even if Encizo had a handgun, the time he'd take shooting one of the guards would give the other the chance to draw and fire, ending whatever assault he'd intended.

The Cuban kept note of the man in his peripheral vision, but did very little to betray his alertness. He wanted to seem tired, scared. "The town, so many hurt…"

"What's it to us?" the guard asked.

"My wife, she needs medical attention. The town doesn't have the kind of medical facilities. I thought that since this was some kind of science expedition…"

The guard rolled his eyes. The other man seemed to relax his stance.

"We're not going to allow those Option Omega psychos to catch us out in the open, or to sneak in an infiltrator," the other man said, pulling Encizo's attention away from the first man.

Encizo lost the first of the guards, just outside of his peripheral vision, but he still had a sense of his position thanks to the sound of his breathing and the crunch of gravel beneath his boots. "The Americans haven't come here?"

The "ready" gunman shook his head. "Maybe they don't care about a stretch of barren land with a few geology nerds hanging around."

"But my wife…"

"We're security guards, not emergency medical technicians," the gunman said. "All we have are bandages and burn salve."

Encizo frowned. "I came all this way... No morphine. No antibiotics?"

"Just bullets to end suffering, and I didn't sign on to shoot people in the head," the other stated.

The phrase sounded too cut, too dried. There wasn't any emotion behind what was a scripted response. Encizo pushed, pleading with the two men, though not moving too near to either, getting into their space and perhaps inspiring them to take a more violent response. The last thing he needed was shooting, or having to bury a couple of eviscerated creeps after he took them out by blade.

These two were professionals. They had the cool, rangy, relaxed stance of men who were ready for action, and had set themselves up equidistant from him. What raised his suspicions about their story was that neither showed a sign of interest in actually calling for help.

There was no call for off-duty personnel to come and try to do their thing. They acted like cops, used to dealing with the rowdy, but they showed none of that instinct that made them true police. Encizo had worked beside lawmen quite often, mostly in Florida helping battle drug smugglers, and the vast majority had compassion for others and would act to the best of their ability to protect and assist those who fell upon misfortune.

This much gave Encizo some idea of who these two men were. They had law-enforcement training. He could tell that by the way their feet were planted in a T-formation, the top line of the tee being one foot. Such footing allowed each man to resist a sudden force coming toward them, as well as to pivot swiftly to avoid contact or face a new as yet unseen threat. It was a principle of martial arts that Encizo knew full well. He had to make certain that he didn't stand like that, lest they recognize his own training.

"Can I bring her here?" Encizo whimpered. No husband with an injured wife was going to be put down so easily. The longer he stayed here with the men, the more he could learn about them and their origins. One thing he was coldly aware of was that these were not the Option Omega thugs that the FBI had files on from Idaho. They spoke Spanish quite well, something that members of a racist, isolationist militia would not cater to. Looking at them, he could tell that they were of European descent, which made it easy for them to pass for whites looking for empowerment.

"Please, in the name of Jesus, my Savior, help," Encizo pleaded. If they were white power, there was a strong chance that they were members of a Christian Identity group, essentially the North American version of the violent radical Muslims that made up terror groups such as al Qaeda.

Yet, even though the so-called Christian Identity thugs believed themselves followers of Christ, Encizo knew from firsthand experience that even a lapsed Roman Catholic as himself showed far more godliness and compassion than they could ever imagine. The Christian Identity terrorists were greedy, self-absorbed and looking for a means of enforcing their will and justifying it, much the same as those who took Islam in vain as the source of their struggle. In all the battles that Phoenix Force had engaged in, very few "holy warriors" showed any sort of love for their neighbors, only spite for those who didn't have the lack of self-control to take what they wanted, no matter who was harmed.

Encizo's very Christian plea didn't move either of these men. In fact, out of the corner of his eye, he could make out a sneer of derision that had more than sufficient spite to wither small plants. These weren't the Option Omega that had sprung up in the isolation of a northwestern wilderness.

If anything, there was a small bit of consolation that at least one group of racist thugs had met its end at the hands of conspirators who didn't want the real bigots raising a stink when their name was used under false pretenses.

One of the guards took a step closer to Encizo, but his hand went from the handle of his pistol to a canister of capsicum spray. "Sir, you're going to have to vacate the premises."

Encizo allowed himself a rictus, grit teeth bared in frustration. Inwardly, however, he was preparing for the onslaught of the sizzling response his mucus membranes were about to experience in relation to several thousand Scoville units of pepper oil solution. While it would hurt, Encizo would still have some sense of himself. He and the rest of the Stony Man warriors had trained to endure riot gas, commonly called "tear gas," which was the same composition as the liquid stream issued from the small canisters. He'd be in agony, and tears would flow, fogging up his vision, but he would not be rendered helpless. He'd have to appear that way, though, and this would be more than sufficient grounds for him to disengage and run from the two guards, disappearing.

He kept his stance loose, avoiding the reflex to brace himself.

"Please…"

That's when the canister rose. Encizo raised his hands instinctively, crossing them in front of his face, but the hot spray flashed between his splayed fingers and struck his face.

The fires of a thousand suns burned under his eyelids, in his nostrils and sinuses. He gave in to his body's request to fold up and drop to the ground. No amount of endurance and training was enough to dispel the pain of capsicum oil concentrate striking one's sensitive membranes. Eyes clenched shut, nose running like a faucet, Encizo rolled around, hating this exposure. Were he less disciplined, he'd actually have allowed himself to get to his feet, and even through the blur of teary eyes, unleash a wave of retribution on the two men.

He'd sparred like this before, in training. Utilizing his sense of touch and his unharmed hearing to compensate for his impaired vision, he'd proved able to trade blows and wrestle with other members of the Stony Man action teams in a fight. Instead, he twisted and clawed at the ground, scurrying away, gasping and groaning in agony. He was going to be feeling the biting effects of the spray for hours, discomfort and swollen sinuses taking a long time to cool from the hot pepper extract's stinging torrent.

Now he felt a boot rise and strike him in the thigh.

Its owner spat an angry epithet to follow. "And don't come back, *scheisskopf!*"

The German term for "shithead" was not lost on Encizo as he scrambled, seemingly blinded, away from the source of his abuse.

He stumbled, allowing himself to trip but recovering before he caused himself real harm, fleeing the scene. He played the part of wounded, frightened civilian perfectly.

What was more, Encizo had a hint of who the two men were, simply by the content of their words.

They spoke Spanish with impeccable fluency, yet lapsed into Germanic curses.

Encizo was going to have to ask for the effects of the La Palma superwave on Argentina, but every instinct showed that these two weren't American renegade Christian Identity gunmen.

They were something darker, far more evil and beholden to a deeper, grimmer god-thing, the dark lord of Ultima Thule.

They were South American Nazis.

Suddenly the alliance of international enemies here on the island had grown far more deadly.

CHAPTER NINE

There was no way that Calvin James could cross back to Tarajal and grab his buried scuba gear and the equipment he'd require to wage a one-man war of attrition on the enemy's disguised missile freighter. Q-ships were nothing new, used from the very beginning of sailing when pirates sought to strike at vulnerable ships bearing precious cargo. In turn, navies and merchants often went with the expedient of making these vulnerable-seeming craft actually bristling fortresses on the sea.

It was first called a Q-ship in World War I, when the British made their sea wolves in sheep's clothing take to the seas, drawing in German U-boats to engage in surface action against an apparently harmless freighter, saving its precious few torpedoes for other engagements.

Mostly they looked like tramp steamers, but cruise ships had been up-armed, as well.

The placement of large-scale missile launchers on the deck of a cruise ship was a shocking extreme, and one that was so blatant, so unlikely that the world hadn't expected it to explode, literally, on the scene in Santa Cruz harbor.

Something like the Q-ship must have been in evidence at the Norfolk shipyard, where the OSHA team had been ambushed and slaughtered. The Q-ship, or something far more sinister. James could imagine half a dozen things that could be built at a navy yard that could be worth murdering a handful of men and that would make conquering a tourist island so much easier. Since it was a shipyard, James doubted that it was a Predator-style drone like the ones soaring above. The Farm was still working on the underwater photographs, but it was taking a little while because of water damage to the memory card.

James wove through the streets to the harbor, staying out of sight, remaining quiet. He knew he was asking for trouble assaulting a ship with only his knives and a .22-caliber pistol, but he wasn't going to take any action that would attract attention. He needed to neutralize any threats to the hostages in Santa Cruz without alerting Option Omega to his assault. It was a tightrope that he had to walk; one error in balance would either end his life or cause the deaths of hundreds in an instant.

Going in fully armed would fit him into the mindset of "having a hammer makes every problem a nail." He needed versatility, and he needed stealth.

Reaching one of the beaches, he was relieved to see that no one was out. He'd be backlit by the sands on this side of the island, and wished he'd had the darker, black volcanic sands from the other side, but either way, he needed to be careful. He was in real danger of being spotted if there were spotters nearby, utilizing night-vision devices.

He did a sweep with his own light-amplification glasses, searching for the telltale sign of nonvisible illumination that other optics often projected to make their views clearer. He picked up two different spotlights of UV or IR illumination, but they were far between.

James slid the shoes and socks off his feet. He was going to be free-swimming to the Q-ship, which meant that he would need the most efficient use of his feet as he swam. Shoes did nothing for that, hindering movement. Also, on the boat, he'd be barefoot, and thus less likely to make a clanking sound when he stalked the decks. He buried the shoes and socks, hoping that no one would go digging through, then removed the waterproof satchel in which he'd brought his clothes and backpack to shore. It had folded compactly into a pocket of the day pack, which meant that it would protect the gear he stored within, as well as his clothing. He could have fit his shoes and socks into the bag, but rather than take up room, he left them behind.

He'd move a little faster through the water with the proportionally lesser weight, and if he needed the room after picking up something on the Omega strike ship, he'd have it in the bag, and then could return to shore and retrieve his footwear if necessary.

Stripped down to his black swim trunks, form-fitting akin to BVDs but giving him room to stretch, James looked as if he were an Olympic athlete, ready to take to the pool for one of the fastest swim laps of his life. Years of swimming had added to his commando training to make him long and lean, without the bulldoglike upper body of Rafael Encizo. James simply had more height to stretch his muscles along, and he was corded tightly.

James checked the timing on the illumination patterns once more, then cinched the waterproof sack over his shoulder. He didn't want his gear bouncing as he crossed the beach at a full sprint. It would make noise and throw off his pace. He perched, ready, breathing slowly and deeply, filling his blood with an excess of oxygen. Each moment ticked in his mind, synchronized with his waterproof watch that he hadn't looked at since he'd cued up his brain to count the seconds in time with it.

Four.

Three.

Two.

One.

In an explosion of compressed spring-steel muscles, he sprang into a lightning-quick run. Long, lanky legs propelled him through the sand, bare feet digging in and providing far more traction than any shoe could hope to. Ten strides, and he was halfway across the beach, arms pumping, an oxygen high tingling through his cheeks.

Fifteen strides and he was nearly to the beach.

Eighteen strides and there was a sudden call of alarm.

Twenty strides and he launched himself, sailing into the incoming surf, body plunging into the foamy waves and disappearing with the crack of the first gunshot.

Now James added the strength of his arms to increase his speed in the water. His shoulders and back flexed as he surfaced, settling into a front crawl. No longer did his gangly legs need to push his entire weight alone, but settled into a tight, swift kicking motion as he stretched out one long arm, then rolled to stroke with the next arm, taking the brief instant when his face turned out of the water to suck in fresh air, expelling it as he twisted to take an alternating stroke.

He estimated that he'd have to make a long crawl, just short of one mile. The Farm had indicated which of the cruise ships was the deadly gunboat of Option Omega, and he'd taken one last-minute glance at the screen to make certain that it hadn't moved from its original position. His course would be long, even grueling.

The world's fastest swimmers had been able to do that mile in just under fifteen minutes, but that was in a swimming pool, and they had brief moments as they decelerated, then flipped off the wall. This was going to be much different. Even at that relative quickness, the fastest human swimmers were tearing through at under four miles per hour for that duration.

James had to keep up a pace, and while he hadn't timed himself in a while, at his best he'd been able to do a mile-long swim, no gear, in the space of seventeen minutes and change. Back in 1960, that would have made him a world-record holder. Nowadays, there were people who lived every minute training, sometimes even taking steroids, who blasted past that time.

James added in the weight and resistance of his bag strapped across his shoulders. His head cut through the water as a break tide for the satchel, but he was going to have some drag off his time there.

Twenty minutes to reach the ship, he figured, if it sat in the same spot.

The gunmen on the shore might still be firing at him, but they had been so far from his point of entry into the surf, they were reaching at the extreme for the range of their rifles. Sure, they could run closer to the shore, but what if they decided that calling in would be the better tactic to take?

The cruise ship might be on alert when he reached it. James also wondered if the cool night waters of Santa Cruz harbor were going to be enough camouflage against infrared cameras on the unmanned drones that would undoubtedly be sent after him.

Then again, James mused, he'd run across the beach with barely even a swimsuit and a watch. The backpack he wore didn't have room for anything more than the tiny Walther he'd tucked in his pants' pocket. Would a naked, nearly unarmed man be worth looking for? What could he do?

A mile from his starting point was an incredible distance for most people to swim. The Option Omega guards might alert the ship, but would any of them take a naked man as a real threat to their operation? There were countless places for a man to swim to. He could even have been crazed with fear, seeking escape to another of the Canary Islands, or to the fleets held at bay by the threat of hostage-killing explosions.

James pushed those thoughts away. He'd find out how badly he'd miscalculated when he got to the Q-ship. As it was, no explosions rocked the air.

The only thing he concentrated on was his stroke, cutting through the black water with each passing second.

He became the water he plowed through, moving on instinct, keeping to a straight line.

GARY MANNING FINISHED rinsing off Rafael Encizo's face with a bottle of water, making certain none of the pepper extract remained on his face or hands. The burning capsicum wouldn't be given a second chance to strike down the Cuban with a careless wipe of his hand across his face. Even so, his mucus membranes were still raw, breaths coming through in little whistles as the sinus passages were swollen. Encizo grimaced, but at least he could deal with this discomfort now that the capsicum had been washed from his eyes.

He could see clearly, even though his eyelids felt as if they'd been stuffed with cotton.

"They're definitely in no-trespassing mode," Manning surmised. "And they don't want to leave the safety of this area."

"What do we see on aerial photography?" Encizo asked, his flannel shirt buried. The extract would stay in the fibers for days, waiting for any opportunity to re-inflict inflammation and pain on the garment's unsuspecting wearer. Luckily he wore a dark tank top, as a white shirt would make him stick out in the darkness. As it was, the knife he wore around his neck now hung freely, and even if he tucked it under the collar of his top, he'd still end up popping it loose with any exertion.

Encizo didn't mind. He couldn't hope to be unnoticed the next time he appeared to the guards. He'd rather have faster access to his blades anyway.

"The camp is operating as it normally was," Manning said. "Your visit didn't raise any alarms."

"The drone?" Encizo asked.

"It's being spelled by a second one. The replacement took off before the first one turned back to refuel and cool down," Manning told him. "That's the feed as I'm getting it from the Farm. Only a minute or two of delay."

Encizo glanced upward. They were currently nestled in the shadow of a rock sticking out over the bicycle path they'd parked in. Farther down the road, the trees were thicker. Up the road, there were fewer places to tuck into the shade from the sun or to get out from under the watchful eye of an orbiting UAV.

"So we're going to be under constant observation," Encizo muttered. He looked at their position. "We didn't come all this way to hide under a rock."

"No, we didn't," Manning returned. "I've been trying to see if the guys at the Farm could spoof their visual feed, but as they're switching off, that's going to be a lot more difficult."

"Who needs a spoof?" Encizo asked. "I'm sure we could fake something else."

Manning narrowed his gaze. "What are you thinking?"

"Solar flares? Those generate a lot of radio interference," Encizo said. "It wouldn't have to last long, just enough for us to find our way inside the caldera work area."

"That might work. It'd have to be brief, though," Manning said. "Otherwise, Option Omega might realize that someone's throwing a smoke screen for people to sneak in."

"Even so, we're going to have to look for somewhere to get in," Encizo mentioned. "Without being seen by patrols or the drone. You don't happen to have a cloak of invisibility, have you?"

Manning smirked. "Well, don't forget, Striker ran into those thuggees who got a hold of that kind of technology."

"I thought that was all confiscated and destroyed," Encizo said.

"It was," Manning answered. "But that cloak of invisibility gave me an idea. You've got your thermal blanket?"

"Thermal blankets are meant to stop the movement of heat. They'll either block it in the sunlight, or they'll contain it in the cold," Encizo mused. "Just like a cloak of invisibility, except it'll work only on infrared cameras."

Manning nodded. "Of course we'll still have to keep an eye out for human patrols."

Encizo opened his thermal blanket package, which he'd taken out of his bag. "That is why you packed the non-Mylar emergency blankets."

Manning nodded. The black, satiny fabric was actually ballistic nylon, two layers, and sandwiched between them was the traditional metallic, mirror-surfaced Mylar. The Mylar was excellent at capturing and absorbing up to ninety percent of normal body heat radiation. However, Manning chose to weave this particular design so as not to be so brightly noticeable in the dark or in stealth situations. However, should anyone look through their day packs, they would resemble nothing more than the standard supplies that hikers would take on their trips in the mountains.

Hermann Schwarz wasn't the only commando in the Sensitive Operations Group who had a knack for invention, Manning thought idly as he folded the blanket into a hooded wrap for himself. Encizo did the same. As the blankets covered close to 2500 square inches, he was able to shield his head and upper body quite well with one blanket, but he took a second blanket and wrapped it around his waist as a sort of skirt. This would provide his long legs with coverage. Despite a six-inch height difference between Manning and Encizo, the Cuban had to wrap himself up with two blankets, as well.

The skirts would make them seem oddly ridiculous, but the Mylar-and-nylon fabric couldn't hide body heat while it was poking out around its limits.

"Friar Gary? Art thou ready for this journey?" Encizo quipped.

Manning managed a smirk. "But take it easy. Although this keeps us from radiating heat to be seen, it'll contain our body heat."

"Exertion could lead us to getting too hot, resulting in dehydration," Encizo noted. "Right."

"We stop, breathe and give a moment to let in cool air every five minutes," Manning said. "More often if our perspiration becomes too much. And keep regularly hydrated."

With that, clad like wraiths from a forgotten age, Manning and Encizo stalked into the volcano, looking for the extent of Option Omega's security in the area.

AFTER THE FIRST TWO shotguns had been restored to shooting condition, things became much easier for T. J. Hawkins. The frightened townsfolk had taken an hour to assemble, but they had arrived in force, bringing whatever they could grab.

He found old Browning Hi-Powers, which were simple to fix for fighting. He even found three old Smith and Wesson Victory revolvers with their long, slender, five-inch barrels and thumbnail-shaped front sights. The six-guns were sleek and beautiful, even the one whose surface was pitted with rust where it had been worn by being pulled and reholstered. The one with the rust had its firing pin intact, and its barrel was clean.

This had been a working firearm, so nothing needed to be done except find ammunition. Unfortunately they were chambered for the .38 Smith and Wesson cartridge, or the .38-200, which was a more massive slug, but pushed along at the same pressures. There was a full box of .38 Special rounds, but they were completely incompatible with the old Victory guns. Of the .38 S&W rounds available, he was able to split five shots between each, leaving each with an empty chamber. Two Webley Mk IV revolvers, also in .38-200, were around, but aside from three shots split between the two, they were not optimal. He could have taken slugs from the others, leaving each revolver with only three shots, but he wasn't sure if he wanted to trust the top-break actions of the Webleys.

Finally, he bit his tongue, made certain that their firing pins operated and thinned out the revolver ammunition even further among them.

By the time two hours had passed, in town, Hawkins had restored or okayed a dozen shotguns for action. The majority were double-barrels, but there was one autoloader and two pumps. They were a hodgepodge of gauges, the autoloader being in 20-gauge, the one-pump being in 16-gauge. The higher the gauge, the less volume per shot shell, and the majority were .410-bore shotguns. The size of the .410 shells was half of even a 20-gauge, and they were best used for taking small pigeons and other fowl. Against a man, Hawkins would prefer something stronger, but the weapon was still dangerous.

"One last thing," Hector said as he brought a box forward. "This used to be my brother's. It's not a Colt .45 like a Texan should carry...."

Hawkins looked down and opened the box. Sitting inside was a battered old revolver with a definitely noticeable front sight silver-soldered to the top of the barrel. He picked it up. It was a Smith and Wesson Model 1917 that had been cut down from five to four inches and the new sight welded on. He opened it, and saw that the action and cylinder were clean and clear of obstructions. It was covered with scratches outside, but inside, it was good as new.

Next to the revolver was a small box of .45 ACP cartridges. He opened it and saw that eleven were still left for the sleek old six-gun.

"Wow," Hawkins said.

"I figured you'd need a .45," Hector said. "We don't have much…"

"No. We're definitely not storming the bad guys, but if you get someone pounding at your door, even a .410 will tear his face off," Hawkins said.

"What is your plan?" Hector asked.

Hawkins looked around. "The people who brought the guns keep at least one that they came with. No one untrained gets a firearm, though. I don't have time, and we don't have ammunition to get your people used to shooting."

"Some of us haven't forgotten," one of the townspeople said.

"Either way, you all are on the defensive here," Hawkins ordered.

The sudden spokesman looked embarrassed. "So we hide?"

"We don't let the enemy notice us," Hawkins explained. "If they come snooping, we don't ambush them. We kill them only when we're certain they've come to try to kill us first. Then, aim, squeeze and lean into the recoil."

"And what about you, Texas?" a young woman asked.

She spoke in English, catching Hawkins off guard. She was a blonde, but with dark brown eyes. Her skin was fair, and her build was lean.

"I'm not going to raise no fuss, if that's what you're asking, ma'am," Hawkins replied. "American?"

She nodded. "Tourist, like you. Natalie Chase."

She extended her hand. Hawkins took it, but his instincts were on fire. He thought back to the list of names of dead tourists, and immediately picked that name off the list of those who'd disappeared, and most likely ended up at the bottom of the Atlantic. He couldn't say for certain if Chase was one of the dead, but that association raised Hawkins's suspicions.

"Thomas Presley."

She smiled, pretty, disarming. If Hawkins weren't paranoid, aware that the Option Omega terrorists could have left a spotter here, he'd have bought her attraction to him.

"I know how to use a gun," she said.

Hawkins nodded. "Really?"

She stepped closer. The clothes she wore looked as if they were painted on. Hawkins was glad for his serious nature, his focus while on duty. She came on as if she was trouble and he was not up to it. Still, if she suspected he was suspicious…

"Here," Hawkins said. He handed her one of the Smith and Wesson Victory revolvers. "You've only got three shots. Use them wisely. And sparingly."

She looked at him, a glint in her eye.

If there was one thing that Hawkins could count on,

it was that they were in front of a group of frightened people, many of whom had guns. Natalie Chase, if that was her real name, wouldn't open fire now. The townspeople's reactions would end with her pounded to a pulp by a salvo of shotgun blasts.

Instead, that mischievous glint was accompanied by a healthy dose of swagger in her voice. "Will do, Texas."

That bravado chilled Hawkins to the point that he was glad that the big .45-caliber revolver was empty.

There was darkness beneath that sunny, bright hair.

CHAPTER TEN

David McCarter stalked the alley behind the hotel and paused, looking at his CPDA, searching for the reservations of the dead he'd discovered in the depths of the Atlantic just off the island. This hotel was the destination for five of those identified as having been on the trip. He frowned. Other suspected dead were placed at different hotels, and all five of the places had been listed as the buildings where hostages had been holed up by Option Omega to keep the world's militaries at bay.

That made things simpler for McCarter. Now he was certain that those murdered and dumped at the bottom of the ocean were victims in this mad plan. He frisked himself with one hand to make certain that the Walther and his knives were tucked away from where people would notice them on a casual once-over. If Option Omega's thugs had full military, police or even department of corrections training, then they would be willing to feel for weaponry in the Briton's crotch and other out-of-the-way places. If not, then he was going to have a chance, but he wasn't going to rely on the incompetence of his opponents.

He was going to have to get into the hotel unseen if he wanted to bring his weapons with him. If he wanted to get inside the hotel easily, though, without raising any alarm, he would have to disarm, stash the weaponry and play the part of helpless civilian. It'd be hard. The fox-faced Briton was as rough and tumble as they got. Even though he'd calmed, gotten more "civilized" as the leader of Phoenix Force, he still was exactly what he'd been when he came to Mack Bolan's crusade against terrorism—he was a Cockney hard-ass.

He weighed the options either way, and decided to do what he used to do best when left to his own devices in the field.

Approach the problem head-on, like a bull in a China shop.

He figured that it wouldn't do much to harm the hostage situation. He wasn't geared up to appear as a member of an outside commando unit, and McCarter was also the instructor at a school for bodyguards, personal servants and hotel detectives under one of his identities in England. He sent a quick text to Stony Man Farm to hook up his current cover identity with his school credentials so that he could better appear to be a trainer for the hotel staff who decided to take a more active role against the people messing with his hotel.

McCarter spent a few moments loosening up, limbering and oxygenating his body for either fight or flight. He checked for a response from the Farm.

"ID confirm. Plan?"

That had to be Price. She knew him well enough to realize that McCarter was going to do something audacious. If it was one thing that he and Mack Bolan agreed on, it was that a good bluff and show of force was more than sufficient to make people buy whatever you wanted.

And McCarter only had one simple, symbolic reply—a smiley face with devil horns.

"Try not to get everyone killed." But on the other end, Barbara Price knew better. She was familiar with the Phoenix Force leader, his prowess and his willingness to take great risks to protect the helpless and punish the evil.

David McCarter was going to bedevil Option Omega to the best of his considerable abilities.

THE BACK OF THE HOTEL, where the supplies for day-to-day operation for a resort were brought in and stored, was a smoky, rubble-strewn mess. The charred remains of four people, burned beyond any recognition, were bent and broken over the wreckage of a smashed delivery van. McCarter could recognize the effects of a hand grenade thrown into the closed quarters of the scene.

Grisly carnage was used as a bar against trespass, but McCarter didn't walk blindly through the mess. While most people would avoid the stench of death, there would be people who would be less than deterred, even attracted by the gore and brutality of such a scene.

He'd passed one body, a young woman, a bullet hole punched through her forehead. That death would be sufficient to drive away stragglers, but there would be other measures against infiltration. Whether it be an actual trip wire, or a motion detector, Option Omega wasn't going to lose its bargaining chip out the back way.

McCarter was comforted and shielded by the darkness, but knew it was only a temporary situation. If Option Omega had access to unmanned drones, then they would also have access to night vision and other senses.

McCarter also didn't intend to stay out of sight for too long anyway.

He just needed to make certain that the enemy didn't think he was coming in from the outside.

With the speed and grace of a panther, he dashed down into the loading dock, sidestepping wreckage that would trip him up. He held his knife in one hand, the spine of the weapon tucked to his forearm and out of sight to a casual first glance, but held so that he could snap it up and around, slashing open a throat in a blindingly quick movement.

McCarter's stalk through the shadows of the wrecked storeroom was even slower. The stink of voided bowels and cloying blood made it obvious that the Option Omega hostage takers were full-blown murderers, even though he couldn't see the carnage strewed behind in the darkness. His foot bumped one lifeless form, then another, but he maintained his balance, continuing on through.

All the while, he fought his imagination, tucked the emotions building up within inside a lockbox of fury that he knew he'd need later. The odds were against him, and he couldn't afford to lose control now, but when he inevitably came into conflict with the enemy, he would need every ounce of motivation and strength that he could muster.

Cold fury over the innocent dead here and outside

was going to grant him more than enough adrenaline to push him through the pain and exhaustion thrown in his path. Nothing like a smoldering rage to motivate you into taking one step more when a broken leg could barely support your weight.

Finally he passed the kitchen, but the smells were of rotted food and souring milk. Those killed within must have been dragged away, and he could see a few lights on, illuminating an empty cooking area. Meals had been abandoned midpreparation, and in the dim light, he could make out the smears of blood where bodies had been dragged away.

McCarter grit his teeth and continued.

There was movement around the corner, and he retreated into the kitchen. McCarter was already in the enemy's den, so maneuvering for position was secondary to gathering intelligence. To the enemy, he might as well have been here since the very beginning. As it was, his CPDA contained a layout of all the floors of the hotel, including annotations where a demolitions expert would place explosives to most effectively destroy the building and kill everyone within.

His first goal was to check out those places, to see if Option Omega had actual explosives on the scene, or if, as James and he had surmised, it was something that they were going to leave up to drones or guided missiles. Once he had that bit of information, things would be easier to plan.

Until then, McCarter intended to avoid direct contact, but if he did, he knew he still had to stuff the corpse of whichever guard he encountered into a dark hideaway. The immediate future was going to be more of the same—corpses dumped aside in corners, leaking blood.

This time, however, it would be the murderers decomposing as opposed to their victims.

The man who stalked into view was tall, with straight hair and dark skin. It took a few moments for McCarter to peg him as South American, which was confusing until McCarter connected the dots. China had been making inroads into South America, working with groups that still held the old feelings of Communist revolution in their hearts, groups like the Sendero Luminoso. It wasn't any far stretch of imagination that they would tap that kind of muscle for an operation in the Spanish Canary Islands.

McCarter lay still, tucked out of sight just under a preparation table. He was able to make out the man in the reflection of a small metal drawer wall. As long as he remained motionless, he wouldn't attract return attention as the stranger scanned the dimmed kitchen.

Shoes creaked, a crushed vegetable bursting at the end of the row of prep tables, and McCarter was glad he'd stuffed his entire tall frame in the space beneath. His back and hair were lying in grease, his cheek squished against the floor, but anyone looking down wouldn't be able to see him from the point of view from just above.

The man came to a halt, shifting his weight from one foot to the other, shoes creaking as leather bent.

"Fucking rats. I knew we should have had some of those bitches clean up this mess before we culled them," the man grumbled in rough, deep Spanish. McCarter wondered at the dialect, but he could make out mixed South American "Indian" words, confirming that this guy was Peruvian.

McCarter knew he hadn't made any sound. As if to confirm the man's complaints, a patch of wiry scruff touched the back of the Briton's forearm. Something warm and wet brushed against his skin, and McCarter knew it was some kind of a large rat, most likely a Norwegian, considering the bulk of the beast. He didn't dare move an inch, not even to shoo the rat. If he did, there was no telling what kind of alarm the Peruvian could raise, let alone what kind of firepower he'd punch into the prone, trapped McCarter's body.

The gunman turned and walked away, moving closer to the refrigerator. With the feet turned away from him, McCarter slithered out from under the table, then scurried onto his hands and knees, moving silently. The knife was still clutched in his right hand, and he glanced toward the Peruvian. The man scratched the back of his head, in consternation, confused at the false alarm that had drawn him into the kitchen.

McCarter rose, lunging toward the Option Omega guard at full speed. He snapped the pommel of his knife hard into the terrorist's right kidney, the steel butt of the blade amplifying the force of his punch to the point that it paralyzed the Peruvian.

McCarter's target dropped his gun with a clatter, hands rising and fingers curling into claws. Stiffened, the Peruvian had little defense as the Briton kicked him in the hollow of his left knee. Both legs folded and the disarmed gunman flopped onto his face, crashing into the rough rubber floor mat that provided chefs traction in case of spills in the kitchen. A third impact was with the knife again, this time the point of McCarter's blade sinking into the base of the man's skull.

Taking him prisoner would have given the Phoenix Force commander someone to interrogate, but McCarter didn't have the room, and certainly didn't have the time or privacy, to question the captured gunman. Seven inches of steel directly into his brain kept the man from suffering.

McCarter, finished with taking down the armed guard, began frisking him, looking for pieces of gear that would help him out. He immediately found a pistol tucked into a belt holster, as well as spare magazines and two cell phones. He quickly stripped this gear from the man's belt, checking everything over. The first cellular unit was bulkier than the other, at twice the size and configured like a brick rather than a flat, sleek touch screen or a compact little folder, and he was able to determine that it was a satellite phone, capable of communicating long distance, likely back toward the European mainland or the East Coast.

The other was a smartphone, all screen with a few buttons along the edges. McCarter took out his CPDA and pulled two small Firewires from an inside spool. Schwarz had installed the spool interface to make it easier for the men of Able Team and Phoenix Force to hijack and read the memories of captured enemy phones. Within moments of contacting the other processors on the two phones, hacking software cut through, broke down the information inside and fed it over a satellite uplink to Stony Man Farm.

He unplugged the phones, then returned them to the man's belt holders. If someone examined the corpse, McCarter didn't want the opposition to know just how much of their communications had been discovered, traced or hacked.

He picked up the guard's pistol and examined it closely. It was a Turkish knockoff of the CZ-75, which itself was a late twentieth-century update of his preferred Browning GP-35. McCarter didn't think too much of the design, if only because it was heavier and bulkier than the Browning or the CZ it was derived from. That meant it would be more solid, and recoil less, but it would be more of a bear to carry concealed, especially in an age where CZ produced a design with a lightweight polymer frame.

Either way, McCarter knew it was a lot better than the .22 he carried, with a better grip, a longer sight radius and a far more authoritative caliber. McCarter pocketed the two spare 15-shot magazines and tucked the pistol into his waistband. He then turned back to the submachine gun the man had dropped in the first moment.

It was an Uzi-style machine pistol, with a central pistol grip and a magazine that fed into it. After a second he remembered the tubular design—the 9 mm Argentinian FMK. He'd used one during an unauthorized invasion into Colombia. There were five magazines, each stuffed into a sleeve attached to the shoulder strap. There was another inside the gun well.

"Hell of a mismatched set of gear," McCarter mused. Then again, he'd received information about Option Omega's setup. The money had to have been passed around the world at least two or three times, and undoubtedly the gear that the conspirators had assembled had been gathered at random, bought in lots from all over, making it harder to trace buying patterns and obfuscating the actual growth of the conspiracy's armory.

McCarter sent digital camera images of the pistol and the SMG to the Farm. The more they knew about where Omega had gathered its gear, the better the chance that the hackers could narrow down where the enemy's money originated and who ultimately was responsible for all of this murder and mayhem.

He also felt the man's chest, but didn't find any body armor. He was about to dismiss that these killers came in relatively unprepared when his fingertips snagged on a burned hole in the gunman's shirt. They had body armor. One of them had taken a bullet to the chest. McCarter rolled him over, then saw the livid bruise where the slug nearly punched clean through.

He sent out a text with this information, a simple line that would be available to the other four members of the team. He wasn't afraid that they'd be unprepared. The first rule in combat was that any shot to center mass that didn't stop the fight was followed up by bullets to the head or the groin, breaking the skeleton's ability to support weight on legs or unplugging the brain.

Still, a little bit of foreknowledge was good for saving ammunition and for the brief instant of surprise where an enemy could take down his friends.

All of this happened with no shots fired. McCarter now had to get to the basement, check out if the explosives were present.

If so, he'd unplug them and begin taking out the hostage takers.

If not, then he was going to have to rely on Calvin James out in the harbor, making a one-man assault on Option Omega's Q-ship.

Things were getting tighter, and it wasn't just the darkness, the stench of death and cluttered hallways that made things more claustrophobic. It was the timetable.

Phoenix Force was running out of time now that McCarter had dropped the first of the terrorists on the island.

Long odds and an impossible deadline.

Business as usual, McCarter thought. He just hoped that he and his team could pull yet one more miracle out of their hat. If not, hundreds, maybe thousands were dead.

CALVIN JAMES CLUNG TO the chain as the Q-ship bobbed in the water. He was several feet below the lowest of the deck rails, so climbing up was going to be impossible, at least along this section of the hull. What he needed to do was to look for another low area, something that wouldn't be guarded.

He doubted that he was going to find anything unattended.

The Option Omega thugs were up to their gills on the wrong side of what could be a bad situation. If they were caught napping, each of the cold-blooded killers on board would end up dead, slaughtered by a former Navy SEAL.

He reached into his waterproof bag and brought out his CPDA. It was designed to be used in sea water, so he wasn't worried about its electronics. James needed to take a breather before he continued to look for a way onto the ship. Maybe he could get the layout of the cruise ship.

That's when he saw that McCarter had made a hard first contact. He looked at the face of the man the Briton had killed, and the thumbprint that had been uploaded to Stony Man Farm.

McCarter set it so that the rest of the team could see that their time was going to get very short.

James didn't waste the energy making a face over that bit of news. Sooner or later, this infiltration was going to get violent and bloody. All they could hope to do was to limit the lives lost in the crossfire. He checked for information on the cruise ship when he caught a glimpse of information drawn up from the shipyard in Norfolk.

It was the interior hull of a freighter, but the OSHA investigator had snapped footage of how the insides had been set up for an in-belly submarine dock.

James looked at the ship he'd swum to. Twenty minutes of paddling across the harbor, dragging his gear bag along with, had been meant to get him here to launch a raid on the decks. During that time, however, he'd gotten a measure of the ship.

It was little coincidence that the hull that the OSHA inspector had photographed was similar to the Q-ship.

He fired off a text to the Farm. Almost immediately, he was answered.

"We're aware of the similarities. That's why we've put this info up for you," Price responded. "Where are you?"

"On its anchor chain."

James bobbed, staying low to the water. There was little exposure in the shadow of the hull, but he wasn't going to make it easier for the enemy to see him. He'd dimmed the CPDA screen, and treaded water with most of his face beneath the waves.

Price's answer was short. "Got that way in."

James nodded, sucking in a breath as the motion of the waves bobbed him upward.

He typed in another line with his thumbs, still holding fast, recharging his spent muscles. "Subs equal bad news."

"We know."

James wished he had a scuba tank. There was no telling how he'd be able to get to that underkeel opening. If it was just a little too far, he'd drown.

If he didn't go for it, though, there was no telling what kind of nightmare would unfold. He began to hyperventilate, building up reserves of oxygen in his blood. At the same time, he reached into the waterproof bag, retrieving the Walther and its holster. This he tethered around his chest. He already had his two knives on hand, strapped to his forearm and leg with waterproof sheaths.

His clothes were drenched inside the bag, but if he had the chance, he'd still get to squeeze them so they didn't drip. He needed to be ready to fight the moment he broke the surface. If not…

Calvin James, fingers humming with blood coursing through them, plunged beneath the waves, guiding himself to the bottom of the ship, giving himself direction by touching the belly of the cruise ship.

CHAPTER ELEVEN

Surrounded by the inky blackness that could only exist in the shadow of a several-hundred-ton cruise ship at night, Calvin James kicked along carefully. If he exerted too much energy swimming underneath the boat, he could use up all of his oxygen and strength before he could reach the underwater bay that the large craft had installed for the minisubs. But if he swam too slowly, even his endurance would flag, and he'd need more oxygen.

He couldn't see. It was just too damn dark, but he didn't dare try to illuminate beneath the water. All he had to go on was the skin of the ship and his knowledge of the best possible position of the port. If James was wrong, the game was up and he'd drown.

He grit his teeth, continuing to kick along.

Then he felt a depression in the hull above him. Controlling his feelings, he slowed himself, gripping it tightly. He turned over, reaching upward to make certain there was something. He could make out the dull red glow of low-powered emergency lights in the shadows between large bulks. James kicked to the surface and gently exhaled a breath. He sucked in fresh air, exercising every ounce of willpower to keep from making any noise.

James raised himself a little farther and looked around.

The submarine bay was relatively empty, but the pool he was in had six of the crafts, yet there were eight berths. James made sure that he got a correct count, and looked around for signs of life inside the bay.

Satisfied that no one was snoozing down here, he pulled himself out of the water and breathed a sigh of relief. He sat on the deck, dangling his legs into the water as he dumped his bag down. The CPDA was out, and he snapped digital imagery all around, getting several shots of the minisubs.

The berthed crafts were not much different from the Swimmer Delivery Vehicle that Phoenix Force had used to sneak onto La Palma. There was room for six people inside, and there also appeared to be provisions for attaching extra equipment underneath or to the sides. They were naked for now, but in his scan around the dimly lit bay, James saw pods that could be attached.

He took pictures of the two empty berths. The subs had to be somewhere else, which meant that they could have been on the other side of the island or on a rendezvous with some other craft in the Option Omega fleet. The fact that the lights were off and no staff were present meant that the two lost lambs were not expected back for a long time.

James grimaced as he realized that the SDV could meet up with a full-size submarine. It wouldn't be the first time Phoenix Force or Able Team encountered a rogue submarine built and sold off by the Russian or Chinese military. That the Chinese were involved, even peripherally in this occupation of the island, meant that an actual Chinese or a North Korean sub could have been used.

He sent a text along with the images back to Stony Man Farm, referring to this concern.

"Informing naval forces of presence of subs around La Palma," came the Farm's response.

James smirked.

It wouldn't be too bad having the combined navies of the U.S., Britain and Spain involved in this situation. If those three fleets couldn't locate a renegade sub…

James dismissed the thought.

Option Omega's leaders had managed to conceal an effort to blow a chunk of an island into the Atlantic Ocean, and the assembly of the forces necessary to conquer the city of Santa Cruz.

Submarines were just too damn hard to track down, especially with the hodgepodge of high technology that Omega had gathered.

It was time to get to work, James told himself. There could be important information on this ship, and the clock was ticking. No extensions would be coming if he failed to find what was necessary.

Even if he found the means of protecting the hostages in the hotels of Santa Cruz, there was still a hell of a tsunami that would be set off by a detonation of apocalyptic proportions. The resulting wave would cause billions in property damage and kill thousands, even millions of people.

James wrung out his shirt and pants, pulling them on. He tested to make certain he wasn't a slopping, puddle-dripping mess, then tucked the Walther away. Knives at the ready, he looked at the CPDA screen.

New message.

"Able reports. New dry dock found. Sub capable."

James figured that there was something to this. He inquired as to what kind of submarine.

"Diesel patrol," was the answer.

As desperate as Russian naval officers could be, there was no way they were going to sell a submarine with a nuclear reactor to another country. That would provide a buyer with more than sufficient material for a dirty bomb. Even so, diesel subs could power up electrical batteries to engage in silent running for days, if necessary.

The subs, originally intended for use in countering American and NATO underwater crafts jockeying for position to attack the Soviet Union, could also deliver troops or launch high-powered missiles, everything from more conventional explosives to full-blown atomic warheads. James chewed his lower lip.

"Armed?" he inquired.

"Undetermined," came the response. "Find out."

James nodded. He made certain everything was set, then checked the door. There was a good chance that he could be locked in, but the latch opened with an uncomfortably loud, hollow drumbeat of metal against metal. He looked out into the corridor. Lighting outside of the sub bay was much better than it had been within.

He closed the door behind him and padded stealthily

along, checking his corners, keeping the compact .22 in his grasp. It would be much quieter to use the knife, but there was little telling how much reaction time or how much of a gap James would have to cross to take down an opponent. His opponents weren't going to have any qualms about remaining quiet, and they would be free to gun him down.

Shooting first, with the low-velocity slugs from the Walther, would at least buy James some time and disguise the fact that there was an unauthorized gunman in the belly of the ship.

Long strides carried him through the hallways, and James kept his head on a swivel.

Movement around the corner caused James to pause and duck into an open doorway. The room he'd entered was a belowdecks storage closet, so rather than a simple hotel-style doorway, it was a more traditional rounded hatch. James tucked himself tightly into the darkness.

"Just check the sub bay," one of the men said in Spanish, but his tone nasal, as if mocking the original speaker of those words.

"They saw someone running on the beach and into the water," another voice intoned. This one had a more singsong lilt and accent to it. James wondered about the origin of the speaker, but kept still. Any movement to figure out who the pair were would call attention to himself.

They passed, and James could make them both out to be dark, swarthy men. Black hair and bronzed skin were about where their similarities ended. One was a more familiar South American native, perhaps a mem-

ber of Sendero Luminoso, as in the original photo that
McCarter shared. The other had a far more Asian caste
to his features. James pegged him as from the subconti-
nent of India, either Pakistani or actual Indian in origin.

He remembered from one of his many Phoenix Force
briefings that the Indian government had troubles with
Maoist insurgents, to the point where that brand of communism was rendered illegal.

It would fit in with the Chinese use of Peruvian Maoists as muscle. James wondered, though, what contin-
gency the paymasters had in mind for when the hostage
situation was breached. It would be hard to disguise that
kind of influence with dead bodies in evidence. Escape
and evasion could only allow so many of the Option
Omega forces to elude capture or death.

James watched the pair pass by. He was glad that he
had left his shoes and socks behind. Few things were
quieter than bare feet. He stepped out behind them,
grabbed an image of them on his CPDA camera, then
set out stalking after them.

"The floor's dry," the South American complained.
"If someone did reach the ship, which I doubt…it's only
a half hour since they saw him on the shore…he'd be
dripping wet."

The Hindi shook his head. "We heard movement
down that way. Someone opened the door."

"Was it really the hatch?" the Peruvian asked. "These
ships make all kinds of racket. They're built flexibly so
they don't snap in half if a large wave strikes."

James allowed himself a smile as the two spoke.
He'd made certain to wring out his clothing to stop

what seawater soaked them to drip. He was damp and uncomfortable, but he wasn't leaving behind puddles where he'd stepped.

The two moved closer to the hallway where he'd first appeared. These crewmen had been sent to look for trouble, but they only had side arms tucked into their holsters. A glance showed that they were likely the CZ-75 knockoff that McCarter had found on the guard he'd killed. James lamented not having something bigger to take on an enemy crew, but for now, he had to ride along in stealth. Being involved in a raging submachine gun battle in the depths of this cruise ship would certainly distract Option Omega, but it would also open up Santa Cruz to reprisal strikes.

"Hang on," the Indian said. The other paused as the tall man strode toward a doorway farther down. He opened the hatch, and the familiar stink of gasoline filled the air after a few moments. James couldn't see inside, but he knew the layout of the ship, and engineering was not in this section of the cruiser. That was why they'd picked this section to cut a hole in the hull.

That might have been fuel for the minisubs, but James's interest was piqued. He remained out of sight as the Indian rejoined his partner.

As soon as the two men entered the submarine bay, James took off. Three steps and he was beside the hatch, which was slowly closing. The pair had turned on the lights within, so when James crossed the doorway, his shadow wouldn't cut into the room. Another sprint on bare feet, and he was quietly at the other door that the

Indian had opened. James waited for the sound of the sub bay's hatch shutting when he opened this door.

His timing was impeccable, and he was inside the room, overwhelmed by the heady, intoxicating rush of gasoline fumes. James tucked his damp shirt to his face to filter out most of the effect, but clicked on his LED torch.

Canisters of fuel, each marked Explosive/Flammable, were packed in here. James scarcely had room to move as he bent and investigated further. He held his breath to allow himself a free hand to bring out the CPDA again, snapping pictures of the fifty-five-gallon drums.

These photos were immediately sent to Manning before James uploaded them into an info-dump to Stony Man Farm. James clamped the damp fabric in place over his nose and mouth and went back to breathing the filtered air. If Manning was busy, at least the Farm would have some information on what was in the drums. James's first instinct, however, was that it was a petroleum-based explosive rather than fuel for submarines or the cruise ship. He did a quick count, sweeping the compact lamp over the drums.

Each drum, if utilized as a fuel-air explosive base, would produce an enormous blast wave. Together they could easily turn the ship into a mass of splinters, raining down as far away as the caldera. James didn't assume that this was a form of self-destruct, but he didn't dismiss that idea, either.

A fuel-air explosion would be exactly the kind of thing to erase evidence of non-white supremacists in the employ of the reborn, renewed Option Omega. James kept his ears open. Obviously there was a reason why these guys were armed with only pistols. There must have been more men, "faces" who could pass for white, or mercenaries who were hired to be the antiforeign thugs who could be caught on camera. The cruise ship likely had more than sufficient needs to occupy the non-Caucasian staff.

Both of the men wore simple coveralls, he remembered. So far, Phoenix Force hadn't encountered enough enemy troops to determine whether they had a uniform or not. Given that both men were dressed similarly, though, it was likely that they were in uniform. James knew that he might be able to pass for one of the sub crew if he could get a uniform and perhaps some boots.

James slipped out into the hall again, not wishing to push his luck with the fume-filled room. He gently rested the door just before the latch snapped shut, barely a bump. The two men in the submarine bay weren't coming out yet, something that the Phoenix pro was glad for. He slipped away to another corner where he could wait in quiet. He took a brief moment to take a whiff of himself, and the faint musk of the petroleum fumes still clung to him. It was nothing he couldn't rinse out in the water, and he was going to look for replacement clothing.

The two guards exited the sub bay, and the Indian man looked back toward the fuel-drum room.

James grimaced. He may have smelled the gas, or he could have just noticed that the hatch was ajar. Either way, James realized that the Indian's suspicions were raised. Sure enough, he noticed the man rest his hand on the pistol in his belt. The one Omega guard nodded to his Peruvian ally, who pulled his pistol, as well.

The Peruvian advanced toward the doorway, and James tucked himself farther out of sight, remaining low and holding his breath. The guard pushed open the door and started to push his pistol into the room when the Indian stopped him.

"Are you insane?" the taller man asked. "You fire a single shot in there…this whole ship disappears."

The South American grimaced, then put the gun away. Instead he reached into his pocket and withdrew a small rectangle. With the click of a button, a sharpened, double-edged blade, about five inches in length, snapped out.

The Indian nodded, and he pulled a collapsible baton, snapping it open.

Two deadly weapons in the close quarters of belowdecks. James was good with a knife, actually one of the most experienced blade fighters in the world thanks to his time with Phoenix Force and his work as a trainer at the Farm. He still knew that he was going to need a damn good plan and an equalizer if he was going to handle these two. If they didn't find anything in the drum room, they'd begin searching farther.

James tensed, Walther in one hand, knife in the other. The real weapons, though, that James counted on were his mind and body. He needed a place to spring an ambush, and a means of separating the two partners. He tucked the Walther in his waistband and pulled one of the spare magazines he had for the pistol. Quickly he thumbed out two of the small .22-caliber rounds.

One of them he flicked down the hall with considerable energy. The little bullet clanged on bulkhead and bounced, rattling off down the corridor.

"There!" the Peruvian snarled, turning out of the fuel-drum room.

Both guards burst out of the hatch, starting toward the sound. That wasn't enough to truly separate them, though. As they both rushed past the opening that James hid behind, he leaned out and hurled the second of the cartridges through the closing door. The .22 bullet banged loudly amid the drums, causing the Indian to stop in his tracks.

"What?" the Peruvian asked, almost to the corner where the first sound disappeared.

"Something was in storage. I heard it," the Indian said.

The Peruvian grimaced, then pulled his pistol. "I can handle this."

The Indian smirked. "All right."

The two split up.

As soon as the South American guard was around the corner, James took that moment to spring out behind the Indian man's back. Barefoot, his landing made hardly a sound, at least in comparison to the rattle of metal on metal. James clutched the man's thick black hair and used it as a handle to ram him face-first into the bulkhead. The ugly crunch of nose cartilage crumpling under massive force resounded through the hard thrust.

Stunned, the Indian had little sense of self-preservation. The metal wall had smashed his nose flat and split his forehead brutally. His eyes were unfocused, giving

James the opportunity to bring up the point of his dagger, plunging it under the man's jaw, spearing his mouth shut and impaling his tongue to the roof of his mouth. The point continued on, piercing into the brainpan, ending his life instantly. James wasn't taking chances and wrenched the blade handle to crack neck bones.

Now with a lump of lifeless flesh and bone in hand, James caught the corpse under its armpits and hauled it backward. The only sign of the deadly conflict and end of the Indian's life was the bloody smear on the bulkhead.

"Ranji?" the Peruvian asked. He had the .22 bullet in his palm, looking at it in confusion. "The guy must not have a gun. He's resorting to throwing bullets by..."

The Peruvian looked up when he didn't sense his partner's presence in the corridor. "Ranji?"

The Option Omega muscle raised his pistol, gripping it in a tight two-handed hold. His eyes were wide, sweat beginning to bead on his forehead as he advanced. "Ranji!"

James could see his attention was split between the closed-off storage room and the bloody splash on the bulkhead, a splatter that was farther from the doorway where the lifeless Ranji lay in James's shadow. That kept the Peruvian from believing that anything was between him and the storage room, with its door still ajar. Something had dragged his friend off, and James was too well hidden behind the hatchway as the guard closed in on the fuel-drum room.

James hadn't had time to remove his knife from Ranji's skull; it had been rammed home pretty hard. That

didn't matter. He palmed the Walther, made sure the
safety was off and tensed for his next attack. As soon
as the Peruvian was in the doorway, the Chicago bad-
ass launched himself again, stabbing the muzzle of the
Walther into his target's stomach. The Walther's extended barrel kept the pistol in battery as James angled
the gun up toward the guard's sternal notch. One, two,
three pulls of the trigger, .22-caliber brass tinkling on
the walkway beneath them, and the Peruvian's face went
from surprise to anguish to expressionless numbness.

A .22-caliber autoloader wasn't the most powerful of
handguns, especially a tiny pocket pistol like the Walther, but James made the most of the weapon's power,
applying the muzzle close to his opponent's heart. Three
bullets, still accelerating under the force of expanding
gasses, were able to do a lot of internal damage. In addition, the expanding gasses that pushed those bullets
along gushed out in a blast of heat and shock.

Three to the heart, and the small patrol that had come
belowdecks was down for the count.

James set about taking pictures and stripping the pair
for useful gear to continue his infiltration.

CHAPTER TWELVE

Carl Lyons's jaw was set grimly as he looked at the stripped-down diesel submarine sitting in dry dock at the backup boatyard Option Omega had set up. He'd been on enough missions with submarines to know that when these things were bought secondhand from navies, they were usually in poor condition and stripped of most of their deadliest cutting-edge technology. They were still in Virginia, but miles south of Norfolk, in an unlisted asset of the Jeopardy Corporation.

They'd gotten that information from the prisoners that Schwarz had taken and from the GPS mapping in their smartphones and SUVs. The discovery of the broken-down sub was confirmation that there was at least one other Soviet navy surplus diesel still out and around. Two had likely been bought, and one was carved up for spare parts to get the other into optimum sailing condition.

Schwarz came back from the workbench area, shaking his head. "They've been installing electronic components on the sub."

"New radar and sonar, and probably com," Lyons muttered. "Once the landslide goes, we're right here at sea level. No one would find this place and be able to pick up anything forensic to link it to Jeopardy."

Blancanales nodded. "If anyone was really interested, they've already gone through this place pretty well."

"I expected as much," Lyons said. "No sign of when the sub was last here."

"These are Soviet-era original Kilo-class subs, but they exported over thirty of them to various nations," Blancanales said. Before Blancanales entered the Army to become a Ranger, he had been a big fan of the U.S. Navy and their craft, as well as being interested in the opposition. He still kept up on that information. "Three of them are in Iran…"

"It's possible, but Iran wouldn't cut up one of their boats to supply the others, and they sure wouldn't do it in Virginia," Lyons mused. "That's why I'm thinking this came from a Russian base."

Blancanales frowned. "We've waylaid a couple in our day. Those, along with the official record of five being laid up and two more retired…"

"These could have been the retired vessels," Schwarz said. "Especially if they needed this much space to refit one sub. I've checked the trash bins, and the electronics are the same as those used inside the unmanned aerial vehicles."

"Jeopardy has money, but it's spending it wisely. Not blowing anything they don't need to?" Lyons asked.

"That or they're avoiding traces back to the conspirators," Schwarz said. "Pol, how fast do these Kilos go?"

"Twenty-five knots when submerged, using the original design engines," Blancanales said. "So, thirty miles an hour."

Schwarz grimaced. "So, it'd take a day or two to get to the Canaries."

"No. Not for a long haul like that. If they're going long distance, it's more likely they'll be doing only three to seven knots," Blancanales answered. "The submarine could have left more than a month ago, all things considered. If they were going balls out, they'd only make it about twelve miles."

Lyons grinned.

"What's with you?" Blancanales asked.

The big ex-cop shrugged. "Usually it's me or Gadgets who rattles off the technical details. Good to see you've got a little nerd in you, too."

Blancanales rolled his eyes. "Funny. Wait, that means you called yourself a nerd."

"Gadgets explained that nerddom is attention to details you find important. Or is that geekdom?" Lyons asked.

"Geekdom," Schwarz answered. "Geeks get it done."

"Ah," Lyons said. "Not that I really care."

"So you geek out on gang demographics and police procedure, Gadgets geeks out on science and I geek out on warships," Blancanales replied, nodding.

"What about the Kilo? Any particular way we can track one?" Lyons asked.

"They were designed at the peak of the Cold War, after having years of other subs vetting the technology," Blancanales told him. "They're meant to be the hardest thing to track using antisubmarine warfare."

"And now we've got one with twenty-first-century electronics," Schwarz said. "So we're looking at low-profile communications, passive radar and sonar that won't make the sub easy to track by its pings. And the underwater propulsion is nonscrew electric propulsion."

"What kind of armament could one of these carry?" Lyons asked Blancanales.

"They can carry up to eight antiship missiles, and have six tubes and storage for eighteen torpedoes," Blancanales answered. "The missiles we're looking at are about six to eight meters long, some are capable of supersonic 'sprints' to get past point defenses, and either a two-hundred-kilogram antishipping warhead, or if limiting the speed to subsonic four hundred kilograms for land attack…"

"Four hundred kilos of explosives," Schwarz mused. "That's capable of breaking off a hunk of cliff and dropping it into the ocean."

"Enough to cause the mega-tsunami?" Lyons asked.

"Maybe," Schwarz said. "The crew at the Farm's going over the same information. They're tracking naval-based surface-to-surface missiles. Who might be trading in them, and if any shipments showed up on the radar, then disappeared."

"This could be the suspenders-backup-to-a-belt plan." Blancanales spoke up, looking at his CPDA. "James just reported in. He's aboard the cruise ship and he found fifty-five-gallon drums full of fuel that could be used for fuel-air explosions. Manning and Encizo also have spotted the potential for more containers on the island."

Schwarz added up in his mind. "Each drum is the equivalent of 530 pounds of TNT. But a truckload of drums would add up to half of a MOAB."

"Half of a MOAB?" Lyons asked.

"Call it six and a half tons of TNT equivalent," Schwarz explained. "Massive Ordnance Air Blast bombs go a full 11 ton equivalent with a payload of 8200 kilograms of fuel. You get a complete destruction blast radius of 150 meters from the Mother Of All Bombs...."

"But we're placing the drums for effect, on the side of a caldera," Lyons finished for him.

Schwarz nodded. "And that's only one truckload."

"Is that what Manning thinks?" Lyons asked.

"He's gone silent. He and Encizo are infiltrating the caldera. There seems to be a major buildup in the volcano of Option Omega personnel, either workers or soldiers or both," Schwarz told him.

"Great," Lyons replied. "What about us? Can we get to La Palma?"

"Price says we could be of use, if we want," Blancanales said. "According to James, the Q-ship has a full complement of minisubs. Eight of them, and two are at large."

"And they could hook up with a Kilo, if necessary?" Lyons asked.

"The Russians have their own Swimmer Delivery Vehicles. It's not impossible," Blancanales answered.

"Phoenix Force has its hands full on the island, so our help could be appreciated in hunting for the subs," Schwarz said.

"You've got a few tricks in mind?" Lyons quizzed.

"I've got three or four stored up my sleeve," Schwarz returned. "And the Farm has arranged for us to pop out to the U.S. fleet and hook up with Jack Grimaldi and our own 'borrowed' S-3 Viking."

Lyons wrinkled his nose. "Will it get there?"

"Jack will be flying it," Schwarz added. "If anyone can milk every ounce of speed and performance out of an airplane, it's him. We'll meet Jack at Langley. We'll refuel in flight."

"We'll get there in time for some action?" Lyons asked.

"We're looking at over five hundred miles per hour at height, which is shy of Mach 1. It won't be like getting there via supersonic jet, but we'll be on the scene. And we'll have some serious firepower with the missiles aboard," Schwarz said.

"Great. X-box battle plan," Lyons muttered.

"Don't knock it till you hose them down with three thousand kilos of high explosives," Blancanales replied. "If you don't care for that, there's always the conventional ramp-mounted MGs. We'll even see if we can hook up a Ma Deuce for you."

Lyons raised an eyebrow at the thought of the Browning M-2 machine gun. "I could live with that."

Blancanales and Schwarz grinned.

Able Team got back into their van, peeling out toward their rendezvous with Grimaldi and their flight to the Spanish Canary Islands.

However, the moment the Able Team van was on the move, another set of headlights flashed on, following.

BLANCANALES HAD BEEN driving in hotspots around the world for long enough to instantly get the sense that he was being followed. He identified their tail after a few scans and turns of corners. He identified one of them, but he had the suspicion that there were more in reserve. He alerted his partners.

"Option Omega or Jeopardy is looking to end our part of the investigation here," Blancanales said. "They're on our trail."

"How many?" Lyons asked. He checked his eight-shot .357 Magnum, then the .45-caliber auto in their holsters. In the back of the van, Schwarz opened their weapons cases.

"Two, likely. Maybe more," Blancanales said. "Strange that the company has so many people willing to stay in a tsunami zone...."

"Maybe they weren't told," Schwarz returned. "These are just off-the-cuff hires, armed personnel who don't have a clue that they might be treading water in a day's time."

"A day?" Lyons asked.

"Sundown tonight is when the fleets are in position, surrounding the island of La Palma. What better time to unleash a mega-wave than when you can inundate aircraft carriers and heavy cruisers?" Schwarz asked. "We're speculating that this is a means of bankrupting American and European nations, and the loss of billions in warships..."

"You know when the fleet's going to be in position," Lyons stated bluntly as he accepted his shotgun from his partner.

"I'm keeping an eye on things," Schwarz said. "Just a back door into the system."

"So we have a time line and a countdown," Lyons murmured. "Price aware of this yet? Or the others?"

"I alerted them," Schwarz answered.

"When do you get time to do all of this?" Lyons asked.

Schwarz winked and affected an accent. "I'm a wizard, 'arry."

Lyons shook his head as Schwarz handed Blancanales his UMP .45 SMG. "These kids today, with their multitasking. Just make sure to focus on the bad guys."

"I will," Schwarz said. "We looking for prisoners?"

"Well, your speculation on who these goons are passes the logic test. They wouldn't be here if there was a deadline for the wave to start," Lyons said. "Though, if we're looking at the fleet finally assembled at six tonight…"

"Six tonight," Schwarz confirmed.

"They'd still have time to get to a safe distance from the shore after capping us," Lyons concluded. "Fuck it. We're needed elsewhere. Dicking around with hired guns, info or no, isn't on our schedule."

"Got you," Blancanales said. "This is a nice, empty stretch of road. Going to pull a one-eighty."

"Do it," Lyons ordered.

The Able Team van squealed to a skidding halt, tires smoking as Blancanales yanked on the emergency brake while spinning the wheel. The g-forces inside the vehicle were high, but Blancanales had the forethought to put the SMG's sling over his neck and shoulder. Lyons and Schwarz also gripped their seats and weapons. Loose items flew against the passenger's door, empty coffee cups and spare change, and even though their weapons shifted, secured rifles and shotguns were still accessible.

Now the van was facing the trailing SUV, which had slammed on the brakes itself. Another vehicle that had been trailing farther back continued on, accelerating as the first two slowed to a halt.

"They're going to try to flank us," Schwarz said, noting the headlights zooming toward them.

"Should have let the lead car go past and shut the door on us," Lyons muttered as he kicked open the passenger's-side door, swiveling the collapsed-stock Benelli M-4 out of the seat with him. "Now we can cut them off."

Even as Lyons said it, the sound of gunfire resounded, the windshield turning white with thousands of cracks as enemy bullets poured in, fractures turning glass opaque with damage. Lyons shouldered the Benelli, short stock and all, and opened up with a quick double-tap from the powerful 12-gauge. The distance between Able Team and their Option Omega pursuit wasn't long, and at twenty yards, the buckshot pellets racing downrange had more than sufficient punch to dent sheet metal and break the enemy's windshield, as well.

That blazing opening salvo caused the gunmen to hold their fire, ducking for cover against Lyons's fury. That gave Blancanales and Schwarz the opportunity to unass and get outside of the van themselves. Lyons took the brief reprieve to strip two shells off his bandolier and thumb them into the magazine tube. The action of reloading the shotgun was quick, heavily practiced. The big ex-cop even kept his shotgun reloading skills in condition by shooting in cowboy action events, where even larger capacity shotguns only had to be filled with a maximum of two shells to keep things even with the double-barreled period pieces. There, the shooters had developed fast refill techniques, which Lyons adapted to pump and semiauto shotguns for real action. This kept the Benelli at its full load of eight, with another in the chamber, ready to go.

Blancanales and Schwarz reached their cover, then opened up to give Lyons even more room to maneuver. Their two .45-caliber machine pistols burped out short precision bursts. Blancanales was able to tag one of the gunmen's legs as it was visible beneath his vehicle's passenger door, heavyweight bullets shattering bone and muscle, knocking his feet from under him.

Schwarz's fire was suppressive in nature, short bursts spitting out two or three rounds at a time. The hood and the side of the SUV were peppered with high-powered slugs that kept the enemy on their toes, except for the man that Blancanales maimed.

The screaming gunner begged for help as bright arterial blood jetted from his grisly leg injury. Bone was visible, poking through the torn skin. His partners weren't interested in this as they concentrated on the location where the two muzzle-flashes opened up on them. Luckily, Blancanales and Schwarz made a beeline for a low roadside rail made of masonry. Stone chips flew as the Omega guns ripped out full-auto bursts, but the Able pair were behind cover and repositioning to return fire.

While the gunners were distracted, Lyons swept around the other side of the enemy SUV, stock to shoulder, sights locked onto the driver, who clumsily brought up a machine pistol to nail the man moving toward him. The Benelli bucked twice more against Lyons's shoulder, booming flares of fire and lead discharging from the other end of the gun.

The driver's head snapped back violently, face and hands shredded by the brutal butchering power of double-ought buckshot at a range of only fifteen yards. Mangled and dead, the driver bounced off the headrest of his seat and flopped against the steering wheel, setting off the SUV's horn. There were cries of consternation as the other SUV squealed on the road, blowing past the stopped vehicles.

The driver of the second SUV hit the brakes, drifting into the turn to bring himself and his gunners into position to trap Able Team, but even as the SUV swerved, it came under assault from twin streams of .45 ACP on full auto. The Omega gunners inside either ducked out of sight or were hammered by shattered glass and deformed slugs. The windshield, now that the SUV came to a halt, facing Blancanales and Schwarz, was drenched in blood and chunks of crushed meat.

Able Team had little time for mercy as they dumped their empty magazines and reloaded. Schwarz kept on the newcomer, fanning three bursts into the windshield of that SUV while Blancanales tagged a gunman from the first vehicle who had popped out when the Able pair revealed their new position. The unfortunate Omega shooter caught a face full of copper-jacketed 230-grain slugs that blew off half of his skull.

Blancanales ducked down and shifted closer to that group even as Lyons pressed his attack on the SUV with his shotgun.

Lyons snapped a shell into place with his free hand, then triggered his Benelli M-4 at close range, five yards now. A swarm of heavy buckshot caught a retreating gunner in his left hip, shattering his pelvis. Cut nearly in two, the assault rifle in his hands slipped free. Lyons ended his suffering with a follow-up 12-gauge charge that struck the doomed mercenary between his pectorals. Dumped to the ground in a bloody heap, he would not feel any more pain or menace the Stony Man warriors again.

The last man at the back of the first SUV let out a curse as he realized that Blancanales and Lyons had eliminated the rest of his truck crew in a matter of moments. The shooter grimaced and threw something round over the top of his SUV, too scared and too smart to expose even a small part of his anatomy to the deadly gunmen coming for him as he had hoped to overwhelm them.

It was a hand grenade, and it plopped to the ground only yards from Lyons's feet. He swung the Benelli's muzzle toward it and fired off three shots as fast as he could pull the trigger. The thunderous wave of buckshot struck the grenade and kicked it off to the side of the road, away from him and against a backdrop of stone and mortar that would protect Blancanales. Both men took cover, Blancanales down behind the stone roadside wall, Lyons at the front fender of the Omega SUV.

The blast shook the ground, shattering stone, but only harmless dust rained down atop Blancanales. Lyons wasn't even subjected to that much debris from the explosion. He had other things on his mind, however. He let the shotgun drop on its sling and drew his big Smith and Wesson Magnum.

The last gunman, assuming that the grenade bought him a distraction, spun around the back of the vehicle, firing from the hip.

Lyons flopped onto his stomach, bullets sizzling through the air over his head. He stabbed the R8 Magnum up until the big front sight bisected the shooter's center mass, then opened fire with a pair of .357 Magnum man stoppers, screaming out of the revolver's five-inch barrel at 1500 feet per second. Both rounds struck the gunman in his breastbone, blowing it to splinters and severing his aorta. Cored out by Lyons's magnum salvo, the Omega gunman folded over, blood vomiting from his lips, and died before his forehead bounced off the asphalt.

Lyons rolled onto his back, looking at the second SUV that had tried to flank Able Team. Schwarz's UMP burped out quick, precision salvos that left the driver dead, and a gunman flopped on the ground at the opposite door. He took aim at a shadow bursting from cover and fired a pair of rounds at him.

The big Magnum bucked, but his target was too swift and fleeting to catch more than a glancing shot. Lyons knew he'd hit thanks to the ugly grunt he recognized from a lifetime of battles. He'd hit home, but it was a nonvital impact. Not bad for on his back and in the dark, but that meant there was still a wounded shooter on the loose.

"More headlights," Blancanales announced. "No bars."

"Not highway patrol," Lyons returned across the road. "Gadgets?"

"I'm on the runner," Schwarz called back.

Blancanales spent a moment to finish off the wounded man he'd shot in the leg, even though he looked as if he were well on the path of bleeding out. Better a quick end than long suffering on a lonely road in the night.

It was the third gunfight in twenty-four hours, and despite only a quick two-hour nap, Schwarz was wide awake, adrenaline pouring through his system and making him as mentally and physically sharp as ever. Any aches and bumps he'd received in the earlier combat were dulled by the pain-deadening effects and razor focus he was locked in to. The enemy runner stumbled along crazily as he cut into the trees, smashing a path that a blind man could follow even in the dark.

Schwarz kept up the pursuit, pausing every few moments to scan his flanks with the night-vision scope mounted atop his UMP. He wasn't going to be outmaneuvered by an opponent, which was why he kept up a steady pace, fighting down his urge for further action. If he got reckless now, he'd open up his partners to disaster and ruin.

Something big sounded off to his left, and Schwarz whirled. He thumbed on the LED lamp-mounted coaxial with his gun barrel, putting out a blazing spotlight that illuminated the wounded gunman, his shirt wet and red where Lyons's bullet had struck him through the lateral abdominal muscles.

Schwarz spotted the handgun in the killer's fist. The Omega gunman's snarl of rage mutated into an agonized wince as the gun light blinded him. It was as if he'd struck a brick wall. Schwarz nailed him to that wall with a short salvo of .45 slugs that ripped him from navel to throat.

The ambusher dropped into a messy pile at Schwarz's feet. A less trained man would have relaxed, but Schwarz swept the area with his spotlight before reloading and flicking on the safety. There was still enemy action out in the night, but a sudden crescendo of shotgun and SMG fire blazed back at the road.

There had been a few extant pops of rifles and handguns in the melee, but the sudden wave of violence could only have been his Able Team partners opening up. The third part of the pursuit and ambush set up by Option Omega had come to an end as it ran into the fully loaded guns of Lyons and Blancanales.

Schwarz jogged back to the road, flashing his light to signal the others of his arrival. Sure enough, he saw the third SUV smoking as it sat on the yellow line, every bit of glass punched out of the windshield and doors, wisps of steam rising from the holed hood and the slumped corpse of a gunman hanging out the window.

Schwarz looked at the mess. "Barb's going to flip over this one."

"We'll call it in," Blancanales said. He went and checked the van, which still was running and, after a little fiddling, still felt in good driving condition. "What can she do, ground us and keep us from helping Phoenix?"

"We can always handle the paperwork later," Lyons added, getting in.

Schwarz tilted his head. "We've got paperwork now?"

"If she assigns us homework on this mission," Lyons replied with exasperation. "Let's go."

Able Team sped off, heading to complete their rendezvous with Stony Man pilot Jack Grimaldi and the first leg of their trip to La Palma.

CHAPTER THIRTEEN

The Peruvian slithered into the water bonelessly, and Calvin James was done cleaning up the corpses he'd put behind him. He had donned the jumpsuit of the taller man, its sleeves and ankles short on his slender, long frame, but James compensated by rolling up his sleeves and tucking the cuffs of the legs into his boots. It wasn't the most fashionable of looks, and the Indian's jumpsuit left plenty of room around James's lean, rippling torso, but that only provided him the means of improvising straps to hide his second AR-24 pistol between that and a borrowed T-shirt, with room left over for the web belts that made up his tanker harness. He located a baseball cap and pulled it down over his head, then returned toward work.

All the time he was setting himself up like this, he hoped that there were African Maoists in the entourage running the ship out of sight of news cameras and intelligence network surveillance. At least he was good on skintone; the Indian man's flesh was nearly as dark as his own. If anything, he could always throw on his Spanish and pretend to be a Cuban or a Dominican.

He checked the CPDA once more. The identification of the submarine that Option Omega had acquired was a Kilo-class, diesel submarine from the 1980s. James clenched his jaw tightly. Those were powerful, stealthy craft, and even if most of the systems had been gutted, there was room for considerable firepower and technology to be installed. That sub must have been near enough to rendezvous with the two minisubs. He didn't know why they had gone out with it, but it was that long trip that had given James the time he needed to get aboard and to take out two of the guards. Their bodies were on the way to the bottom of the harbor, weighted down with chains that had been on hand.

He patted the one Turkish CZ knockoff in its holster, hammer cocked back, safety engaged, just like on his favored Colt 1911, one of the reasons why the CZ-75 had become so exotically desirable when it was first introduced. The single-action, locked-and-cocked mode overrode the uncomfortable hammer cocking trigger pull on most wonder-nines such as the Beretta or Smith and Wesson, not that James himself ever felt hindered by the Beretta 92's initial self-cocking shot. Still, consistently uniform, crisp trigger pulls from beginning to end appealed more to the veteran 1911 fan. The one concealed under his top was hammer down, so it wouldn't snag in the folds of the coverall. If he was in the middle of a gunfight and ran out with the first AR-24, he could pull the second one and fire right away, ignoring the longer first trigger pull.

He still wished that he had access to explosives and a submachine gun or a rifle. The armed cruise ship, the wolf in sheep's clothing, had the potential for causing too many deaths, especially with the surface-to-surface missiles that Blancanales and the Farm crew hypothesized were in use by the enemy. The Soviet-era Klub missiles were heavy-duty hammers meant to blow holes in enemy warships or cause massive destruction on shore. If only one missile was fired at a populated section of Santa Cruz, the entire block could easily be leveled, and hundreds killed in an instant.

James's hope was to blend in with the crew and find some form of ship's armory. A pack of plastic explosives and a remote detonator could do more to cripple the Q-ship from within than a cruise missile launched by one of the enemy fleets.

The CPDA informed James that there was now a countdown. Schwarz surmised, and the Farm agreed, that Option Omega would actually wait until the American fleet set up a blockade position and completed the ring of steel around La Palma. Having done that, scores of ships from three navies would be in the path of the initial landslide shock wave.

Dressed like one of the natives, James now had a little wiggle room to search for the kind of firepower he wanted. If he could arrange for a massive blast to cripple the cruise ship, or even blow it to smithereens, he'd at least give the people on shore a chance to survive, maybe even delay the detonation of the hotels or the charges placed in the volcano. So far, there was no word on what Manning and Encizo were accomplishing on their penetration.

That was good news. If they had been discovered and pegged as commandos, the whole boat would be on red alert. They would be seen as the tip of the spear, and Option Omega would have to spring into action to deter further encroachment by NATO or U.S. special operations.

They'd kill the hostages in the five hotels.

James couldn't accept that. He stalked off through the bowels of the ship, putting on the airs of belonging, all the while keeping his eyes peeled for signs of the enemy.

T. J. HAWKINS HAD MADE certain that the people of the town were all armed and ready to protect themselves should Option Omega determine that leaving them alone would simply be too dangerous. As Tarajal was only a few miles from where Phoenix Force landed and the grisly body dump had been discovered at the bottom of the sea, the conquerors of La Palma wouldn't be interested in a stranger preparing the locals to fight.

Hawkins still thought of the beautiful young woman who called herself Natalie Chase. Now that he was alone, he hooked up with Stony Man Farm and requested an ID photo for the American tourist. Looking at the digital image, she was only nominally similar to the woman who had introduced herself as Natalie Chase.

Hawkins's instincts and vague memory were on target. And he'd given her a revolver with three bullets in it. It wasn't as if she was prancing around the town with a loaded assault rifle and grenade launcher... Or was it? Just because she asked for a weapon didn't mean she didn't have access to her own firepower. This just would have been a way to wheedle down the locals' weaponry by one.

She was a good-looking woman, the fake, but as she had stepped into the identity of a murdered young American, Hawkins could feel any amorous feelings disappear with that grisly knowledge. The Chase woman was an imposter, and she was in collusion with cold-blooded murderers who thought nothing of ending young lives as they were on vacation, or dropping a missile into the middle of a quiet town. As well, Option Omega's ultimate goal was to unleash a powerful tidal wave that would strip the East Coast of the United States, the islands of the Caribbean and even have disastrous effects on Central and South America.

The Jeopardy white paper listed tens of millions of potential lives lost in the initial wave, as well as a sweeping epidemic of poverty, homelessness, joblessness and the potential for plagues to strike the wave-stricken areas. Japan, India, Thailand and Sri Lanka had all been hammered by deadly tsunamis in the past decade, and the loss of life had stretched far beyond the initial destruction. With cities wrecked, epidemics and infections crossed the swamped survivors.

Japan's population had responded without internal strife and looting, but there were pirates and other predators who'd thrived in the Indian Ocean tragedy. Considering the gang populations of coastal cities such as New York, Baltimore, Atlanta and Washington, D.C., Hawkins could see a lot of criminals taking the opportunity to engage in wanton looting, murder and setting up small empires in lands scoured of law by a force of nature.

Again, recent history showed the kind of mayhem that occurred in New Orleans as gangs opened fire on the Army Corps of Engineers who came to alleviate the troubles of the hurricane-smashed city. Nothing short of the arrival of the Marines had done anything to smother most of the violence, and even then, vast sections of the Louisiana Gulf Coast had been emptied, providing safe havens for criminals for years afterward. Hawkins couldn't help but think of a classic old movie where New York City had been walled off and turned into a prison wasteland. Stretching that out to encompass the whole East Coast would be more than America could hope to bear.

He hefted the .45-caliber that had been given to him. Six rounds in the cylinder and five in reserve. Hawkins felt comfortable with this, even with its sliver-thin grips.

He tried to imagine shooting Natalie Chase. It was hard. The murder of an unarmed civilian was something every piece of him rebelled against. Now that he knew that she likely was an armed terrorist, though, he tried again, but once more he couldn't stomach the thought of shooting someone who didn't look like an enemy.

Hawkins shook it off. He'd joined Phoenix Force to protect the world from the monsters that hid among normal men. Natalie Chase and her allies had been responsible for hundreds of deaths and several times that in wounded innocents. They had little problem opening fire on noncombatants.

That was the major difference that existed between Hawkins and the woman.

She was on the street, walking toward Hector's house, where Hawkins was staying. The older man had fallen asleep, mouth open, nose stuffed up, snoring loudly, the double-barreled shotgun only a few feet away from him.

Hawkins hadn't slept, but he'd forced himself to relax. Perfect stillness and meditation, allowing his mind to wander as his body drained off its tension and the aches he'd accumulated during the day, all of this was nearly as good as sleep. Not quite, but Hawkins sat up, feeling ready for trouble.

Chase looked in through the window, pressing her forehead against the class. Hawkins smiled in the dimmed firelight of the room, and she returned the unspoken greeting. It was an act. His fist clenched around the handle of the .45-caliber revolver, finger resting on the frame just above the trigger. The lanyard ring had been tied off with a small leather strip to keep it from clattering against the butt of the gun. Hawkins liked the idea of having an actual lanyard on a side arm, but he didn't have a holster for the gun, just his belt.

Still, the leather strip kept the revolver quiet as he moved to the door, opening it. Chase stood in the doorway, part of her body out of sight, one hand hidden, her right hand to be exact. Hawkins remembered handing her the revolver earlier, and she'd accepted and hefted it with her right hand. He wondered what kind of more modern weapon she had on hand.

She was dressed in hip-conforming jeans that accentuated the length and grace of her legs and the narrowness of her waist. Her hips were a curvaceous swell, though she wore a poofy, oversize sweater that was just warm enough for a tourist-season night such as this. If anything, the rolls of cable-knit yarn did little to take away from the promises of her figure above the waist.

Hawkins always did like a little bit of mystery in a woman. The trouble was, the mystery that this woman hid could be solved with a bullet in his gut. He crossed both hands behind his back, off hand wrapped around the wrist of the hand with the revolver in it.

"Miss Chase," Hawkins said, accentuating his Texas drawl, greeting her with a polite and courteous nod. He tried to make himself sound delighted to see her, but wasn't certain if he'd pulled that off.

"Mr. Presley," Chase answered, her lips turned up in a comely smile. "Would you like to take a little walk?"

Hawkins glanced back toward Hector, who was still sound asleep. The snarl of a sputtering chainsaw engine escaped his snoring nostrils. Chase wanted to pretend that she wasn't interested in disturbing the old man's sleep, insinuating that there could be a romp of naked, athletic bodies somewhere else, somewhere in private.

Hawkins almost could welcome that, but the real Natalie Chase had been dumped, mostly naked, overboard, killed via a deadly nerve toxin so virulent that not even carrion crabs could taste the preserved corpses without dying themselves. The real Natalie Chase had just finished college and was en route to Europe for the experience of a lifetime, only to be murdered for the sake of some mad goal of economic terrorism or international blackmail in the wake of a major disaster.

This Chase imposter could have the body of a goddess, but the rotting stink of evil clung to her even more tightly than the painted-on jeans and the bright, wide-lipped smile she wore.

"Let's take a trip, lovely lady," Hawkins answered, winking at her. He turned, still keeping the Smith out of sight as he leaned over and extinguished a lamp, allowing Hector to rattle on in complete, comforting darkness. As he stood, he pushed the muzzle of his weapon into his belt, then tugged down his shirt over the butt and frame.

He turned to her, and she rested her back against the door jamb, showing off the curves of her tight little ass. "Hurry up, Texas."

"I'm coming," Hawkins answered.

Chase smiled, eyes glinting. "Not yet…"

Hawkins passed her by. The bulky cable-knit sweater, he noticed, had more than enough room to conceal something small like a Micro-Uzi or a full-auto Glock 18 without altering or interfering with the rest of her figure. His instincts were on fire now as he noticed that she had her right hand on her hip, thumb hooked into the waistline of her jeans, just in the right position to push up under the hem of the sweater and pull out a powerful weapon.

The door closed and the two walked, exchanging small talk about where they came from. Chase tried to sound nervous about the presence of terrorists in a vacation paradise, but even as the words left her lips, she could see the confidence on his face. Her fear faded as the charade seemed more and more ludicrous.

"We're not going somewhere private, are we now?" Hawkins asked as her features grew grim, determined.

"No, Texas," she said. "What are you? Delta? Rangers?"

Hawkins didn't answer. "How many are waiting for us?"

Chase bit her lower lip. "Enough."

Hawkins shook his head. "I ain't got time for this, woman."

"The name is Natalie…"

"Bullshit," Hawkins said. "You're a cheap three-dollar fake."

Chase stopped. Hawkins looked up the path, then noticed a pickup turn on its headlights.

"You're giving these spineless Europeans some hope, Texas," Chase said. "If they have hope, they might think that they can do something. They'll go and investigate up at the volcano, even."

"So what's there?" Hawkins asked as the pickup closed in on the pair.

Chase shook her head. "You don't get to learn that, dead man."

Hawkins shrugged. "It was worth it to ask."

The imposter smirked. "Just get down on your knees. And throw that old dinosaur of a pistol into the dirt beside the road."

Hawkins plucked the M-1917 from its resting place just behind his belt buckle. "This dinosaur?"

Chase glared at him. "Don't try anything. You're outnumbered and outgunned."

The Phoenix Force warrior glanced toward the approaching headlights. The truck was still about two hundred feet out. Hawkins stared at Chase.

"I've been there before, honey," Hawkins told her. "I'll be there again."

The Option Omega woman's lips peeled back in an angry rictus. She yanked up her sweater, revealing a flat, toned stomach and the butt of some kind of pistol with an extended magazine. Hawkins lunged in close, bringing up his shoulder to slam it into her face. He struck her jaw and nose with the body block, his free hand clamping and snarling up the machine pistol with her sweater. The impact caused the Chase imposter to stagger backward, then lose her balance as Hawkins held on to her gun and her gun hand.

She pivoted and landed on that tight, curvy little ass in the road. She screamed in rage, trying to free herself and her weapon. In the distance, there was a shout as the pickup crunched to a halt on the gravel road. Hawkins yanked hard on Chase's hand, pulling her up and across his body, taking cover behind her. An initial burst of enemy gunfire chewed at the gravel to the side of the entwined pair, Option Omega suddenly loathe to gun down one of their own, no matter what the threat of the man standing with her.

Maybe it was some semblance of hope for romance, or maybe they thought she was too pretty to shoot, or maybe it was actual loyalty among the replacements for the murdered tourists. Either way, that moment of hesitation allowed Hawkins to bring up his Smith and Wesson, leveling it at a spot above the left headlight, compensating for the fact that European vehicles had their steering wheels on the opposite side as American cars and trucks.

That old World War II era craftsmanship turned the first two trigger pulls into the smoothest things that Hawkins had ever experienced. If it hadn't been for the roar and the recoil of the big .45 in response to the pulls, Hawkins would have thought that the action didn't work at all. Instead, two massive bullets rocketed downrange. Windshield glass burst audibly but invisibly behind the headlights of the truck.

Curses and a dying scream erupted from the truck, and in a moment, those who hesitated to open fire on Chase and Hawkins were suddenly fanning bursts of autofire toward the two of them.

"Goddamn it!" Chase shouted, suddenly letting go of her machine pistol and allowing Hawkins to throw her to the roadside ditch. He followed after her, bullets snapping and cracking through the air over their heads.

The blond imposter glared up at Hawkins, who punched her hard across the jaw, adding the weight of his revolver and the irresistible steel ring and mount of the lanyard to the force of the blow that knocked her out cold. Hawkins felt something crack on impact, and if she woke up, her jaw would be broken.

That didn't bother him any. Not when he'd seen how vicious she'd become as she tried to pull her weapon and gun him down. He pushed up her sweater and grabbed the machine pistol out of its holster. It was a Glock 18 as he'd figured, identical to the standard police Glock 9 mm service pistol, except for a select-fire lever and an elongated 33-round magazine that poked out beneath the butt of the gun.

She hadn't had the opportunity to pull it, but Hawkins press checked to see if she had a round chambered. She had.

Now Hawkins had something with a high rate of fire and a large magazine capacity. One of the group of ambushers was dead, the driver catching two .45 slugs through the windshield and likely his upper chest to start this wild melee off. Hawkins had noticed the presence of four more muzzle-flashes, and from the crackle of supersonic bullets, they were packing assault rifles, not submachine guns, which the Glock 18 approximated.

No matter. He plucked the two spare magazines from the Chase imposter's offside magazine carrier, pocketing them. If they wanted to kill him, Hawkins was going to make every effort to kill them and cost Option Omega first. One of the enemy gunners suddenly leaped into the roadside ditch ten yards north of him and the unconscious woman. Hawkins pivoted, clenching the Glock in a two-handed grip. He was used to the machine pistols service handgun counterpart, so he was on target with the initial rip-saw burst. At over 1100 rounds per minute, his brief trigger pull unleashed four rounds that turned the gunman in the ditch into a tumbling corpse.

Two down, three muzzle-flashes to go, and that was only if there were only three other men shooting. One could have been jumping or taking cover, not firing his weapon. He couldn't count on his initial poll of who was trying to kill him. He double-checked that the unconscious Chase was still out cold. She hadn't stirred after he hit her.

So he hadn't shot her. It wasn't for lack of her lethality. He'd simply had more important things to kill than her at the moment. Incoming fire always had the right of way.

Hawkins shifted position, closing in on the first of the gunmen. He hoped that the enemy would think he would retreat, flushed out of his original spot by an attack from one area. He kept the Glock gripped firmly as he advanced, ears straining for the sound of footsteps on the gravel.

Sure enough, his reckoning of their intent held true as two shooters opened up on full-auto, spraying a section of the ditch farther down, toward where anyone else would have retreated when confronted by at least one gunman. Hawkins held his fire, and heard the scrunch of feet on the country road. He stopped, crouching deeper, anticipating the path of the enemy. As soon as a shadow appeared in the darkness, Hawkins leveled the auto-Glock, ripping off another burst that illuminated the newcomer.

The muzzle-flash showed off the assault rifle he carried, which meant that he hadn't inadvertently gunned down an innocent man. The Glock spit out a spurt of five or six bullets that spread upward as the recoil forced the weapon to rise. Opened up, the rifleman exhaled a cloud of crimson, then shambled into the ditch, crashing headfirst and lifeless at the bottom.

It was an ignoble end, but Hawkins didn't have time to reflect on that gunman. He popped up, scanning the area. Sure enough, there had been six men in the pickup. This one must have held his fire, but the eruption of the Glock machine pistol had drawn him toward Hawkins. The Phoenix pro dropped to the ground, almost bonelessly, landing on his back as the enemy gunman opened fire, bullets slicing through the air over his head.

The Option Omega killer lurched into view of the ditch and Hawkins cut loose with one more full-auto stream, hammering off another half-dozen rounds that stitched their way across his upper chest, a sideways cant of the Glock causing the weapon to recoil and spread horizontally. It was as if a buzz saw were raked across the man's rib cage, a line of gore and burst tissue opening up before the gunner went down.

Hawkins let the Glock drop into the dirt. His experience with the side arm and the machine pistol variant told him that he could pick it up later, and it wouldn't be any the worse for wear. Instead, he turned back to the terrorist who had fallen headfirst into the ditch. The gunner's rifle had fallen free, not trapped under his bulk, enabling Hawkins to bring it up. It was an M-4 carbine knockoff, most likely one of the Belgium-built models, considering the wide spread of origins for Option Omega's equipment.

Hawkins didn't know how much ammunition the rifleman expended, but he hoped the guy had reloaded before advancing. If not, this was going to be a very short gunfight. The remaining pair of shooters retreated from the ditch, going for the cover of the truck. Hawkins caught the man at the back of the duo, 5.56 mm rounds zipping through his lower back.

The impact made the target fold backward, almost bent completely double from the hail of impacts. Hawkins turned toward the other gunman, triggering his captured rifle once more. The carbine chattered off a few rounds that were stopped by the front of the pickup, and then the weapon stopped cold.

"Fuck," Hawkins exclaimed loudly. He made a show of tossing the empty rifle aside.

With a swagger of bravado, the last rifleman stood and leaned on the hood of his vehicle.

"You're dead," the man grunted in heavily Germanic English.

After noisily ditching the carbine, Hawkins had transferred to the Smith and Wesson, which still had four shots in it. He stiff-armed the revolver and fired as soon as the thug proclaimed his premature victory. Three fast shots exploded in the darkness, then the flare of the enemy's rifle muzzle as a death reflex tore through his body.

The final issuance from the dead man's rifle dug into the gravel road, coming nowhere near Hawkins.

Bruised, sweaty, but still alive, T. J. Hawkins thumbed in his five spare rounds for the .45, then looked toward Tarajal.

This brief, violent exchange had roused the town. He knew that Option Omega knew about a Texan being present, all thanks to "Natalie Chase," the murderous imposter. When their gunmen didn't come back, there was going to be hell to pay.

Nothing less than a trained commando could have gone toe-to-toe with heavily armed adversaries. By surviving this battle, Hawkins realized that he may have just damned hundreds, if not thousands, to death as Option Omega collapsed the hotels in which they were held hostage.

Hawkins keyed up his CPDA, informing the Farm of this latest development, all the while cursing the blond bitch who had forced his hand.

If a hostage died, he was going to kill her, helpless or not.

CHAPTER FOURTEEN

Rafael Encizo was worried about the loaded pickup that had torn out of the Option Omega camp. The gunmen packed into it seemed to be in a hurry. As Santa Cruz was too far away, and probably already had a huge contingent of gunmen, he could only surmise that their destination was the town of Tarajal.

Hawkins's presence, the information he gave out that he was openly gunsmithing for the Spanish locals, had attracted the attention of the mercenary force operating in the caldera. Encizo looked over at Gary Manning, who remained grimly impassive. The only sign of emotion he showed over the situation was to pick up his pace, scurrying along in the dark.

Through their night optics, the two had determined the setup of the camp. Fifty heat signatures suggested a little over forty men and various heat sources such as computer processors and generators to run the camp. The men in camp were all armed, with pistol belts, submachine guns and rifles.

Compared to the enemy force, Encizo and Manning might as well have been naked.

Thankfully, both of them were wrapped in the thermal blankets, which kept them invisible to the unmanned drones that the two Phoenix warriors had spotted earlier. This close to enemy electronics, they didn't dare use any of their communications back to the Farm. Satellite imagery might show where the predators were patrolling, but the information transmitted to them, even over encrypted signals, would still betray their position and penetration of the island.

Of course, all of that would go straight to hell if Hawkins ended up in a gunfight. So far, it had been an hour since the truck left. Perhaps the Omega team had found nothing.

If they did, then Encizo and Manning's infiltration would be in vain. Even so, it was only an hour and a half until sunrise. The thermal blankets negated their visibility to airborne infrared cameras, but in daylight, things would not go so smoothly. Armed with an air rifle and two .22-caliber pistols, the two Phoenix veterans were behind the eight ball, and the caldera was akin to a moonscape, providing very little concealment from the air or even over ground. There were ruts and cracks that they could hide in, but it was hard traveling if they wanted to sneak up on an enemy force and secure their weaponry. Encizo remembered his throwing darts, the flying blades of shurikenjutsu, and that they would give him a little bit of reach in addition to the puny Walther.

"We have movement," Manning said. They'd bypassed the main camp to an area where gunmen and technicians were working on the drums of explosive fuel, attaching detonators to their sides before the drums were loaded onto trucks. From a distance the exact type of detonator was hard to make out, but it was some manner of electronics embedded in a cake of plastic explosive, more than enough to burst the drum and set off whatever concoction was within.

Manning and Encizo watched the pickup take off out of the camp, but knew that they had to trail the transports that had gone out.

"They're working to meet a deadline," Encizo muttered. "No one is stuck doing busywork. Either they're standing guard or they're working on moving the explosives. Any idea what could be in those drums?"

"Could be anything, as the detonators are simply shaped so as to rupture the drums and release the insides," Manning said. "Thus, we could be working with anything that could cause a grain silo explosion. They could be jammed with sawdust, coal powder, magnesium…"

Encizo frowned. "There are dispersal charges—what about the ignition spark?"

"Those are probably on-site. A radio-controlled electrical discharge, set within a particular confined space, such as a lava tube," Manning said. "This way, Omega could bring in whatever they wanted, fertilizer or petroleum, or even a mix."

Encizo and Manning were closing in on a truck that was laden with ten barrels. Other trucks zoomed back toward the camp. So far, they'd spotted five pickups that had been making the deliveries. Manning looked worried at the amount of material being moved.

"Two tons of explosive material at a time, so while

we've been watching, Omega has put ten tons into position," Manning said. He looked over at Encizo.

"And since they intend to use it as a fuel-air explosion…" Encizo said.

Manning put his hand on Encizo's biceps. "All right. We're looking at the landslide as igneous volcanic rock. My experience with rock blasting says we need a high-velocity explosive because we need to shatter the stone to cause the landslide to set off the tidal wave. That means an ANFO type of explosive, not a fuel-air blast."

"ANFO…ammonium nitrate and fuel oil," Encizo clarified for himself.

Manning nodded. "I'm tempted to see if the Jeopardy Corporation obtained aluminum powder. ANFO is usually only ninety-three percent as effective as its weight in TNT, but with added aluminum, that increases the energy and sensitivity of the explosive by up to thirty percent. A 950-kilogram bomb used in the terrorist attack on Oslo was about 150 kilograms of aluminum added to 800 kilograms of ANFO. We saw ten tons of drums deployed already."

"Is that bad?" Encizo asked.

Manning nodded. "It's enough to blow the side off the volcano and dump the millions of tons of mass into the Atlantic necessary to unleash the wave. And we're looking at the end result of the transportation. There could be ten times that already in place."

"The equivalent of a low-yield nuclear weapon," Encizo muttered.

They looked at the truck. There were four men who had ridden up with the drums in addition to the driver.

There were also eight men on hand, with roll carts, ready to load the drums. The driver had one man on hand with an assault rifle who wasn't busy handling the explosives.

The rifleman was alert, even a little on edge. Manning consulted his watch. "We've got a little over an hour of darkness left. If we hope to get something done…"

"We act now. What's the plan?" Encizo asked.

"Can you take down the rifleman?" Manning responded.

"You won't use the air rifle?" Encizo returned.

"We need hands on that M-4 right off the bat," Manning said. "I'll be using the Walther to keep the others busy."

"So, I close in, use my knife, get the rifle then cover you," Encizo replied. "I see a good approach to the truck."

With that, the veteran Cuban warrior began pulling off the thermal blanket. Manning followed suit. They needed to move quickly and the blanket parkas were too constricting. Besides, exertion would only cause them to overheat.

Now both men were exposed to airborne thermal cameras, armed only with the smallest of pistols and regular fighting knives.

"Good luck," Manning whispered.

Encizo nodded, then took off. The path he took was across the craggy, broken ground of the fused, long-dead volcano. The depression was a crack, long since worn smooth by centuries of rain and wind, just deep enough for him to disappear into as he crouched.

He slid the rubber handle of his knife into one hand, then pulled one of the nail-like throwing darts from his forearm sheath. Both weapons were dull, painted with black phosphate so no moonlight would reflect off them. His approach was a balance of stealth and speed, and he knew that Manning was making a longer circuit around. The greater distance he took allowed him to move a little more quickly without fear of being seen.

Together, the two men were flanking the group of Option Omega workers.

Encizo paused and checked the group more closely. Two of the men who were operating the handcarts had compact machine pistols hung around their necks on slings. That kind of firepower would be useful. They looked like his preferred Heckler and Koch MP-5 SMGs, but something was off about the shape. They looked a little too cartoony in their furniture, like something out of a comic strip drawn by an artist who wanted to make their guns look cooler. That helped him settle on the knowledge that these were SAFs, Chilean-made weapons that were based on the Swiss SIG assault rifle, which itself was an update of the Kalashnikov mechanism.

Either way, the SAFs were simple, robust and reliable by reputation. The folding stocks halved the length of the chatterboxes, giving them a little more maneuverability, and the ability to be carried while performing other tasks, as the men armed with them displayed.

Manning would notice them, he hoped. There was no

way to contact the brawny Canadian now. Encizo had already exposed himself enough to infrared cameras, so transmitting a radio signal would only compound his blatant presence.

Encizo edged toward the rear of the rifleman. His gun was a typical M-4 carbine, one made by dozens of companies worldwide to the point where the term for the knockoffs was a simple abbreviation of M Forgery. He couldn't tell the brand, but it didn't matter. The manual of arms was the same for all of these rifles—same magazine drop, same safety, same bolt operation, same iron sights. He kept the rifleman between himself and the two subgunners. Encizo also had the further opportunity to get the bulk of the pickup between him and the mass of Omega barrel movers.

With luck, he could get cover behind the engine block and front axle of the vehicle before the two SAF-armed shooters could deploy their weapons. The rifleman's head was on a swivel, but he was looking for incursion by vehicle.

Encizo was short and compactly built, and he clung to the bottom of the rut that he was advancing through. A larger group would have been more noticeable to any sharp-eyed sentry, but one man, moving on feet as sure as a cat's, was able to edge through the blind spots in his perception. He got within five yards of his target and stopped.

Manning needed to get into position now. There would be some kind of signal, a small distraction that would attract the attention of the workers, at least for long enough for Encizo to cross the open ground and deal with the rifleman.

Encizo simply had to wait for it.

Then there was a sharp crack. One of the headlights on the pickup shattered and went dark. A second snap split the night, and the rifleman in front of Encizo tensed, turning toward the truck. Both headlights had suddenly died. The man chattered in Spanish and the rifleman shouldered his weapon, scanning the shadows.

Manning had either used the air rifle to put the enemy in disarray, or he was utilizing some form of improvised flash suppressor for the pistol. Either way, there had been no muzzle-flash in the night to call attention to the Canadian marksman's position.

Just the same, that brief moment of confusion was all Encizo needed to rise, spring forward and latch one brawny forearm under the throat of the rifleman. In the next instant his cold steel sunk into the Omega guard's right kidney, paralyzing him with renal shock. There wasn't even a gargle of pain; that had been cut off by Encizo's powerful choke hold.

The Omega workmen were still looking for the possible attack. One man brought his radio up to his lips when two snaps of a pocket pistol cut through the sudden babbling confusion. This time there was a dim muzzle-flash, as Manning was utilizing the Walther at the pistol's extreme range to keep the radioman from speaking. The component flew from his fingers and shattered on the rock at his feet, and his other hand rose to his face, a bullet having torn his cheek, but deflecting off his skull.

"There!" the driver called. He, too, had carried a

Chilean submachine gun, but the driver waved to his rifleman ally, who suddenly had disappeared. "Gunter?"

Encizo jammed the paralyzed, dying man against the ground, ripping the M-4 carbine from his clutches. He didn't want to betray his presence yet, so he rose up and let fly with the shurikenjutsu dart in his left hand. The three-inch-long spike of steel flew straight and true, its hard tine point punching through the bridge of the driver's nose hard enough to embed straight up.

In agony, the driver wailed suddenly, triggering the machine pistol in his hand, blowing chunks of stone out in 9 mm divots. The spasm of gunfire suddenly attracted everyone's attention toward the wheelman, and by extension, Encizo.

Time to get to work, the Cuban thought as he shouldered the rifle, thumbed off the safety and cut loose in semiautomatic mode, as much to conserve ammunition as to lower his profile in the darkness. His first target was one of the handcart operators with an SMG. Two 5.56 mm rounds pierced his upper chest and hurled him to the ground like a flopping fish. The other man raised his chatterbox and got off two rounds before something smacked him, spinning him.

It was Manning again. He'd moved, then come to his partner's rescue with a precisely placed air rifle dart. This time Encizo realized that Manning was doing work with the lethal krait venom, as the man spun not from the force of impact, but from the body-wrenching agony caused by a powerful neurotoxin. Normally the amount of venom delivered by an Indian krait was enough to kill within twelve hours via respiratory paralysis and

asphyxiation, but each of the darts was loaded with a
man-killing dose. It would be as if someone had poured
fire into his lungs, but the target didn't even have the
time to claw at his throat before his arms and legs failed
him. He was out of the fight immediately, but he was
still alive. Thankfully, the time until death was much
shorter, but it was still measured in minutes, not seconds.

Encizo would have ended the man's suffering, but
the driver opened fire, blind with pain, or with spurt-
ing blood, or just plain rage, fanning the night with
a magazine-long burst from his machine pistol. The
Cuban whirled and pumped two shots into the wheelman's center of mass, 5.56 mm rounds shredding his
heart.

That's when the pickup's cab suddenly exploded,
windows shattering under a hail of handgun fire. Encizo ducked down, using the engine block and the tires
of the pickup to shield him. Pistol rounds were nowhere
nearly as powerful as a rifle, and against the sheer mass
of a truck's front end, they had little chance of cutting
through the thinner sheet metal of the doors or fend-
ers to reach him.

This was only a temporary solution. Encizo dumped
the partially expended magazine from his rifle, moving
the dual-clipped magazine over one, snapping a full box
in place. He scurried back to the ditch, dropping low as
handgun fire chased after him. Two men followed him,
their pistols barking as they did so. They hoped to keep
their assailant's head down by dint of sheer volume of
fire, but Encizo wasn't going to let barely aimed fire

stop his response. He rose, shouldered the rifle and fired in one single, smooth movement before dropping back behind the rock lip of the crack he hid in. Encizo's lone 5.56 mm round hit one of the gunmen high in the chest, expelling a bloody cloud of darkness from the impact.

The other gunman froze in his tracks, watching his friend jerk violently backward, gasping as one lung was destroyed, or at least severed at the bottom of the bronchial tube. That brief pause gave Encizo the opportunity to rise once more, then cut loose with another single shot, this one catching the gawking, distracted Omega gunman in the left ear.

As the second gunner fell, Encizo could see that the right side of the man's head had opened up like a grisly flower, brainpan excavated of all matter, simply a black, empty hole. Encizo had literally blown the gunman's brains out.

Brutal and bloody efficient, as his friend David McCarter would say.

Trouble was, the less armed workers had reached the fallen subgunners. Encizo could see one of the Option Omega gunmen wrestling the machine pistol out of a dead man's hands. Before the guy could get the weapon free, Encizo fired three rapid shots, bullets tearing into him, puncturing his thoracic cavity, blowing heart and lungs into shredded meat before dumping him lifeless on the ground.

That was one more down, but there were two other full-auto weapons out there, just out of sight behind the bulk of the pickup. By the time Encizo moved into a position to open up on them, they would have been braced and ready for several moments, laying down streams of autofire to rip him to pieces.

Encizo knew that he had to push ahead. Manning was on the other side of this melee, and it was likely that he was going to catch hell, too. He could hear the crack of handguns as Option Omega's gunmen tried to tag him. Encizo saw a grenade-size rock within reach. He scooped it up and called out, "Fire in the hole!"

He hoped that the bluff would ease the pressure on the Canadian as he lobbed it over the truck. Sure enough, there were shouts of dismay as the enemy thought that a hand grenade had just been hurled into their midst. Figures scrambled away from the truck, one of them packing a Chilean subgun. Encizo targeted him first, triggering the M-4 as fast as he could pull the trigger. Two rounds hammered into the armed gunner, transfixing him across the width of his body, entering under one armpit and blowing through to the other side of his rib cage.

The subgunner whirled under the impact, spiraling down to the hard rock, never to rise again.

Encizo didn't have time to celebrate his marksmanship as another man cut loose with his handgun. One 9 mm bullet leaped across the space between the two men, striking the frame of Encizo's shouldered rifle and smashing it hard into his face.

Cheek split by the hammering effect of steel and bone colliding with skin in the center, the Cuban dropped dazedly to the ground, shock setting off flashbulbs behind his eyes. Encizo remembered being shot in the head once before, and this was nowhere near as traumatic. However, the pain was all-encompassing, filling him with an inability to focus on anything more than breathing. He was down and an easy target now.

The only thing he could hope for was a quick and easy death. That and the strength to meet his murderer with a growl on his lips and defiance still in his heart.

The gunman didn't advance, though. Encizo's rattled brains couldn't process outside information, so he was clueless as to what was happening. He fought to move his limbs, and after what felt like a year, he lurched, rolling over onto his stomach, pushing with both hands against the ground. It was as if gravity had quadrupled, but he shoved himself up to his hands and knees. Blood splattered on the ground from his gashed cheek.

All of this transpired in a skewed, wildly distorted time. He could tell because he saw a figure seeming to bend next to him. He thought the man was bending, but instead, he was falling, one eyeball a greasy red mess that spewed out viscera. The whole thing was happening in what felt like slow motion, but Encizo realized that it was simply his brain, his perceptions warped to the point that he was experiencing the world one frame of film at a time.

It was the man who'd shot him, side arm still clutched in his fist, jaw slack. It had to have been Manning's dart that had taken him out, a direct hit to the eye, tail fins jutting through the orbital, a needle-sharp point puncturing the soft, squishy orb and penetrating deep into his brain cavity. Encizo pushed himself hard, lunging toward the falling corpse, hands clawing at the pistol locked in the man's hand. He pried the weapon free, and saw that the slide had been locked back on an empty magazine. Another magazine was in the guy's other fist; he had been in the middle of reloading when he'd been hit.

Encizo cracked open lifeless fingers, plucked up the magazine, then slammed it into place. It was some kind of CZ-75 clone, and when the slide closed, it stripped the top round off the fresh magazine. It was cocked and ready to fire with a light, swift pull of the trigger. His senses were returning to a normal time stream. He spotted the enemy gathered on his side of the truck, aiming at a bulky figure that had a slender little rifle in his hands.

It was Manning with his air gun.

The thing was, that air gun only held six shots, and Manning had obviously burned off four of them so far, if not all six. He was under pressure now, and the chatter of a Chilean submachine gun rattled on the other side of the truck.

Encizo had a 9 mm pistol and the element of surprise. He had to act now before his partner was gunned down brutally. Lurching to his feet, he fought to maintain his balance. The blow to his face must have shaken him more than he'd realized, but his brother in arms was in danger.

There were three men left, using the pickup for cover, and their backs were to him. Gritting his teeth, Encizo spread his feet, took aim at one of the subgunners and cut loose. The pistol barked and jumped in Encizo's grasp, his perceptions still out of whack, senses operating at different time scales. He trusted his body to follow the same commands it always had before, muscle memory putting him in the proper position, his eyes confirming that front sight and rear sight were aligned. The Omega gunman writhed as 9 mm slugs punched into his back, slamming him against the pickup.

The sudden blast of gunfire from their rear and the violent spasm of their partner caught the attention of the other two guards. They whirled toward Encizo, and he felt himself pivot, front sight coming into alignment with the head of the next gunman in line. The CZ clone thundered again, jumping four times in his grasp, but Encizo's strong fingers crushed down on the grip, hard plastic dug into his palms and the pads of his fingers, wrists snapping back straight as the slide closed back into battery.

Four trigger pulls and the turning Omega terrorist's head bounced wildly on his neck like a speed bag. Craters were blown out of the gunman's head, one over his right ear, another sinking into his temple, a third obscuring the center of his face, the fourth chipping away the bottom of his jaw. The turning man was operating on momentum, Encizo's rapid salvo striking him so quickly that he was still moving even though his brain was dead, transected three times before he began tumbling backward.

The third man started firing before he was lined up on Encizo, but the stream of gunfire was leveling toward the Cuban. The Phoenix Force vet was going to catch some full-auto slugs in the gut or chest, and no amount of shooting was going to do more than avenge his own death.

Encizo braced himself anyway, tripping the trigger on the CZ-75 clone as soon as he brought the handgun to the third target. Even as his first bullet slammed into the shoulder of the Omega murderer, the man's head jerked violently forward as if struck from behind by a sledgehammer. That impact didn't tense up the gunman, but left him a jellied sack of meat in a human skin.

Gary Manning, top sniper and marksman, had destroyed the man's medulla oblongata with a direct injection of krait venom from the high-powered air gun. The dart lanced into the slight gap between skull and top of vertebrae, discharging its payload of neurotoxin into the juncture of nerves that let the body tense. It was a target of police snipers, vulnerable from the front in the triangle between the bridge of the nose and the corners of the mouth. A shot there hit so hard and so fast, it simply unplugged the body, preventing the possibility of a reflexive death spasm.

Manning's shot dropped the gunner, his body gone completely relaxed, the SAF's trigger released. Encizo still had felt one bullet pluck at his hip, grazing through the fabric and searing his skin.

It was a close call, but it didn't matter to Option Omega because Encizo was still alive and able to fight. He'd be hurting, and he'd need to take care of the bleeding when he had a chance, but he was on the move, fighting and killing.

Encizo had taken the pressure off Manning, and the superb rifleman returned the favor by saving Encizo's life.

The gunfight was brutal, loud and violent. Even

this far from the Omega camp, it was likely that someone would have heard. While Phoenix Force had managed to assemble a small arsenal from the effects of the dead, the terrorists were going to know danger was on the way. What was worse was that they would inform the hostage takers in Santa Cruz about the arrival of a trained operations team.

Option Omega's threat of murdering a hotel full of innocents was about to come to fruition. And if they didn't act, the very explosive drums that Encizo and Manning now hoped to remove from the equation were going to be the target of Jeopardy's engineers to protect their ultimate plan.

Either way, despite this victory, despite what they had gained, things grew tighter for the Stony Man warriors.

CHAPTER FIFTEEN

David McCarter consulted his CPDA as he stalked through the basement of the hotel, looking for the demolitions charge Option Omega would need to collapse the building at first sight of an intrusion by special operations teams. Santa Cruz was a vacation paradise, a destination for travelers from both sides of the Atlantic, meaning that the people who were in these buildings were still considered valuable to American and European governments.

As the Phoenix Force leader approached the stress point that demolitions expert Gary Manning indicated would be the best spot for an explosive, he could smell the stink of diesel fuel. As he approached the central support of the hotel, he saw four drums around it. The smell of diesel meant that Option Omega was using the deadly mixture of ammonium nitrate and fuel oil.

McCarter grimaced. Four drums meant that he was looking at about three-quarters of the equivalent of a ton of TNT around the center mast. That was if it was simply conventional ANFO, and not amplified by accelerants, which would allow for faster oxidization and thus quicker burning. He hadn't hung around Gary Manning without learning lessons about high explosives, and this was all that McCarter needed to confirm that Option Omega was keeping explosives on site.

It made sense to utilize ANFO. The vast majority of the supplies could be transported as simple high-nitrogen fertilizer, or as components for any dozens of things. Diesel fuel was a common source of power for many European vehicles, which meant that fixing it together would be easy and relatively cheap. Even so, five hotels with four drums of ANFO a piece...

It was a little under four and a half tons. McCarter looked for fresh news on the CPDA.

"Firefight caught on orbital surveillance. Location—caldera," was a posting that McCarter picked up from Stony Man Farm's data ticker. If there had been a gunfight that big, then it was certain that Phoenix Force had encountered the enemy. He was fairly certain his allies had been successful, but even so, he sent out an emergency message to Manning and Encizo.

As he did so, he switched over to the digital camera function and took photos of the drums assembled in the basement.

There were radio transceivers with explosive charges attached to the sides of the drums. He grimaced as he realized that Manning would know whether or not it was safe to pull off the detonators, but even if he did so, he wasn't certain that taking out the charges for this central support would do enough to stop hundreds from dying.

The CPDA vibrated, announcing an incoming message. McCarter looked at it.

"Made it through," Manning relayed.

McCarter immediately sent a digital image of the

first of the drums to him, following it up with another text. "No response here."

Even as he did so, his CPDA popped up an inset into his text conversation with Manning. It was the cloned cell phone that he'd gotten off the dead man. It was a general announcement among the whole Option Omega group.

"Incursion to caldera. Step up timetable."

That didn't sound good. Not in the slightest.

McCarter added another message to Manning. "They know you're active all the way over here in Santa Cruz. They want the timetable stepped up."

Due to the nature of conversation by instant messaging, Manning's first response had nothing to do with his warning. Not that Manning needed to be told that he'd awakened the whole neighborhood.

"Charges seem safe. Simple blasting packs. Disarm."

McCarter set about peeling the detonation charges off the drums, though he held off from completely tearing them away until he was certain there were no trip wires in evidence. He now had four small bombs added to his supply of stolen weapons, but he wasn't sure what he could do with them. They were radio-activated.

"We were here. We heard the gunfight. Not sure what the advanced timetable could be."

If it was one thing that Manning was, he was straight and to the point.

"Two questions—are there other charges? Are there other ways to set off these drums?"

"A surface-to-surface missile might be able to do some damage. That means drums on other floors. Doubtful.

They have at least one hundred tons of ANFO here at the volcano. Possibly more."

McCarter grimaced. "If they have that much more, why not spare some to make sure they can knock out buildings?"

"Have the surface-to-surface missiles on the Q-ship. Fast, nearly as effective with much more dense explosives."

"Great. Lied—have a third question. What can I do with the C-4?"

"Find some electrical detonators. Otherwise, you can mold an ash tray out of them."

McCarter snorted in a restrained laugh. He looked toward the drums. "Can we do something with the ANFO?"

"Unless you're able to find a frequency to set off the charges, same problem. Except you should keep them away from fire."

McCarter nodded at that answer. No way would things be so simple that he could take a drum full of high explosives and convert it into a weapon capable of taking out enemy forces in one fell swoop. "What about you? Got a plan for the camp? Delay the landslide?"

"Setting something up. May also be seen from orbit."

McCarter knew that access to the kinds of explosives that Option Omega wanted to use to blow open the side of a volcano would make Manning one of the most dangerous humans on the planet at this moment. If anyone could improvise a knockout punch, it would be the burly Canadian, with help from Rafael Encizo.

A second text cut into McCarter's conversation.

"Any word from Gary?" It was from Calvin James.

"Got him on other text," McCarter sent back.

"Got explosive fuel in storage on the Q-ship. What can I do?"

The Phoenix Force commander forwarded that text to his partner. McCarter could swear that he could hear Gary Manning's chuckle all the way from the other side of the island.

"Will give Cal instructions," Manning advised Mc-Carter.

McCarter grinned, then informed James of the enemy's knowledge and need to update their timetable. Things were closing in tight, but if anything could be done to the missile cruiser that was in the harbor, James would mastermind an act of sabotage involving drums of ANFO on board.

"Miguel?" a voice called from the stairwell, cutting into McCarter's musings. The Briton put away his CPDA, snatching up the FMK-9 machine pistol from where it had hung on his sling.

A gunfight in the basement would be bad. A stray bullet could hit the drums. ANFO was something that could be sparked off by a sufficient ignition, and if things went as they usually did on a Stony Man operation, the bad guys would be able to set off the ANFO in a way that McCarter couldn't repeat even if he tried.

"*¿Qué?*" McCarter answered with a slur to his voice.

There was a rapid-fire distant rattle of a voice. Up close, McCarter had a passable command of Spanish, more than enough to handle himself in South America or Spain itself. The trouble was, the other man was far away. There was something wrong with the way he spoke Spanish, as well, as if there were some other accent at work here.

"I can't hear you!" McCarter snapped in Spanish. *"¡Ven acá!"*

The last command was forceful, hardly the more friendly *ven aquí* used among friends. However, the dead man that McCarter was impersonating would not be happy with the mushiness of language used, nor being interrupted.

"I said," the newcomer stated, coming closer in answer to McCarter's summons. "Quit playing with yourself down in the basement and get up top. We don't want to be in the building when the drums go off."

"I got the message, too," McCarter said, bluffing, still keeping himself just out of sight of the Omega messenger. "We've got a few minutes."

"No, Karl said that he wants us out and on the street by sunrise. That's fifteen minutes. Miguel, quit screwing around!" the newcomer said.

McCarter kept in motion, keeping racks of supplies and tools between himself and the gunman. "I'm coming!"

"That is what I am afraid of, you pervert," the man said.

McCarter was behind him, and he had the metal stock of the FMK open and locked into place. With a sudden burst of speed, he cracked the half-inch-thick steel wire and the eight pounds of loaded weapon against the back of the gunman's head. The blow sent him stumbling forward, knocking off his knit cap and betraying a shock of ginger hair that was quickly growing darker as a scalp laceration opened up.

"The…" was all the groggy gunman managed to get past his lips when he saw McCarter move close again, whipping down the muzzle of the machine pistol hard, raking it across the Omega terrorist's forehead. Skin peeled open, revealing pink bone, and the sentry staggered backward to the ground, eyes unfocused.

McCarter dropped onto him, knees slamming into each of the man's shoulders to pin him down. He pressed the FMK under his chin, sneering with disgust.

"Fifteen minutes?" McCarter asked. "Then you kill hundreds?"

"Don't shoot me!" he sputtered in Flemish. He repeated the plea in French. No wonder the man's Spanish was so bloody awful. McCarter wrapped his fingers around the man's throat. The last major group of Maoist terrorists in Belgium were the Communist Combatant Cells, but that was back in the mid-'80s. A more recent group, however, was a Belgian group called Black November, operating in concert with their brothers in Greece.

"Belgian?" McCarter growled in his much more fluent French.

The man's eyes widened.

Red hair, blue eyes, it wasn't hard to place this man as European, but also as a good candidate for Option Omega's face men as they took hostages. If he was a Maoist who had been recruited for this operation, then this must have been one of the few who had slipped through the cracks when that group had been rounded up.

"I take that as a yes," McCarter said. "How many others are upstairs, minus Miguel?"

"I won't…"

McCarter tossed the SMG aside, then pulled out his automatic folding knife. The snick of the blade opening riveted his prisoner's attention. "I wouldn't shoot you, but I disarmed the drums down here. I've got more than fifteen minutes to kill you."

"Please…"

McCarter squeezed, then rested the point of the switchblade against the lid of his prisoner's left eye. "I'll cut off your eyelids so you can watch the whole show."

"Eight!" the Belgian gurgled. "Don't cut my eyes! Don't cut my eyes!"

McCarter brought the knife back, sneering at the man. He reoriented his fist and punched the man unconscious with a hard shot to the jaw. "Thank your god I'm not as sick as you bastards."

He grabbed the Belgian's cell phone and a walkie-talkie.

He thought back to the larger, stranger phone that Miguel had on his person upstairs. He'd been able to plug the CPDA into it, which had given him access to its programming, or at least any signal that the phone was operating on.

He hoped that he wouldn't have to waste time explaining what was going on, but just to make sure, McCarter took a few minutes to tape the unconscious man's wrists and ankles together with duct tape. Another swatch went over his mouth to keep him from making noise when he woke up. Then he headed back upstairs, to the kitchen where he'd stuffed Miguel's corpse.

On the way, McCarter opened an instant messaging conversation with the Farm.

"Home, did one of those first phones have detonation codes?"

"Checking."

If that were the case, there was hope that the other four hotels wouldn't be affected by basement detonations that would demolish the buildings with hundreds of innocents trapped inside. Reaching the kitchen, McCarter pulled Miguel's form from under the table, patting him down for the unusually large and bulky device that he'd assumed was a satellite phone.

"You're right, Phoenix One," Price replied.

McCarter grinned. "Can you find a way in to block any detonation signals?"

"We're working on it now," Price answered.

"You've got eleven minutes to do it," McCarter warned. "Gary and Rafe set the ball rolling."

"Figured the new timetable," Price responded. "Were at work as soon as we knew. Been monitoring their phones the moment you captured the first one."

McCarter tucked the CPDA away and pocketed Miguel's unit. It was some form of smartphone that had been retasked to work as a central detonator at least for this hotel, if not the others.

Eight gunmen were still on the loose in this hotel, and likely another forty to go with the other four hostaged buildings. Eight-to-one odds were long enough.

But quintuple that, and then spread it across a city, and things would be impossible for McCarter to handle all on his own. If only the whole team were present in Santa Cruz, then maybe he'd have a chance to stop a massacre once Option Omega realized that their planned explosions had been aborted.

He was about to exit the kitchen when he heard the hushed conversation of a group of men down the hall and around the corner.

"Hey, Miguel! Elio! Hurry up!" a voice called. McCarter tensed, then realized that he had a chance to even the odds until they were a little closer. He had the element of surprise, and he had an SMG on hand. The others didn't realize that there was an enemy among them, here in the hotel.

All he had to do was to strike fast, strike hard and hope for the best.

He remembered the lifeless eyes staring back at him from the bottom of the ocean.

"Hold up!" McCarter shouted, emulating Elio's shitty Spanish accent. "Miguel's still beating off downstairs!"

That elicited a peal of laughter from the others.

One of the gunmen, sporting a mop of black curls and an equally dark mustache over a chin shadowed with stubble, leaned into the kitchen, eyes bright and a smile on his face as he was expecting a friend. Both hands were on the doorjamb, and away from his weapons, especially the machine pistol hanging around his neck.

That smile was frozen on his face as the others passed behind him. There was a dull moment of recognition, a long pregnant pause that McCarter didn't let slip away without a sudden explosion of automatic fire that ripped from the muzzle of his weapon. Bullets hammered into the smiling man hard and quick. He hadn't even had the opportunity to cry out in pain, just simply grunt as he was hurled against the far wall across from the door.

The hallway suddenly filled with the sound of scrambling feet and curses, one man screaming in pain as he caught a couple of bullets through the Sheetrock of the wall. McCarter focused on that sound and compensated for the reflexive movement of the shot man and he triggered the FMK once more. Sheetrock crumbled under a dozen 9 mm impacts that pulverized the wall.

A dying wail filled the air, accompanied by another injured grunt.

All of this happened so fast that the man in the doorway was still sliding down the wall, friction holding him up even as his lifeblood smeared a trail behind him. McCarter pivoted with the machine pistol and opened up through the Sheetrock once more, only on the other side of the door. There had been a shadow crouched at the doorjamb, but McCarter's third salvo of full-auto thunder hurled the kneeling man out into the hall, back peppered with pulverized plaster and bloody splotches where deformed bullets hammered into him.

The cries of pain and fear filtered in through the hall, and those were a grim form of music to McCarter's ears. The gunmen who had terrorized a hotel filled with hostages were now themselves subjected to fear. That had a form of justice to it as McCarter popped out the nearly emptied magazine and replaced it with another. At least two were down for the count, most likely three, and there was an injured man among them. By his calculations, he'd almost halved the odds against him, and he still had three full magazines to work with.

The only problem was that now he no longer had the element of surprise. Those first three were as free as he was going to get, and even then, the third gunman downed had been perched, ready to fight back had not the wall at his back failed to shield him. McCarter's fears were realized as two streams of gunfire chopped windows through the walls and into the kitchen.

Bullets bounced off metal surfaces, forcing the Briton to the floor to avoid death by ricochet. Sheetrock had been punched through, fist-size cavities blown in the wall where the gunmen stood back and reloaded, replaced by partners with full weapons.

Bolstered by the knowledge that they could shoot through walls, the Omega terrorists felt nearly invincible, as long as they could cut loose with their own guns. The trouble with that theory was that while they might have had a hint of where McCarter had been at the beginning of the fight, they had lost track of him during the opening seconds of their retaliation. McCarter scurried on the floor out of his old position, and now reloaded, he spotted the muzzle-flashes of subguns firing through holes blasted in Sheetrock.

McCarter let the FMK hang on its sling, opting for the Turkish CZ pistol. He fired two shots just below each of the firing ports that the terrorists had blasted for themselves. He would have fired higher, but he didn't know if his enemies were crouched or if they were kneeling in the hope of peering through the wrecked wall to see their opponent. Either way, McCarter would nail them in the groins if they were firing from the hip or in the chest if they were kneeling.

One let out a cry of bloody agony and staggered into the open doorway clutching at his bullet-blasted crotch. The other hole fell silent as McCarter's double tap punched into him. It wasn't the blatant, tragically comic display of the 9-mm-castrated gunman who wailed at the loss of his manhood, but it was information that McCarter could use.

The Briton stiff-armed the pistol again and punched three rapid shots into the badly wounded man in the door. Rocked by 9 mm slugs, he was dumped atop the smiling, mustached man, cries forever silenced.

More bullets punched through the Sheetrock wall, chasing after McCarter, but he was back on the floor, crawling away from the incoming fire. He could hear a few shouts in a muddle of Spanish and other languages. The gist of the conversation was if there were one or two men inside the kitchen. McCarter decided to further confuse the issue by cutting loose with his captured machine pistol from a third position, hammering a spot where a salvo of gunfire had cut through on the other side. He hit nothing, but there was the sound of someone jumping with surprise. McCarter did a shoulder roll and came up with the pistol, firing toward the sound of that hop, blazing away with five shots before another submachine gun ripped through the Sheetrock on the other side of the door.

There was a call for a retreat as the Option Omega gunner cut loose, spraying the kitchen left and right. A ricochet tagged McCarter along his triceps, making him flinch and tumble to the messy floor. Rubble and rotted food surrounded him, and he decided that he did have another option to make them think that they'd nailed him.

McCarter grabbed Miguel and pushed him upright with a powerful surge of his legs. As the dead man swayed in the kitchen, erect before gravity tugged at him, another burst of bullets ripped across the kitchen, peppering the dead Peruvian. Miguel toppled with a mighty crash, breaking dishes and hurling steel utensils to the floor.

"Did you get him?" one of them called.

"Why don't you go take a look?" someone else snapped.

"Fuck it, we've got grenades. I'll fix this shit!" a third declared.

McCarter rolled to his hands and knees, looking for movement at the wall. A single grenade would be the end of his part in this fight. Even if he survived the wounds, he'd be left deaf and stunned, easy pickings for the Option Omega death squad.

That's when he heard the ping of a spoon by the doorjamb. McCarter was up and firing, hammering out a long burst from the FMK machine pistol. The grenadier jerked violently under a rain of full-auto copper jackets. The grenade fell to the ground at his feet, rolling away, but farther down the hall.

There was a loud curse and the sudden clatter and stomp of feet. McCarter grabbed Miguel's corpse and quickly threw it over him as if it were a blanket of lifeless, rotting meat.

The grenade went off, the world shook around him, and darkness filled McCarter's vision as the deadly blast ripped through the hallway and the kitchen door.

CHAPTER SIXTEEN

Barbara Price knew something was wrong when David McCarter didn't log out of his CPDA conversation with the other members of Phoenix Force. Since Stony Man was the main chat line for the team, and there was a countdown for the detonation of the explosive charges placed in five hotels across the city of Santa Cruz, she knew that the Briton was most likely in combat.

The worst thing about it was that police response was hours away, thanks to the brutal missile assault from the cruise ship that Calvin James was aboard. She turned to Kurtzman.

"Please tell me that you're cracking the detonation programming and signals off that phone detonator," Price said breathlessly. She'd been up for more than twenty-four hours straight, and even with a jolt of caffeine buzzing through her system, she was starting to run low on energy. This had been a marathon sprint ever since Phoenix Force had gone ashore on La Palma just before sundown the night before. It was ten minutes until dawn now. The previous day, she'd been working with Able Team on their investigation through Norfolk to track down Option Omega's operation in America. Four and a half hours ago, they'd gone wheels up on an antisubmarine S-3 Viking after a third brutal gun-fight with the Jeopardy Corporation's hired guns, racing across the ocean for a rendezvous with the other team.

"We've got it," Kurtzman told her, looking back over his shoulder. "We're checking to see if the other hotels are on the same frequency, or if there are other codes for them."

"Ten minutes, Aaron," Price reminded him.

"We do this right, or we just have one hotel safe," Kurtzman grumbled.

Carmen Delahunt stood at her station. "Explosion at the hotel."

Delahunt didn't have to specify which hotel was the target. McCarter was likely engaging the rest of the hostage takers in the building he'd defused, and if the gunfight was more than a few minutes, the terrorists had already demonstrated that they had access to hand grenades. They'd used them to kill dozens as they'd taken over the hotel. Price had gotten close-up digital confirmation of the carnage off McCarter's digital camera.

"David…" Price murmured. "How'd you hear that?"

"We've got open coms on the enemy thanks to the phones McCarter confiscated," Delahunt replied. "The gunfire's abated for now."

"Put it on the main speakers," Price ordered.

"He's faced worse odds before," Kurtzman said, trying to reassure her.

Barbara Price had come into this job after being recruited from the NSA, where she'd served as a capable mission controller. It was her job to send men into places where they could die for the sake of others. It still didn't make it easy to not know when one of her team members was injured or dead. She gnawed on her lower lip, brows wrinkled in concern.

She turned back to the feed between Manning and James. They'd ended their conversation, but she saw the setup that Manning had given to the Phoenix medic to begin neutralizing the enemy cruise ship. James hadn't gone far in the craft, barely out from the deck where he'd entered through a submarine port in the belly.

Now, he was going to have to set a bomb, and then escape before it went off. In the meantime, on the other side of the island Manning, Encizo and Hawkins had engaged in their own firefights with Option Omega's forces.

So far, Stony Man had confirmed that the whole operation had been assembled by rogue elements within the Chinese and Saudi governments. The operation had no official sanction from Beijing or Riyadh, though much of the money laundering had been traced along a web of launderers all the way back to the bank accounts of one Diwala bin Lohs.

Price was particularly grim as she realized that Diwala had disappeared, along with his brother Fahd. They must have gone somewhere, and Stony Man needed to track down the two renegades. This operation must have cost them plenty, but there were other factors at work that made the two men dangerous. They already had ties to China, at least for this one operation.

Even if they weren't capable of another conspiracy of terror, the death toll attributed to the brothers was rising. Police stations across the city of Santa Cruz were blasted to smithereens, lawmen slaughtered before they'd even had a chance to respond to the violence inflicted upon their city. Tourists had been murdered and replaced with operatives who had sneaked onto the island in their place.

Should the hotels collapse, thousands would be added to that number. Should the tidal wave be triggered, the number could reach into the millions.

The weight of their crimes against humanity had been measured, and it was worth a death sentence before they took another step. But where could these conspirators hide where they wouldn't be followed?

"Hunt, any progress on tracking down the bin Lohs brothers?" Price asked.

It was something she needed to ask. She had to distract herself from the ever-encroaching countdown to devastation.

"We can't find travel arrangements for either of them," Wethers responded. He chewed the stem of his pipe in frustration. "It's as if they disappeared on a slow boat to China."

"That's pretty likely, except that the SAD group that's working with the guys posing as Option Omega have gone to ground, as well. Their bosses have shoot-to-kill orders for them," Tokaido added. "We're not going to find them alive."

"They should know how to evade their own," Price returned. "Damn it. And what is up with the Q-ship and the Kilo-class sub that Blancanales identified in Virginia?"

"Not to mention the minisubs," Kurtzman added.

Price's eyes narrowed. Everyone else in the War Room also hit a sudden realization.

"They wouldn't be there at ground zero, would they?" Delahunt asked.

"Once the landslide occurs, or the hotels go down, the eyes of the world are going to be elsewhere, especially in Idaho where Omega supposedly hails from," Price said.

"Do you think that they'd be aboard the cruise ship?" Tokaido asked.

"Not likely. I don't think that a Saudi prince is going to jam himself into an SDV to get away from the law," Price said. "That, plus their proximity to the ANFO drums, means that they're working subs. Not escape pods for masterminds."

"We've got a Kilo-class sub in the area. That's what Gadgets and company are rushing out to intercept," Kurtzman replied. "Maybe they're on one of the SDVs, or maybe they're not. But you can't get much more secure than a full-blown Soviet diesel patrol sub."

Price frowned.

"Break radio silence," Price ordered. "Try to raise McCarter. We also need the team to either get back to their Swimmer Delivery Vehicle or to take a minisub and look for that Kilo class before they make for open water and disappear."

A gunshot split the air in the War Room, transmitted from the speakers. Everyone paused for a moment.

McCarter reported in. "Still alive."

"Carmen, give me speaker on their phones," Price asked. "David!"

McCarter's voice was more gravelly than usual, a sign that he'd taken a pounding. "Barb. You were listening in?"

"You went offline. Can you meet up with Cal?" she said into her microphone.

"I can try," McCarter answered. "Why?"

"Able's coming in to try to intercept one, maybe two submarines. I want people in the water already," Price said. "If you can get the subs before they get past the fleet ringing the island, we might catch the leaders of this organization."

McCarter cleared his throat. "Let me tool up some more. Tell Cal to meet me at the pier. Rendezvous SC-2."

"Got it," Price replied.

Tokaido nodded that he'd forwarded the information to James.

"What's the deal on stopping detonation at the other hotels?" McCarter asked.

"We're working on it," Price said. She turned to Kurtzman, then looked at her watch. Three minutes remaining. She ground her teeth.

"Don't cut it close to show off, Bear!" McCarter snarled. "Phoenix One out!"

The speakers went dead. Price looked to her cybercrew. "What's wrong?"

"Each of the charges not attached to the detonator we have has its own black ice. All four of us are working on the rest, trying to crack through, but they've got some good stuff," Kurtzman told her. "We're making progress, but it's going to be close."

Price looked at Tokaido, whose fingers were flying. The young man's hands were a blur as he was in his environment. High stress, pulse-pounding tension compressed his usual mental need for distraction into a diamond-hard, razor-sharp focus. His eyes seemed as glassy as black marble, reflecting the glimmer of his computer screen in them.

Price stood back, realizing that all she could do was watch. She'd gotten the teams to where they needed to be, but even then, there were too many variables on hand. There were loose ends abounding, like the yacht that the terrorists had taken over and replaced dozens of young people. Where had that boat gone?

Yacht, she repeated to herself.

Suddenly she had an outlet for her frustration. She flew to her workstation and brought up satellite imagery of the Tarajal harbor. Price searched for information on the yacht that the tourists had taken, looking for similarities. Top-down views weren't going to be ideal for identification, but she suddenly had an idea where the Option Omega and Jeopardy Corporation manipulators had gathered.

Even the finger of land that surrounded the inlet where Tarajal was located would be the ideal shield against any surge of the Atlantic should a landslide occur to the north. It was easy and simple.

She fired off a text to Hawkins, Manning and Encizo.

Maybe they would have a chance to intercept the Kilo-class sub, especially if it was near the yacht, which was likely. Its presence would provide a shadow to hide the sub, even if the submarine was longer than the boat above.

She looked at her watch. The countdown for the hotels in Santa Cruz was just under a minute now. She grimaced. The others were working their asses off. She could see their concentration, the sweat forming on brows.

Price pulled herself away from idle speculation and checked Grimaldi's progress across the Atlantic. Somewhere along the way, he must have found a tailwind at altitude, picking up speed to the point where he was only a half hour out from the U.S. carrier group where the Marines had promised to give them access to a V-22 Osprey.

Knocking off a third of their travel time was just the kind of thing that Grimaldi could manage due to his mastery of all things aerial.

The clock still ticked down, and Price offered up a silent prayer, hoping that her teams could get this job done.

The woman that T. J. Hawkins knew as Natalie Chase opened her eyes. She winced in pain as she tried to open her mouth, and Hawkins regretted breaking her jaw, if only because it made communication with her a little more difficult. As it was, he had taped her jaw shut with duct tape, which he'd also used to fashion manacles for her wrists and ankles. He had then secured her to the chair he'd put her in.

He showed her a picture of the yacht that the real Natalie Chase had been aboard before she was murdered to provide a cover identity.

"It's in Tarajal, right?" Hawkins asked.

She grumbled something in Greek. Of course she was Greek! Stony Man Farm had assembled a list of possible Maoist terrorist groups that would have been pulled into this plot. One of them was a Greek group that had committed dozens of violent acts and, as well as a group from Belgium, was still being hunted by the authorities.

It was a scattered recruitment effort, but Hawkins knew that the Chinese had sterilized these groups so that their trails wouldn't lead back to their involvement in this operation, even if SAD weren't appreciative of their renegades' efforts.

Hawkins pushed the screen closer to her, tugging on her hair. He could see her roots showing. She'd dyed her hair blond, not that it really mattered. The disguise was merely a cursory one. Price had given him the heads-up about the presence of a possible Kilo-class submarine in Tarajal's inlet, possibly beneath the yacht.

Even as he watched her face for signs of recognition, he could see anger and defiance in her eyes.

"Talk to me," Hawkins growled. "I can make this easier for you."

"Imprisoned in a capitalist dungeon?" the woman asked. She shook her head, glaring hatefully at him. "Sooner die."

Hawkins grimaced. "Oh, that's the point. I'll make it easy on you. You won't see a prison cell."

The imposter's eyes narrowed. "Americans don't..."

Hawkins pocketed the CPDA, then pulled out his .45-caliber revolver. "This isn't about Americans and communism. This is about you taking advantage of the murder of an unarmed, helpless person to get onto an island to cause the death of thousands, millions more."

The fake tourist saw the anger in his eyes.

"If I wanted to be nice to you, I'd let you die easy with a bullet through the brain," Hawkins continued. "But if you feel like putting up a fight, then fuck it. I'll let you live. You'll be dragged before a kangaroo court of whoever wants to take your carcass, and you'll rot at the bottom of a prison cell. And most prisoners, they don't give a fuck about your politics. You're just a leech and a psychopath, not killing for money, which is something they can understand. And because you're crazy, they won't flock to your side as students, they'll torment you. They'll beat you. Maybe even rape you with broken broom handles or whatever they can mutilate you with."

The imposter's steely gaze began to soften.

"You have one way out of that. Tell me how to get the real monsters running this show, the bastards who took an idiotic, crazy little dupe like you and turned you into a tool for making them richer and more powerful," Hawkins said.

"Richer? Powerful? That's not what they said. They said this was for the great revolution, just as Mao envisioned it," she answered.

"Really? So billions of dollars in damage to American and European infrastructure isn't going to be paid for in loans from Red China?" Hawkins asked. "How do you think the U.S. financed much of the second Gulf War, you little twit?"

The woman swallowed.

"They borrowed the money from China. It got so bad that one political party was turned upside down by people upset over that administration's waste of cash," Hawkins pressed. "Now China has the weapon to cripple the United States, but then they can make a huge profit. They and the Saudis are capitalists underneath. Scratch them, and they bleed the ink used to print money."

"It's a lie," she sputtered, but her will was buckling.

"Then why are you so worried?" Hawkins asked. "You were a disposable tool. I bet you even vowed to give your life for the People's Revolution, ensuring that the evil capitalist empire collapses under the weight of its own debt. But that debt is what is going to make China a fatter cat than you've ever imagined."

She looked down.

"You'll make it quick?" she asked.

"Only if you talk fast," Hawkins replied. "The greedy fuckers are going to escape once they pull off this plan."

She told Hawkins where the yacht was anchored, in the inlet where the water was just deep enough for a skilled crew to park a submarine. The people of Tarajal hadn't seen any sign of the sub, but it had been the Omega spy's job to keep an eye out for such betrayal of the truth. The enemy had lucked out, at least until the Texan showed up and tore through those sent to kill him.

She looked up at him. "Make it quick, please."

Hawkins shook his head. "I lied. I'm not someone who can murder an unarmed victim."

He stepped back, and Hector and the other people of Tarajal stood, bloody fury in their eyes.

"However, the people of the town you dropped a missile on might feel differently," Hawkins said. "I don't do favors for cold-blooded killers."

"Oh, God," she whispered, realizing the irony of her desperate plea.

Hawkins turned and left the angry Canary Islanders to their vengeance. He had to connect with Encizo and Manning.

GARY MANNING AND Rafael Encizo loaded the fourth drum onto the handcart, their powerful upper bodies aching and sore from the brutal effort of lifting the heavy loads of ANFO. Once the cart had been loaded to the top, Manning went to work on the detonators atop each drum, slaving them to his own radio detonator built into the CPDA. It took only a few moments to assemble this for each pack on the cart.

In the meantime, Encizo made certain that they had transportation. Luckily, the crew who had been here to receive the drums had their own pickup, which had avoided becoming the centerpiece of a blazing gun battle. The vehicle that he and Manning had attacked was badly damaged, its engine hammered by 9 mm and 5.56 mm bullets, its tires and axles chopped by the same high-powered slugs. Even if those parts hadn't been blown into useless messes, the dashboard and steering column had absorbed so many slugs that the wheel was broken to pieces, the electronics for the ignition reduced to multicolored spaghetti.

There was no way that the truck they had followed and ambushed could be driven again. The second truck, already on the scene, was gassed up, and they'd also found spare submachine guns and ammunition. It was a good addition to the arsenal that Encizo and Manning had picked up, but the real weaponry was eight hundred kilograms of ANFO.

Manning confirmed that the ANFO was mixed with aluminum powder, which accelerated the combustion of the ammonium nitrate and fuel oil. With the detonation packs in place, the Canadian demolitions expert had a beast of a bomb, equal to 2300 pounds of TNT.

"It's almost dawn," Encizo said. "We better get going."

"Dawn. That's when Omega planned to set off its bombs early," Manning pointed out. "I gave the Farm the frequency I wanted to use to detonate my little parting gift. I hope it works."

"You think that the drums here will be on the same set of circuits as the ones at the hotels?" Encizo asked.

"It makes sense. But if not, then we're screwed," Manning said. "Well, we'd be safe at the compound."

"But the East Coast goes under," Encizo concluded.

Manning nodded. "That's why I'm not concerned with holding back on these bastards. Either the Farm blankets Omega's detonation channels with interference, or we're avenging everyone killed by the tsunami."

Encizo clenched his jaw. He crawled behind the wheel of the truck, then looked back as Manning finished strapping down the drums to the handcart with steel bands. With the cart hooked to the pickup's tow hitch, it was time for the two Phoenix Force warriors to unleash hell upon the men who'd worked hard to shatter one of Cumbre Vieja's slopes and drop it into the Atlantic.

Manning got in, riding shotgun—literally. He'd picked up a Benelli Nova shotgun from the arsenal of the group they'd defeated. With a magazine tube filled with six rounds of buckshot and a bandolier of fresh shells, the 12-gauge was going to be everything he needed for close-quarters mayhem, as opposed to Encizo, who preferred the SAF machine pistol. Long-distance death was to be delivered by the cart behind the truck.

Encizo double-checked his setup to turn the pickup into a guided missile. He had nylon rope to secure the steering wheel, and he had sawn a shovel handle to the appropriate length to keep the gas pedal engaged. It was going to hurt like hell when he bailed out of the cab, but not as much as being caught at ground zero of the blast.

"We're ready," Manning said. "Let's hit them."

Encizo revved the engine, realizing that the deadline for detonation, the bombs set for a deadly seismic surge, had slipped past only five seconds ago.

CHAPTER SEVENTEEN

Calvin James clenched the mouthpiece between his teeth, sucking oxygen from the scuba tanks as the seconded minisub plunged into the murky shadows beneath the cruise ship. The waterproofed CPDA was tethered to his wrist, speed dial set up to reach the small cell phone he'd taken off one of the dead men. On his other wrist, his tritium-dialed watch allowed him to see the seconds ticking down to damnation.

He knew that Stony Man Farm was only able to handle one part of the equation to prevent the murder of innocent hostages in the hotels. They were working on jamming or deprogramming the detonators that would set off the high-powered ANFO drums in their basements. The explosions caused by those massive detonations would result in countless deaths.

But if the bombs didn't go off, Option Omega had another plan. The Q-ship had been loaded with Soviet antishipping missiles with warheads as large as four hundred kilograms of high-intensity explosives. Yielding eight times the power of normal TNT, those missiles could easily take up the slack in Omega's threat to murder innocents should the allied forces of the U.S., Britain and Spain act to rescue the hostages in Santa

Cruz. Unfortunately, Phoenix Force had reached the point where battle had been unavoidable.

And Option Omega's response was "detonate at sunrise."

That was in one minute, according to James's watch. He pushed the minisub, nothing more than an underwater sled, making it dive as deep and fast as he could push it. Above, he could see that the inky blackness had lost some of its opaque intensity. Gray predawn light penetrated to turn the world around him into a murky cloud in which he could barely see his limbs and the underwater sled.

James knew that the ship was packed with ten drums of ANFO that hadn't been offloaded. It was among them that he'd set down a charge according to Gary Manning's instructions, hooking it up to a cell phone as a detonator.

Forty-five seconds before the deadline to detonation, and James knew that he had to touch off the bomb he'd set aboard the ship. He couldn't count on the Omega crew not to immediately cut loose with a salvo of surface-to-surface missiles to wreak havoc on Santa Cruz. He feared they would launch missiles at other parts of the city and the huddled, frightened people trapped on damaged cruise ships still stuck in the harbor.

Thirty seconds, and James pressed the enter key, dialing up the cell phone aboard the Q-ship.

The eruption of the equivalent of five tons of TNT tore through steel bulkheads and struck incompressible seawater. Shock waves radiated off outward, ripping through the distance that James had built up between himself and the terrorist boat, and it felt as if he'd been tackled by both Gary Manning and Carl Lyons in a game of "murder the guy with the ball."

The powerful hammer blow shook James's brains and sent the minisub spinning through the depths. The regulator popped from his mouth, and his swim goggles were yanked off by the violence of the blast that threatened to burst his skull like a watermelon struck by a sledgehammer.

Blind and cut off from oxygen, James clawed through the murky dark waters, seeking breath and life. If he could breathe again, he'd reset his goggles and look for the controls of the minisub, if they still even worked.

Desperate fingers wrapped around the hose that led to the tanks, and James worked his way backward from there. His whole head was throbbing with the overpressure at being so close to such a powerful detonation. Up above, the ship must have looked as if it had been struck by the thunderbolts of the gods, because James had taken enough backwash that it jarred him to clumsiness.

The regulator and hose slipped free from numbed fingers, as if a living thing, an eel squirming for the liberation of the bottom of the harbor. James clutched at the hose again, working to insert the regulator again, but this time as he brought it up, he missed his mouth, gouging his cheek.

James grit his teeth, cursing himself for being so inept, but he couldn't help it. Water had amplified the shock wave produced by a five-ton bomb blast, and he was lucky he could still focus on holding his breath, let alone pushing the regulator to his lips.

Finally he clenched the regulator in place, blew out the stale air in his lungs and inhaled deeply. Oxygen rushed into his lungs, sweeter than the richest honey. James took three deep breaths before he readjusted the swim goggles over his eyes. He felt along himself for the flashlight he'd stolen from the boat, and swept the minisub.

The scuba tanks he'd stolen for McCarter were still strapped into place, as well as the trash bag that contained his confiscated pistols and submachine guns.

Light struggled to penetrate into the depths of the harbor as James gunned the engine, rushing the minisub to his rendezvous with McCarter.

He would get a look at the effects of the bomb blast on the Q-ship when he met with the Phoenix Force commander, and after he made sure that his efforts weren't in vain.

DAVID MCCARTER STAGGERED out of the hotel, still feeling the effects of being too damn close to a hand grenade's detonation. He'd finished off the one man who hadn't been blasted to lifeless meat, spoken with the Farm and looked down the boulevard to see one of the other hotels that had been targeted for destruction by Option Omega.

He stood and waited, pistol clenched in one fist, forcing himself to stand straight despite his body's request to sway and flop down on his ass.

By his estimate, he'd ensured that one in five hostages in Santa Cruz would see the sunrise. That still meant eighty percent were doomed to death because he'd been too damn slow to realize that he'd had access to a detonator that could defuse the other bombs.

Saving only two hundred out of a thousand wasn't a victory. And they weren't the kinds of results that the teams of Stony Man Farm fought for. Phoenix Force could have been seen as doing their job by killing every single bastard responsible, but failing to save lives was a loss. McCarter ground his teeth, waiting for the doomsday clock to reach zero. He could feel his pulse pounding in his veins.

The sunrise crept closer, and McCarter checked his watch.

Ten.

Nine.

From out in the harbor, a peal of thunder washed ashore. It echoed off edifices, vibrating sickly through the streets.

Calvin James had done his job on the Q-ship.

But what about the other hotels?

What about the hundreds trapped in their rooms, frightened and terrorized by Option Omega's jackbooted thugs?

Three.

Two.

McCarter took a deep breath, stiffening himself, bracing for the ugly roars that would signal he was a consummate cock-up. Eight hundred or so lives were to be decided in the next second.

The silence was deafening as the first beams of

bloodred sunlight pierced the dawn skies. McCarter waited. He didn't want to relax.

He didn't want to be wrong.

The checkering on the rubber grips was grinding against the skin of his palm. His index finger ached from where he pressed it against the frame over the trigger guard. His other hand's palm was screaming as he jammed his nails into the pink, callused flesh.

Ten seconds.

Fifteen seconds.

After forty-five seconds, he realized he wasn't breathing, and he gulped down air.

His CPDA vibrated, and he plucked it out.

"Frequencies jammed," Price said.

McCarter didn't have the strength to smile. "Thanks, Barb. What about the gunmen?"

"We've got a surprise for them," the Stony Man mission controller told him. "We can't get Marines and SEALs deployed to deal with them…"

Movement cut through the air over one building. McCarter could make out the slender, broad-winged shape of an unmanned aerial vehicle. After the night before, with the Option Omega drones sailing through the city, his first reaction was to bring up his pistol, no matter how useless it was at this range, to fight to bring the drone down.

But this UAV wasn't alone. There were others flying through the sky, like a flock of mechanical geese floating silently in the orange dawn. They were big, larger than the drones that McCarter and James had spied the night before. Each was about forty-five feet long.

"I didn't think that the Navy had Reapers," McCarter said absently.

Price must have heard him on speaker.

"An early squadron of MQ-4C," she said. "Merry Christmas to the U.S. Navy."

Distant booms popped and crackled through the streets of Santa Cruz. McCarter winced at the sound, but these were precision-guided munitions, not the wanton, deadly blasts of terrorist missiles and bombs. He surmised that they were Hellfire MACs—metal augmented charges—which were eighteen-pound bombs designed for antipersonnel use after being laser guided. With the cameras on an MQ-4C unmanned aircraft system and the laser target designators on the MACs, they could strike a single man on the ground, or air-burst over a group of enemy soldiers, scouring them from the earth in a wave of shrapnel.

"Are they doing their job?" McCarter asked. "What's the sit rep?"

As soon as the rattle and crack of MACs detonating across the city died out, Price spoke again.

"No gunmen retreated to the hotels. All were neutralized by air-burst munitions. No civilians in sight, no friendly casualties," Price announced.

McCarter loosened his grip on the Turkish 9 mm pistol. His knuckles pulsed from the tension. He let out a long breath.

McCarter thought of the name of the warheads that rained justice down upon the forty terrorists across Santa Cruz. MACs.

That's what his mates called him back when he was in regiment: Mac.

McCarter smiled at the irony. "I've got a date with Cal," he said."Phoenix One out!"

The Phoenix Force commander pocketed the CPDA and rushed toward the docks.

La Palma was not out of danger yet. Not until McCarter made sure that Option Omega was wiped out to the last man.

THE PICKUP BARRELED DOWN the road toward the Option Omega compound. The night before, Gary Manning had taken a careful account of the occupation of the camp. Stony Man's satellite infrared imagery had told him that there were nearly fifty men in the camp, something he took the time to confirm. Of course, that was before the battle where they'd picked up the drums that were bouncing behind them on a cart.

Those drums, packed with improved ANFO, were the equivalent of a one-ton bomb made from TNT. Luckily, the prilled ammonium nitrate and fuel oil were in a shock-resistant form, so the jostling caused by the rapid transit along the rough road on the floor of the Cumbre Vieja caldera didn't have an effect on it. That was the job of the C-4 packets strapped to each of the drums. Packets set to go off at a command from Manning's radio detonator.

Encizo was at the wheel of the pickup. It was either the tension of beating a deadline or the rockiness of the road, but he seemed to be driving akin to McCarter on a bender.

"Are you aiming for the potholes?" Manning asked.

Encizo grimaced, his knuckles white around the wheel. "Driving slow is not going to make it easy for us. They know something's up—we caused enough of a ruckus."

"We'll make some more," Manning said, looking back. While he wasn't worried about a premature detonation, he did have a concern that the tow hitch on the pickup might not be able to withstand the kind of forces exerted by Encizo's breakneck pace.

Luckily, the Phoenix Force commandos had picked out a path along a relatively straight and flat road leading down to the center of the camp. Manning made certain he had a firm grip on his equipment as he watched Encizo make one final maneuver, then locked the gas pedal to the floor by wedging a sawed-off shovel handle against it. He'd already slackly strapped the steering wheel so that it could be held straight on a final course.

Encizo pulled the nylon cord taut, anchoring it.

With that, the two men threw open the doors of the cab and rolled out onto the ground.

Manning landed and tucked his muscles into a tight ball so that he presented the least resistance to the volcanic plain. A less compact form would have snagged on an outcropping to the point where he'd shatter his bones. Encizo was treating his exit from the pickup in the same manner.

One wrong landing, and neither would be able to get up. Even so, with his head shielded by his brawny arms, Manning could feel a sheen of bruising all along his body as he tumbled. Finally, his forward momentum bled off, and he rolled flat onto his back.

Even as he came to a halt, he closed his thumb over the trigger to the detonator in his hand. The ground shuddered, heaving up as if it were taking a wheezing breath. On the heels of the minor quake released by a ton of TNT going off, the air suddenly snapped in two, breaking loudly as high pressure ripped through it. The thunder of the blast rolled through his body, feeling like a wave surging from his tucked head down to his heels.

He scrambled to his hands and knees and looked up. A thick column of smoke rose from the camp where the cart had crashed into the back of the pickup. For a hundred feet around it, tents and temporary huts were flattened, crushed by the force of the massive blast. There didn't seem to be much movement down here, but Manning didn't want to take chances. The wave of overpressure could have just missed killing all of the Omega gunmen in the camp.

Manning reached for his shotgun, checked to make certain it was undamaged then snapped off the safety on the blaster. Encizo was already on his feet with his submachine gun. The two advanced slowly toward the blast crater blown by the ANFO bomb.

Bodies were strewed amid the wreckage, pounded flat by the sudden increase in air pressure at the heart of the explosion. Eyeballs had burst and intestines bubbled out of mouths of those who were closest to the blast. Others lay as if they had simply gone to sleep on the ground, not a mark on them. More than a couple of severed limbs and dismembered torsos littered between the two groups, showing just where they had died in relation to Manning's bomb blast.

A gunshot cracked in the distance and both Phoenix Force warriors dropped prone. More gunfire followed.

There were survivors, and they were up and back into the fight.

Manning traded his shotgun for his pistol, the Turkish CZ knockoff, simply because his pellets wouldn't have the spread necessary to reach the enemy. They had bailed at 150 yards out, and had only advanced about 25 yards when the Omega survivors shook off their initial shock and began to fight back.

The dawn had arrived, leaving Manning and Encizo out in the open, but instead of having to battle fifty gunmen, there were only five or six left. However, as the survivors had held on to only their handguns, all of their shots were either high and wide or far too short to reach the Stony Man pair.

Encizo shouldered his SMG and triggered a short burst that caught one of the enemy shooters. One hundred yards was stretching things for such a weapon, but Encizo was accurate enough to put sufficient fire on the target to drop him.

Manning fired a few shots to engage the enemy, but as accurate as the CZ-75 platform was, he still didn't have the reach to nail an enemy gunman with enough power to end the fight. The same went for his opponent. The Omega survivors broke into a run, staying low and heading to the cover of the blast crater that used to be their camp. They wanted to be closer to more effectively engage Phoenix Force.

Manning did likewise, transitioning to his Nova shotgun as he rushed across thirty yards.

Inside of 100 yards, he shouldered the 12-gauge and fired two quick shots as fast as he could pump the action. Buckshot sizzled through the air, smacking one of the Omega gunmen, spinning him with the first swarm, then anchoring him to the caldera floor with the second burst.

Manning dropped prone and thumbed fresh shells into the tubular magazine. To his left, Encizo let the SAF subgun rock, fanning the enemy survivors with suppressive fire.

That must have cut the enemy numbers in half, Manning presumed as he advanced.

Autofire rattled again, but it didn't come from Encizo's direction. Instead, a row of bullets spit up chips of igneous stone too close to Manning to be friendly fire from his Cuban friend. Someone was still alive in the Omega group, and he had access to an assault rifle. Manning hurled himself prone once more, supersonic cracks snapping above his head as bullets passed through the air he'd once stood in. Encizo gave a shout of warning, turning his SMG toward the newcomers.

Retaliatory fire ripped toward the Cuban, forcing him into the cradle of cracked, cooled lava. Rifle rounds screamed and yowled as they ricocheted off stone, tumbling into the dawn sky. Manning turned and fired his shotgun at the newcomers, emptying 12-gauge shells, but the rifleman was too well concealed and too far out of range to be hampered by Manning's attack.

Instead, he'd caught the rifleman's attention, bullets

snatching at the ground near the burly Canadian. He found his own cover on the broken ground.

Pinned down by an enemy sniper, Manning couldn't help but recognize the irony of his situation. Now he was terrorized, left impotent by a foe who had superior range and position. Unless a miracle arrived soon, he and Encizo would be rooted out by the rifleman or his allies on the ground ahead of them.

More rifle fire resounded, but the gunshots were unaccompanied by near misses. Manning poked his head up and saw that a second force had recently entered the battle. It was the familiar outline of T. J. Hawkins, holding a confiscated M-4 carbine. Using his own assault rifle on this plain, Hawkins had the range and precision to deal with targets at a longer distance than either of his two Phoenix Force partners.

"The cavalry to the rescue," Encizo said, reloading his spent SAF magazine.

"Some days I could just kiss that boy," Manning returned.

"Remind me to tell him," Encizo quipped.

Manning shook his head. "Let's back his play."

The two men rose from their cover now that Option Omega's hired guns were distracted by Hawkins's sudden contribution to the battle. Even as they did so, Manning made a count of the enemy, realizing that nine had survived the initial bomb blast, four having fallen under the initial efforts of Encizo, Manning and Hawkins.

Manning closed another twenty yards, then dropped to one knee, firing his Nova shotgun. His 12-gauge shells bellowed out the barrel once, twice, and another of the Omega gunmen dropped, chopped to ribbons by swarms of copper-plated pellets. Encizo's SAF ripped loose its own storm of similarly sized projectiles, except these were directed by the spiral of an eight-inch rifled barrel. The Cuban cut through two more enemies even as they were alerted to Manning's reentry to the battle with his shotgun.

The double-spray bought Manning the time he needed to thumb more shells into the sleek Benelli shotgun's tube magazine, not even bringing the stock down from his shoulder. Another target of opportunity appeared and he took only a heartbeat to identify that it was one of the enemy, then triggered the 12-gauge. The man's face and much of his head disappeared in a cloud of gore and bone chips as a half dozen pellets struck his skull at once.

Manning turned toward another gunman, but he was dancing under the crossfire of rifle and subgun bullets directed by Encizo and Hawkins.

"Clear!" Hawkins announced.

Encizo echoed that assessment, but the two men waited for Manning to be certain that no one else had been playing possum.

Satisfied, Manning added his announcement to the group consensus. "Clear!"

"Damn, Gary. How pissed were you at these bastards?" Hawkins asked.

Manning shrugged. "I don't let emotion guide my actions in combat."

Hawkins looked at the blast crater, surveying the

carnage. "Good, but I'd hate to see what happens if you ever do get mad."

"Nice of you to come join us," Encizo said. "How'd you get here?"

"The people of Tarajal lent me a Jeep so I could come help you. I figured you might need a ride back to the inlet so we could go after the bastards who planned this," Hawkins said. "You two still game?"

Manning tilted his head. The chance to find and eliminate the maniacs who had planned the chaos that struck La Palma put the ache of his bruised form to rest, at least for the moment. He'd lied to Hawkins. He did allow anger into his thoughts. Like all soldiers had learned, sometimes negative energy and cold rage were useful to ignore personal discomfort, especially when leashed by self-discipline.

And Gary Manning knew he wasn't the only member of Phoenix Force who was interested in bringing punishment to the conspirators. "Drive, T.J. We've got one last appointment to make."

Hawkins nodded and led them back to his Jeep.

CHAPTER EIGHTEEN

The harbor's crystal-clear waters sluiced around the minisub as Calvin James guided it along. David McCarter strapped his scuba tanks firmly in place, then double-checked his load and gear for the submachine gun he carried. How they were going to deal with a submarine if one were still in the area was going to be a good trick, but McCarter had a few plans for that.

The terrorists who had tried to take him out back at the hotel had been carrying hand grenades, one of which had nearly punched his ticket for the rest of eternity. McCarter decided that what was good for the goose was especially good for this particular Cockney bastard, and he gathered the lot into a sack. He had five of them, as well as the RDX military-grade explosive charge that had been set up to detonate four drums of fuel oil and fertilizer to collapse the hotel. Even before James pulled the minisub to the dock, he'd assembled the package into a pliant square that he could attach to a hull and rip it open.

Would it be enough? McCarter intended to find out.

"We've got another floater," James said.

McCarter pulled his 9 mm Turkish pistol and aimed at the object that James announced. The Option Omega terrorists littered the harbor with what looked to be a dozen inflatable rafts, each carrying a drum. Each drum had a strange disk adhered to the side, something that a good commando or amphibious operative would be familiar with—a magnetic Limpet mine.

The rafts had been set loose the moment that the timetable for Omega had been forced up by the actions of Phoenix Force across the island. It was their idea of an aquatic-scorched Earth ploy, one that would cause serious damage to anyone trying to get out of Santa Cruz by boat, or to naval crafts that entered the harbor to begin rescue operations.

It took little debate for McCarter to adopt a shoot-on-sight policy for the floating bomb rafts. He didn't fire at the drums themselves, but instead blasted holes in the inflatable tubing that kept the rafts afloat. One weakness of ANFO was that it was mostly an oxidizer for a violent, chemical reaction. With a good dunking, the drums would be effectively neutralized as the prilled ammonium nitrate wouldn't be able to interact with the fuel oil or ignite under water.

McCarter had burned off two magazines taking down six of the rafts as they'd found them, but there was still the possibility of others. He'd informed Price, and the U.S. Navy passed on that information to the Spanish and British fleets.

In the days since the *Cole* bombing in the waters of Kuwait, the navies of the United States and its NATO allies had become accustomed to dealing with such improvised bombs. As well, the maritime MQ-4Cs had been requested to stay on station, spotting for other rafts.

The Q-ship lurched, tilted to one side as its hull was burst open, metal peeled back like flower petals. Still, it sat on the water as men worked frantically to release lifeboats to get themselves off the wounded, sinking death trap. Smoke gushed through the ugly wound and through hatches above deck, and McCarter could hear the groan and screech of bending metal as the massive craft's weight shifted. Gravity was the ship's worst enemy, a close runner up to the tide in the harbor. With its hull integrity blown, the Q-ship was being bent, waves pushing it up, gravity hauling it down, the two implacable, omnipresent forces torturing the craft.

Already, McCarter could hear the crack of steel beams and support structures. The pilothouse collapsed in on itself as the antenna mast toppled into it. Decks unaccustomed to the heavy antishipping missile launchers buckled under the added mass.

"How much did you blow up?" McCarter asked.

"Gary estimated it was close to a ten-ton bomb," James answered. He kept an eye on the waters. "I'm surprised the damn ship is still floating."

"They probably armored it up to resist incoming fire, just in case the allied navies weren't held at bay by the threat of killing hostages," McCarter mused. "Either way…"

An Omega lifeboat, brimming with soaked, angry gunmen, cut into view. McCarter grimaced at the sight of the craft, seventy-five yards away. "Company's here."

"See them," James returned. He pulled out the spare

submachine gun McCarter had brought for him and shouldered it. The escaping terrorists hadn't noticed the minisub riding low in the water. They were too busy making sure that all of their comrades were aboard and in good condition, or marveling over the destruction of their former base.

James also noticed that some of the lifeboat crew were looking on the surface of the harbor, seeking out signs of allies. They were looking for a submarine to come pick them up.

Unfortunately, the minisub didn't resemble the craft they were looking for. Farther out into the harbor, the black conning tower of a true military-class submarine broke the surface.

"Found the enemy sub," James said. "At least one of them."

McCarter nodded. "Give the lifeboat a quick rake."

James had the minisub operating on autopilot, allowing both Phoenix Force commandos to shoulder their weapons and cut loose with their submachine guns. Bullets leaped across the distance between the two craft, the soggy, bewildered Option Omega gunners in the lifeboat suddenly under attack by an aquatic drive-by.

Bodies jerked violently under full-auto streams of 9 mm slugs. One or two men fired their weapons in response, but they were so snarled up among the bodies of their friends crowding them in the packed boat that their bullets flew skyward or splashed into the water.

It was a ruthless display of marksmanship, but considering that these men had been part of a crew that had launched missiles at four cruise ships, killing dozens and wounding hundreds, McCarter and James didn't feel sorry for them. Cold-blooded murder was what they had been hired for, and cold-blooded murder was their penance. The Phoenix avengers took neither satisfaction nor relief in the task they performed, only knowledge that they wouldn't have armed killers at their back.

The two men took advantage of their foes' distraction and their low profile, ripping the lifeboat with short, concentrated bursts that struck with the precision of a scalpel and the brutality of a jackhammer. Full-metal-jacketed rounds struck one man and still had plenty of power to slice through his body and cut into another gunner, wounding or killing him, as well. By the time the two Phoenix Force veterans were finished, twelve corpses lay sprawled in the Omega lifeboat.

"Barb, spotted the sub," McCarter said into his com link. "Do the Mariner drones have it?"

"It's jamming them," Price responded. "Schwarz was right—they refitted the damn submarines with good electronics."

"Submarines?" McCarter asked. "As in multiple?"

"Yes," Price responded. "There's one on the other side of the island, just off Tarajal."

"Right where we parked our own sub," James muttered. "But still to the south of the slope where the landslide was set up. The inlet would provide shielding from the tidal surge for anyone in there, just like the harbor here."

"I've got a second lifeboat!" McCarter announced. "They're out of small-arms range, on the other side of the Kilo-class sub."

"Good and bad news for us," James replied. "We can't take their fire, but we can't deal with them anyway."

"Barb, can you nail the Omega lifeboats?" McCarter requested. "I have an idea how to mark the Kilo."

The diesel submarine continued to break the surface of the harbor. James steered toward it, pushing the minisub into top gear to catch up with the breaching craft. He looked back at McCarter, who had set aside the SMG for his improvised mass of grenades and plastic explosives.

"The Mariners aren't under our direct control," Price replied. "And we're giving them a blind eye to the individual craft in the water so that they don't target you two."

McCarter grimaced. "I'm going to scratch that Kilo. Think that will be a good enough 'hit me' sign?"

"That should do it," Price said. "In the meantime, I'll get on the line with the U.S. Navy."

McCarter grunted his sign-off in assent.

"That other lifeboat is going to give us hell," James said.

"I don't care. That sub is venting ports on top," McCarter returned. "Missile silos."

"Surface-to-surface missiles. Backup to the Q-ship," James realized. "Why not just fire from under water?"

"They have to pick their mates up," McCarter answered. "That, and maybe you knocked something off when you blasted the Q-ship. It could have been operating in the boat's shadow."

"Two with one stone, except not exactly," James concluded. "They probably had damage done to the silos or the pressure valves."

The second lifeboat moved closer to the big diesel sub as James and McCarter's minisub crawled closer to its opposite bow. The crew of the Kilo-class sub started to deploy up top, gunmen rushing toward the edge of the deck to target the Phoenix boat.

James flicked on the autopilot once more, withdrew his SMG and opened fire on the deck gunners, driving them to cover with a stream of 9 mm slugs. McCarter, riding behind him, palmed his pistol and cut loose, firing with his right hand as he hefted the pillow of explosive death in his left.

James's gun ran empty as the sled slid alongside the larger submersible. Rather than struggle with a fast magazine change, he transitioned to his own pistol, firing quickly to keep up the pressure on the Kilo's deck crew. The other lifeboat's gunmen were out of sight, blocked by the hull of the large sub, giving McCarter and James a break even though bullets speared into the water from above.

McCarter punched two shots into one of the Omega riflemen on the sub's top, catching him in the throat and right cheek, both bullets crushing bone as they cored through his head. The dying man didn't scream, merely gurgled, but he toppled into the water, rifle splashing into the harbor alongside of him. McCarter saw that the distance between their minisub and the Omega submarine was only two yards now. He climbed out of his seat, then knifed into the water, kicking to reach the side of the enemy boat.

"David!" James shouted as the mini pulled away from where McCarter clung to a handhold on the big diesel's hull.

"Swing back later!" McCarter shouted back.

James pivoted and opened fire, his pistol barking rapidly.

McCarter winced as a body toppled off the deck, crashing into the waves only a few feet away.

"Watch your ass!" James bellowed. He turned back to the controls of the minisub, hit the throttle and peeled off, swinging wide of the diesel sub.

McCarter grimaced as he knew he'd bitten off a hell of a lot. Whether he could chew was dependent on the next few moments. He scurried up the side of the sub, using handholds meant for just such an oceanic rendez-vous, and saw that there were only a couple of gunmen who were still aboard.

For the moment, the two shooters were confused. Had this been one of their own who had toppled into the water?

McCarter didn't give them time to make out the truth. He rushed toward the nearest of the missile silos and jammed the pliant blob of explosive putty onto the lip. As soon as he was sure that it was secure, he plucked the cotter pins from two of the hand grenades. He didn't have time for all of the minibombs, but at least the rest of the explosives in the lump would detonate in sympathy with the first two explosions.

With that, he turned and made three quick strides, leaping off the submarine and into the harbor. Bullets passed close enough to McCarter that he could see their trails of bubbles spiral into the water. McCarter was fully aware that the faster a bullet entered fluid, the more shallow it would be when it expended its energy. As it was, he was glad that the enemy was equipped with assault rifles as their bullets smacked the ocean surface and decelerated violently.

McCarter kicked deeper into the water, ticking down the last of the five seconds on the hand-grenade fuses. Through the water, thanks to the explosion spreading into open air, not detonating close to him under water, the blast was dull and distant. McCarter hoped the burst took out the last of the gunmen on deck, but he wasn't going to count on it.

Rather, he scooped up his regulator, bringing it to his mouth, and kept swimming, keeping below the surface as the hail of bullets entering the water increased dramatically. He turned, looking up to see the belly of the second lifeboat swinging overhead, casting him into shadow.

McCarter cursed as handgun rounds ripped dangerously close to him. Slower, they had a better chance of keeping their course under water. He dived deeper, realizing that he was screwed.

Suddenly the water shook around him. He pivoted, looking upward to see bodies splashing into the waves above. There was another bright flash, another rumble of an explosion overhead.

The MQ-4C drones were on the case now, spearing missiles into the Kilo-class sub. The lifeboat was reduced to splinters by its proximity to the impacts. McCarter grimaced as shock waves ripped through the water, buffeting him, but he was luckily far enough away that he wasn't hurt, just left sore and battered.

With another kick, he started for the surface, heading toward a flashlight dipped into the water. It was James, giving McCarter a beacon to guide his path to the surface and to a safe berth on the surfaced minisub.

He reached up, and James's hand locked around his.

Pulled up top, McCarter spit out his regulator, looking toward the Kilo-class submarine. Smoke boiled from several wounds in its hull, its conning tower crushed and deformed by a direct hit. The drones had done their job.

"Did it launch?" McCarter asked.

"No," James answered. "The drones smacked it before it had a chance."

McCarter breathed a sigh of relief. "We got it."

James nodded.

Even as that happened, the Q-ship, finally folded in two, crumpled like a tin can in the fist of a huge, angry redneck. It finally slurped beneath the waves, sucked down by a compression of its mass in comparison to the water below it. A powerful wave was created as the Q-ship went under, one foot in height, but to the minisub-mounted Phoenix Force members, it was bad. Neither had the time to take a breath before they were splashed, bowled over and knocked from the seats on the minisub.

Paddling madly, James watched as the sea craft crawled away, its throttle still open. He wanted to catch up to it so that they could have a ride back to shore.

That's when he noted a bobbing raft in the distance, crossing into the minisub's path.

"Shit," he grumbled, turning and grabbing McCarter.

Before the Briton could complain about being manhandled, James pulled them both under the surface, just in time to feel the rumble of an explosion through the waves.

James pushed McCarter back to the surface, and both of them sucked down air. They looked to see that their borrowed ride had impacted one of the drum-laden, mine-triggered rafts. The impact produced a violent explosion, and pieces of debris continued to splash into the water.

"Water, water, everywhere," McCarter mused. "But it's still not extinguishing all these damn fires."

"They'll die down," James returned, blinking seawater out of his eyes. "You good?"

"Aching all over," McCarter answered. "You?"

"I think we'll just have to tread water," James admitted. "I couldn't paddle another stroke if you put a gun to my head."

McCarter shook his head. "I'm not going to do it. In fact…"

He turned on a flash beacon attached to his scuba harness, then rolled over onto his back into a dead man's float, the easiest way to tread water.

James followed suit.

"We're in bloody Santa Cruz de La Palma," McCarter said. "If we haven't earned the right to laze on our backs in the fucking pool, then I think it's time we switched jobs."

James chuckled, letting his exhausted body bob in the harbor. "I dunno. All the times we complain that the bad guys don't set up in a comfy island paradise, we finally get our wish. I like this job."

McCarter grinned back to his friend. "Well, it does have its perks."

They waited for search and rescue to spot their beacons and pick them up, letting the morning sun warm them in the tropical waters of the harbor.

DIWALA BIN LOHS WATCHED as communications from the Santa Cruz harbor blinked out, one by one. Their missile cruiser had disappeared, and now so had one of their two Kilo-class submarines. He turned toward the captain of the yacht, Raul Espinoza.

"Do you think it's time for us to get out of here?" bin Lohs asked.

Espinoza's face was cast into a long, deep frown. "If we bolt, they'll recognize us. Besides, there's still the opportunity for the sub to set off the charges on the slope. Santa Cruz was just a distraction, a huge mess that would get the Westerners into position to suffer even more losses."

Diwala bin Lohs shook his head. "You heard the explosion, even from here. The Cumbre Vieja operation has to have been shut down, struck by a missile."

"So?" Espinoza asked. "We've still got one more Kilo class in our pocket. Give the order to fire, and we'll finish this and reap our rewards."

The Saudi grimaced. He'd owned the Jeopardy Corporation as a puppet, a cut-out that would give him access to research grant money in the West. When they'd discovered the potential for an Atlantic mega-disaster, one that could cripple not only the hated United States, but also oil competitor Venezuela, he'd searched for someone who could give him the opportunity to make the most of it.

That was when the man from SAD, Espinoza, had come to him. Espinoza had started as a low-ranking member of the Sendero Luminoso, but his drive and ambition had pushed him not only to the top organization but also to the position of Communist China's top asset in South America. When the Chinese learned that Venezuela was not interested in assisting the FARC in controlling Colombia, they'd turned on the communist puppet state and sought their own alliance to punish the South American oil-producing country.

That was what had brought them together.

"All right. Give the order," bin Lohs returned. "Even if we don't profit, we can still cause our enemies agony that they never expected."

Espinoza smirked, then raised the radio to his lips. "Chong, you have the firing solution. Launch!"

"Aye, aye, sir…" came the response from the submarine commander. Even as the words echoed in the air from the radio, a loud ping rocked across the radio. "Oh, hell…"

"Chong?" Espinoza asked.

"We've been spotted. Someone hit us with a sonar contact," Chong explained.

Espinoza grumbled. "They knew about the other sub. They must have anticipated another…over here?"

The Saudi grimaced, looking at his erstwhile partner. He plucked his cell phone from a pocket. "Fahd. I've been discovered."

There was breathing on the other end of the line.

"Brother? Did you not hear me? The Americans have found us out. You have to go into hiding," bin Lohs said.

"I'm sorry," a grim voice said on the other end. "Fahd bin Lohs has faced his judgment. And from the nerves you're showing, you're about to join him."

"Who is this?" bin Lohs asked.

There was a moment of silence on the other end. "His executioner."

Diwala bin Lohs felt the blood drain from his face, cheeks prickling.

"Goodbye, Diwala," the cold voice said on the other end.

The Saudi turned back to Espinoza. "We have to go. We have to go!"

The Peruvian nodded. He broke from the small command center and ran toward the pilothouse. The Saudi followed, coming out on deck.

That's when bin Lohs saw a strange aircraft zoom into view.

There was a blond man at the back, standing at the top of a loading ramp on the hovering hybrid of airplane and helicopter. It took a moment, but bin Lohs recognized it as an American tiltrotor, a V-22 Osprey.

"Shoot that thing out of the sky!" the Saudi ordered.

Bodyguards and hired guns posing as crew and passengers reached for their guns and brought them up, triggering a cacophony of automatic fire, spearing it toward the hovering, brutal craft floating a hundred feet away off the stern.

If bin Lohs didn't know any better, he would have sworn that the blond man was smiling as they opened up.

CHAPTER NINETEEN

Carl Lyons checked his communicator, even as he spotted Jack Grimaldi zoom past, dipping the wing of his S-3 Viking in a salute to the Able Team commander on board the Osprey. Though he couldn't see into the cockpit of the airplane, he knew that Hermann Schwarz was on hand, likely reconfiguring the electronic antisubmarine sensors on board the Viking on the fly, setting them up to locate the Kilo-class submarine that was parked in the inlet just off Tarajal, La Palma.

He turned to look at Rosario Blancanales, who was beside him in the back of the V-22 Osprey the Marines had lent to the superspooks who had arrived on their aircraft carrier. The United States Marine Corps bird had been stripped down, and would have been packed with riflemen, but for the request of Stony Man Farm.

"The others are still in the caldera," Blancanales said. "It'll take them a half hour to get to the harbor."

"That leaves this to us," Lyons said. He smirked. "Glad Barb asked the Corps to let us retrieve our teammates in secrecy."

Blancanales looked toward the cockpit. "Also glad we have a blacksuit in Marine aviation. He won't say anything about our little detour over to the yacht."

"Nope," Lyons said. "Diwala and his brother are toast."

"His brother already is," Blancanales answered, looking down at his CPDA.

Lyons glanced over. "Striker?"

"Wouldn't you know? He tracked Fahd bin Lohs down in France," Blancanales told him. "We have confirmed digital imagery of the kill."

Lyons smirked. "Didn't even know that Mack was in on this case."

"Bolan works in mysterious ways," Blancanales joked. "There's the yacht dead ahead."

"Strap in," Lyons ordered.

The elder member of Able Team hooked himself to the harness as the ramp on the Osprey opened. Their blacksuit pilot pivoted the Osprey around.

Sure, there was a multibarrel, high-rate-of-fire minigun mounted in the belly of the hovering transport, but Lyons hadn't come all this way to sit idly by. Not when he had an M-2 Browning heavy machine gun on a pintle mount at the ready.

A whole nine-yard belt was ready to feed into the main mechanism. All that was necessary was to push down the spade handle and unleash a torrent of half-inch slugs toward the yacht.

He could see movement on the deck. One was heading to the pilothouse, but the other, an Arab man, paused on deck. The blacksuit pilot had brought them close enough that Lyons could make out his facial features. Blancanales scoped him out through the optics mounted on his grenade launcher.

"That's Diwala," Blancanales said.

There was a distant shout, barely audible above the roar of engines.

Carl Lyons watched as a dozen men went from shock and awe to scrambling for their rifles.

"Yup, it's a hostile craft," Lyons confirmed.

"That's a lot of guns," Blancanales noted. "Big guns."

The Able Team leader smiled even as muzzle-flashes flickered in the distance. The Osprey picked up altitude about two hundred feet as he shouted "Evasive maneuvers!" over the microphone attached to his headphones.

Rippling streams of gunfire lanced into the air. Blancanales and Lyons held on in the face of the rapid ascent, but still kept their eyes on the yacht below.

"They're resisting arrest and opening fire on a U.S. military craft," Lyons said, as if he were reading from a telephone book. "We're weapons-free at last."

Lyons thumbed down the spades on the Ma Deuce. Eighty-three pounds of precision machined metal jolted as the first of hundreds of rounds of .50-caliber hurtled through it, the flex of the pintle mount absorbing recoil to spare Lyons the energies released by the bucking weapon. Every tenth round was a tracer, and at 750 rounds per minute, those glowing bullets were visible even in the dawn's first light.

The stream of heavy-metal thunder ripped out of the barrel, spraying across the rear deck of the yacht where riflemen were adjusting aim to keep up with the Osprey's ascent. As such, they were out in the open when a deadly rain of half-inch-wide bullets swept down onto them.

Limbs exploded, shredded away from torsos that burst like ripe tomatoes smashed on the white decks. The Browning's bellow raked across the gunmen in the open and literally blasted them into pieces. At this close range, the human body wasn't meant for such incredible forces released against it.

There were other gunmen who took cover behind railings and in doorways. The ant that Lyons had identified as Diwala bin Lohs rushed off to belowdecks. As the Browning had been proved to cut through stone like a knife through butter, there was little on the yacht that could resist one slug, let alone a whipsaw stream of automatic fire.

Beside him, Blancanales was operating the 7.62 mm GAU-17 Minigun, a device that, where it lacked the power per bullet, made up for that deficiency with the ability to launch more of them. Much more of them, from 2,000 to 6,000 rounds per minute. For every one bullet put out by the Browning, Blancanales with the GAU-17 could have launched five of them.

Able Team had a full five seconds of raking the decks, and between the two of them and the powerful guns at their command, they had unleashed enough firepower to take out three-quarters of the gunmen on deck, shredding them under a rain of high-velocity lead.

Then the Osprey jolted violently, banking hard as a column of water, steel and fire erupted from the harbor's surface. Even over the sound of the twin rotors that allowed the V-22 to hover, the growl of the 3M-54 Klub antiship missile was amazing. A solid-fuel motor was what was necessary for the Klub to launch from one of the Kilo-class sub's missile silos, punching it skyward.

Had it not been for the Marine aviator at the controls and his reflexes, Lyons and Blancanales would have been falling hundreds of feet to the waters below, or clinging to the hull of the deadly missile as it accelerated to reach its normal flight speed of 0.8 Mach, 600 miles per hour. The Klub's solid-fuel engine disengaged, that stage of the missile falling away as its in-flight Turbojet engine kicked in, applying the phenomenal force necessary to push it toward its target.

"Pol!" Lyons bellowed. "Shoot it!"

Blancanales and Lyons both swiveled their powerful machine guns in unison. The bullets fired by the twin guns were going to be much faster than the high subsonic missile, but neither of them knew if the force of those slugs would be enough to take out the deadly weapon while it was in flight. What they did know was that the four-hundred-kilogram warhead on board the Klub was enough to destroy a hotel complex full of innocent souls, or it was enough to start a chain reaction of deadly detonations of ANFO drums to set a landslide into motion. This knowledge was instinctual: they didn't need to put their thoughts into words, just action.

The M-2 and GAU-17 roared in unison, except this time, their target was not the fragile life forms on the yacht below, soft human bodies that would detonate and fall to pieces on contact with hypervelocity slugs. Their target was a deadly hunk of metal, two tons, with a nose packed with enough military-grade explosive to destroy a city block, the equivalent of three and a half tons of TNT. The 3M-54 shuddered as it was raked by a Mutt-and-Jeff stream of autofire, one composed of big chunks of lead moving at a rate of 750 per minute, the other composed of smaller projectiles, but traveling at 3000 per minute. That Lyons and Blancanales could track the missile as it boosted through 450 miles per hour was an act of considerable training and experience, but even so, their rounds intersected with the path of the zooming Klub as it topped over 500 miles per hour.

Their only spark of hope was the sudden gush of thick, ugly smoke that burst from one side of the deadly surface-to-surface weapon. Its path started to turn, curving to one side, slowing down.

A lucky, once-in-a-lifetime shot, Lyons thought as he chased the missile down, pouring fifty more into its length before it connected with a marina full of parked boats hundreds of yards toward the shore. As it landed, the warhead went up, a blazing explosion that cracked the sky above it, splinters flying everywhere in a cloud of destroyed sailboats and wooden walkways.

In between feeling his teeth vibrate from the chatter of the massive fifty, Lyons felt the pressure wave from that blast slap him in the face.

"They're shooting north," Blancanales said, triggering his com link. "Barb, get to Gary! They're going to start the landslide!"

"I'm on it," Price answered. "Gary has something in mind, but he needs you to harry the submarine."

"We're on it," Lyons told her. "But there's what… seven more tubes? We were lucky we could catch one of those bastards. They fire more, fire them faster…"

"Where the hell are Gadgets and Jack?" Blancanales growled.

As if in answer, the S-3 Viking that had carried Able
Team to the U.S. carrier group zoomed into view, skim-
ming low over the water, a pair of five-hundred-pound
bombs tumbling off two of the hard points on its wings.
Up front, the Marine aviator cursed up a blue streak,
language that didn't surprise either of the two Able veterans, but it was indicative of how closely Jack Grimaldi
had threaded the needle between the Osprey and the
harbor below.

Blossoms of water gushed skyward as the bombs
connected. Each one detonated with more than 162
thousand tons of pressure per bomb. Under water, the
shock waves put off by that amount of energy would
move proportionally faster. There was a reason why
depth charges were generally in five-hundred-pound
amounts. Even at a distance, the forces released pushed
against water that did not compress. As it didn't compress, it moved in a solid wave, the same kind of seismic
surge that would cause the tsunami when a fifty-
million-ton landslide struck the ocean. On this smaller
scale, any submarine within three to ten meters of detonation would be damaged or instantly burst open. Considering the depth of the harbor, the close confines of
the shallow seabed, the twin blasts would prove deadly.

Even so, the force of those blasts produced enormous plumes of foamy water that rushed into the open
ramp of the Osprey. Lyons and Blancanales cursed as
they were drenched, left gasping for oxygen as the V-22
shuddered under the proximity to the plume.

Lyons coughed out seawater, rubbing his eyes against its salty sting. "Gadgets! Watch out!"

"Sub!" Blancanales croaked, pointing down the ramp. He coughed, sea foam erupting from his nostrils as he did so. He clung to a handhold against the inner hull of the Osprey.

Lyons grimaced. The Kilo looked as if it were still in one piece. What was worse was that he saw a sudden vent of smoke coming from a silo on the back of the deadly submarine. He lurched back toward the Browning, pivoting it as another Klub burst from its launch tube, picking up speed.

This time Lyons was behind the curve, the solid rocket motor not having to battle against water pressure to accelerate. The M-2 bellowed impotently, but the blast of spray burning his eyes and the temporary lack of oxygen both caused by the bursting plume slowed his reflexes just enough. Blancanales was still reaching for the Minigun.

"Gary! We lost the missile! One is coming at you!" Lyons bellowed into his throat mike.

There was nothing on board the Viking that was set to shoot a missile out of the sky. All the Viking could do was loop back around. Something erupted from under its wing mount.

It was a Maverick AGM missile, designed for turning tanks into charred hulks. This one ripped along at 700 miles per hour, literally a giant bullet fired at the sub. The Kilo groaned violently, bulkhead peeling apart as the antitank warhead erupted against the armored hull. A deadly jet of copper packed into a shaped charge released a blazing tongue of flame that incinerated anything inside, splashing off interior surfaces and boiling through the submarine.

Lyons and Blancanales had recovered now, aiming their heavy machine guns at the sub and pouring on the firepower, even though they realized that nothing they could do could stop the Klub from striking a cliff packed with high explosives. This was blind vengeance, no question about it. It was better than crying and wringing hands over something they couldn't control.

The roar of the Browning was echoed by Lyons's own rage as he swept the submarine and the yacht.

GARY MANNING AND Rafael Encizo held on to the drums filled with ANFO explosives as T. J. Hawkins drove the pickup toward the position that Manning had marked on the GPS.

"You're sure this is going to work?" Hawkins asked.

"We're going to use the force of the explosion to deflect any missile coming in to detonate the charges," Manning said. "The benefit that we have is that we're bracing the detonation against the surface. When the missile comes in, it'll punch into the ground and its shaped charge will jet through the ground and into the tunnel to have an effect on the other drums."

Encizo kept his hands clenched around the drum on his side of the pickup bed. His hair was matted to his scalp. He, Hawkins and Manning had spent fifteen minutes running from ANFO drum to ANFO drum to assemble enough packets of charges to detonate their own antimissile.

"The concept is like reactive tank armor," Hawkins mused. "The force of one detonation takes out the incoming explosive."

"Right," Manning returned.

Hawkins hit the brakes and skid to a halt.

Immediately, he was out and to the tailgate, even though Manning and Encizo had worked together to unload both of the heavy fifty-five-gallon canisters. Their enormous strength was more than sufficient to heft a 450-pound container between them.

Hawkins leaped into the cab to pick up the detonation packets.

Manning froze, touching his earpiece. It was Barbara Price from the Farm.

"We had a missile launch in the harbor south of Tarajal," she said. "It crashed, and I think Carl and Pol shot it down."

"Just have them keep up the pressure. We need a few more moments," Manning returned.

"They— Hold on, getting word from Able Team," Price said.

Manning looked at Encizo and Hawkins. "We need to set this up ASAP. They've already launched one missile, but it was taken out."

The two drums were stacked together. The tops of the drums were punctured to provide a vent release for the explosives inside. It was a simple thing to do. Pressure would take the path of least resistance. This was where the rock was thinnest above the mine tunnel dug for the other drums, but with the vents cut, Manning could direct the blasts skyward.

All three members of Phoenix Force were trained in demolitions, which was a good thing as they couldn't waste any time setting their detonation packs. Manning knew that there was a Kilo-class submarine out there, and in general, antishipping missiles from submarines operated at speeds from half a Mach to a full 600 miles per hour, some of them going supersonic to deal with aircraft carrier groups and the point defenses meant for the huge craft.

They would have seconds to respond to the incoming launch to set off the charges and save the cliff from the blast.

"Gary!" Price stressed.

The urgency in her voice needed no explanation. The next missile was up just as Hawkins plugged in the last radio detonator into a packet of RDX.

"Go!" Manning ordered.

"The Jeep?" Hawkins asked.

"Run!" Manning snapped. He grabbed Hawkins by the upper arm, and the three men were off, racing as fast as their feet could carry them.

The drums were set to fire in only one direction, but even so, it was dangerous to stay within even a dozen yards of ground zero. They skidded down the slope, kicking up volcanic sand as they dropped. Manning gripped the detonator to his chest, listening beyond the racket the three of them made.

The roar of the turbojet engine in the missile reached

Manning's ears, and as soon as he heard it, he flicked off the safety on the detonator.

"Firing!" Manning bellowed.

He squeezed the trigger. A heartbeat later, a landslide of sand gushed after them, tumbling and sweeping the three men along. Even as he tumbled, Manning looked up to see a jet of fire rise from the top of the cliff. The column of force and light rose, a metallic snow fluttering from the center of the powerful jet.

Encizo punched up from beneath a pile of black sand, coughing out a cloud of the crap. He looked up to see the confetti of a shredded missile. Hawkins grunted, trying to sit up, though he had no leverage in the soft sand beneath him.

"Did we stop it?" Hawkins asked.

Something clattered in the distance, and Manning turned to see that their pickup had literally been lifted by the force of the blast and hurled down the slope. It rolled to a halt, mashed and crushed by its explosive journey.

Manning looked to the sky. "Barb?"

"No more missiles to launch," Price said. "They tore the submarine to pieces when they fired the second missile."

"What does the satellite say about the integrity of the cliff?" Manning asked.

"It's still there," Price said. "It's still there."

Manning wiped his brow.

"It's over," Manning told Hawkins.

Hawkins grimaced. "I'm sure there's still some mop-up to do."

Manning helped him to his feet. "We just went through a landslide of our own."

Hawkins nodded. "I'm as tired as a one-legged man after an ass-kicking contest, but I'm not going to sleep until we make sure all of the assholes involved are corpses."

Encizo gestured that he agreed.

"No rest for the righteous," Manning groaned.

The three men turned and began their walk back to Tarajal.

RAUL ESPINOZA PULLED himself from the water, absolutely surprised that he had stumbled onto a swimmer delivery vehicle. That must have been how the enemy had gotten onto La Palma. He grimaced at the sight of the thing, then realized that there was scuba gear on board and there was fuel in the tanks.

"Lucky," Espinoza said. "I am lucky…"

He turned back to the waters behind him. Somewhere out there, he'd passed by the floating corpse of Diwala bin Lohs, or at least a half of it. Whatever had hit him had ripped the Saudi apart, leaving only his torso from the rib cage up. Where the rest of him floated, Espinoza hadn't seen, nor did he want to.

Espinoza began to strip out of his wet clothes.

The yacht was supposed to be an unknown asset. The only way that they could have known about its presence…

Espinoza looked at the SDV.

The men who came to La Palma must have passed the corpses on the ocean floor. He hadn't expected for the bodies to remain, relatively preserved, but the cold of the depths must have had something to do with it.

"A few weights, and that should have been it, but these bastards crawled along the ocean floor and found them," Espinoza said. He pulled on one of the scuba harnesses. He looked around and saw that there were guns and gear in lockets on the underwater sled.

"At least I can make a profit from this," Espinoza mused, realizing he'd stumbled on a small treasure trove that could fetch him a few thousand dollars. A little cash in pocket, and he could disappear, maybe even make a new identity that the Chinese government couldn't see through.

"This isn't so bad," he muttered.

He looked up at the sound of rotors. It sounded like a helicopter, but it actually was an airplane hanging from two tilted wing engines, ridiculously large blades spinning and keeping the craft aloft. It was a V-22 Osprey.

The same damn gunship that had shown up and raked the yacht, dumping corpses into the harbor.

Espinoza wondered if he should go for one of the guns in the SDV, but decided against it.

The Osprey was an American aircraft. And Americans would put him in a prison, and he would be granted rights. No torture. The U.S. Government didn't have the stomach to punish its enemies, all rumors about Camp X-Ray to the contrary. Espinoza knew what his enemies would do, and unless they chose to rendition him, he would be fine.

Someone was going to have to pay, publicly, for the deaths of the young students.

The Osprey hovered, its tail ramp open.

"I surrender!" Espinoza shouted.

He hoped they could hear him. Even so, he waved a white rag as a flag of surrender.

They'd take him prisoner, and he'd live comfortably. Three meals a day and a warm place to sleep. Things wouldn't be that bad.

Then he looked at the drenched pair of men standing in the back of the Osprey, each of them manning the controls of a huge machine gun.

Espinoza lost the enthusiasm for waving his white flag.

He started to scream as he saw the first muzzle-flash.

An instant later his lungs were completely gone, burst from his body by the impact of a .50-caliber slug.

In another moment the world turned off in Espinoza's mind. He was hurled into oblivion.

BY THE TIME LYONS AND Blancanales stopped firing, the Peruvian agent was a smear of gore on the rocks.

Lyons leaned against the mounted Browning, looking at Blancanales.

"He must not have noticed the silent alarm on the SDV," Lyons said.

Blancanales shrugged. "That's why it's a silent alarm. I'm just glad we caught up with him when we did."

"Carl, I just got a call from Gary. He's wondering if you could mop up in the harbor," Price said over their communicators.

Lyons smirked. "We got the last one from the yacht."

He turned and looked at the greasy smudge of smoke that served as the gravestone of Option Omega's submarine. "And no one got out of that sub."

"Yeah, satellite infrared confirms that," Price returned. "Go pick up the rest of the team and return to the carrier group."

Lyons nodded. It had been a long night. "That sounds like a plan."

The V-22 Osprey tilted its rotors, accelerating up toward the caldera of Cumbre Vieja. The next stop was Santa Cruz harbor.

And after that…home to Stony Man Farm.

If Lyons's luck held up, they might even get a day or three of rest and recreation before the next crisis.

Until then, he left U.S., British and Spanish marines to hunt down bombs and be first responders for an island filled with liberated tourists and locals.

* * * * *

TAKE 'EM FREE
2 action-packed novels plus a mystery bonus

NO RISK
NO OBLIGATION TO BUY

JAMES AXLER

DEATH LANDS®

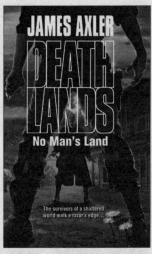

No Man's Land

The survivors of a shattered world walk a razor line.

A civil war raging in the Des Moines River valley forces Ryan and his companions to take sides, or die—because somewhere in the middle of the generations-old conflict is a lost redoubt. But Snake Eye, the deadliest gunslinger in Deathlands, stands between them and the way out...and he won't step aside until he has Ryan's head.

Available November 2012!